"Compared to what our Creator wanted us to be, we are all clowns. And that's what we *koshare* do. We act funny to remind the people. To make the people laugh at themselves. We are the Sacred Clowns."

Officer Jim Chee is making little headway in finding a Pueblo teenager who's gone missing from his boarding school, a task made tougher still by the resentment Chee feels at being asked to play truant officer by his new boss, Lt. Joe Leaphorn. But this truancy turns ominous when the student's uncle, who belonged to the *koshare*, the Pueblo's moral police, is found bludgeoned to death during a tribal festival.

Meanwhile, both Chee and Leaphorn are baffled by the murder of a shop teacher at a nearby missionary school—a crime that seems unrelated to everyone except Chee and Leaphorn. When they do find what links these grisly events, they uncover a deadly web of greed and betrayal at whose center are a ceremonial cane given to the tribe by President Lincoln and a no-holds-barred battle over putting a toxic-waste dump on Pueblo land.

Hillerman is at his apex, with the lyrical depictions of place, impeccable pacing, and gripping evocations of Indian myth and life that have won him many awards and legions of fans across the country. Added to all this are budding romances for both Leaphorn and Chee, a winning combination sure to make *Sacred Clowns* Hillerman's biggest bestseller yet.

SACRED CLOWNS

TONY HILLERMAN

SACRED CLOWNS

HarperCollins*Publishers*

HarperCollins books may be purchased for educational, business, or
sales promotional use. For information, please call or write: Special
Markets Department, HarperCollins Publishers, Inc., 10 East 53rd
Street, New York, NY 10022.

FIRST EDITION

LIBRARY OF CONGRESS CATALOG CARD NUMBER:

ISBN: 0-06-016767-X

93 94 95 96 xxx 10 9 8 7 6 5 4 3 2 1

DEDICATION

This book is dedicated to Fr. Doug McNeill, director of St. Bonaventure, Thoreau, N.M. 87323, and to the volunteers who donate part of their lives to run its classrooms, kitchen, school buses and water trucks. They come from all parts of the country, from different generations and different religions, united only in the desire to help their fellow humans. The volunteers at work as this book was finished were:

Theresa Arsenault, Christine Behnke, Lonnie Behnke, Frances Behr, Ireen Brayman, Jim Brayman, Ken Brewer, Mary Brewer, Barbara Burdick, Natalie Bussiere, Andrew Campbell, Ann Carter, Jan Charles, Maria Cravedi, Ernest Duran, George Erickson, Yoshiko Erickson, Jennifer Farrell. Al Feng, Christine Fitzpatrick, Bob Gallagher, Helen Gallagher, Stu Healy, Cynthia Higbee, Rick Juliani. Julie McKee, Kathy Murray, Bud and Grace Ouelette, Chris Pietraszewski, John Rauch, Carol Rintala, John Seckinger, Dan Skendzel, Bob Sparapani, and Tim Thompson.

I salute you all.

TONY HILLERMAN

AUTHOR'S NOTE

The characters are figments of the author's imagination—representing no one. Nor does Tano Pueblo exist. What one sees of Tano ceremonialism herein is a melding of the author's experience at other pueblos.

The author is indebted for the help and advice of Dr. Louis Heib of the University of Arizona, the author of many works on the Koshare and the ritual clows of the Hopis. However Tano is not a Hopi village and the descriptions in this book do not represent Hopi religious activities.

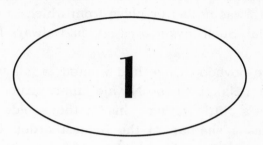

1

AT FIRST, Officer Jim Chee had felt foolish sitting on the roof of the house of some total stranger. But that uneasiness had soon faded. Now this vantage point on the roof had come to seem one of Cowboy Dashee's rare good ideas. Chee could see almost everywhere from here. The drummers directly beneath the tips of his freshly shined boots, the column of masked dancers just entering the plaza to his left, the crowd of spectators jammed along the walls of the buildings, the sales booths lining the narrow streets beyond, he looked down on all of them. And out over the flat crowded roofs of Tano Pueblo, he could rest his eyes on the ragged row of cottonwoods along the river, golden today with autumn, or upon the blue mountains blocking the horizon, or the green-tan-silver patchwork of farm fields the Tanoans irrigated.

It was an excellent perch from which to witness the Tanoan kachina dance–for duty as well as pleasure. Especially with the warm, jean-clad thigh of Janet Pete pressed against him. If Delmar Kanitewa was present, Chee would be likely to see him. If the boy didn't show up, then there was no better place from which to watch the ceremonial. Such mystical rituals had always fascinated Chee.

Since boyhood Chee had wanted to follow Hosteen Frank Sam Nakai. In the Navajo family structure Nakai was Chee's "little father", his mother's elder brother. Nakai was a shaman of the highest order. He was a *hataali*—what the whites called a singer, or medicine man. He was a man respected for his knowledge of the traditional religion and of the curing ways the Holy People had taught to keep humankind in harmony with the reality that surrounds us all. Nakai worked along that narrow line that separates flesh and spirit. Since boyhood, that had interested Chee.

"On the roof is where they like visitors to sit when they're having a kachina dance," Dashee had said. "It gets you tourists out from under foot. Unless you fall off, there's a lot less chance you'll do something stupid and mess up the ceremony. And it leaves room around the dance ground for the Tano people. They need to exchange gifts with the kachinas. Things like that."

Dashee was a sworn Deputy Sheriff of Apache County, Arizona, a Hopi of his people's ancient Side Corn Clan, and Jim Chee's closest friend. But he could also be a pain in the butt.

"But what if I spot the kid?" Chee had asked. "Is he going to wait while I climb down?"

"Why not? He won't know you're looking for him." Cowboy had then leaned against Janet Pete and confided in a mock whisper: "The boy'll think Detective Chee would be over there in Thoreau working on that big homicide."

"You know," Asher Davis said. "I'll bet I know that guy. There was a teacher at that Saint Bonaventure

School—one of those volunteers—who called me once to see if I could get a good price for something some old timer had to sell. It was a little silver pollen container—looked late nineteenth century—and some jerk in Farmington had offered this old man two dollars for it. I got him two hundred and fifty. I wonder if that was the teacher who got killed."

"His name was Dorsey," Chee said, sounding slightly grouchy. He didn't know Davis and wasn't sure he'd like him. But maybe that was just the mood he was in.

"Dorsey," Davis said. "That's him."

"See," Cowboy said. "Officer Chee keeps up on those serious crimes. And he also has time to write letters to the editor telling the Tano council what to do with its old uranium mines."

"Hey," Janet said. "Watch it there, Cowboy. That was a darn good letter. It was good advice. The paper thought so, too. They put the big headline on it." She punched Cowboy on the shoulder. "Do you want to see us being used as the world's toxic waste garbage pile?"

Chee had been ignoring Dashee's needling all morning. At first it had been based on the letter, published in that morning's edition of The Navajo Times. In it Chee had called a proposal to use the open pit of the abandoned Jacks Wild mine as a toxic waste dump "symbolic of the contempt felt for tribal lands." But then they had heard of the homicide on the car radio. A school shop teacher at Thoreau had been hit fatally on the head. Some materials were reported missing and no suspect had been identified. It was a pretty fair murder by reservation standards. Certainly it was more dignified that this assignment. It had happened yesterday, on Chee's day off. Still, Lieutenant Leaphorn might have assigned him to work on it. Or at least mentioned it. But he hadn't, and that burned a little.

What burned more was Janet. Janet had encouraged

Cowboy's needling with amused grins and occasional chuckles.

But now, warmed by her praise of his letter, Chee was willing to forgive all that—even to feel better about Cowboy. He had to concede that he had started the exchange by kidding Cowboy about the Hopi tendency to grow wide, instead of high. And he had to concede that what Cowboy had said about the roof was true enough. If Kanitewa was down there in the crowd watching his pueblo celebrate this autumn feast day, the boy would be feeling secure among family and friends. But, on the other hand, kids who run away from boarding school know someone will be coming after them.

Chee had been just such a kid himself, once. That feeling of fear, of being hunted, is one he could never forget. You can't relax even when, as in Chee's case, the hunt was brief and there was little time for the fear to build. The man from the boarding school had been parked out of sight behind the sheep pens waiting when Chee walked up to his mother's hogan. Seeing him had been almost a relief.

"Kanitewa, he'll be nervous," Chee said. "He won't be easy to catch."

"Tell you what," Dashee said. "We'll sit on the roof. If we see him, you watch him while I climb down. Then you signal me where he is and I grab him."

Chee thought about it.

"It these people were Hopis we wouldn't have to worry about this. They have the men all sitting on the roofs and the woman and children on the chairs down there around the dance ground," Dashee said. "That's the way its supposed to be."

"Not at all Hopi villages," Chee said.

"At mine, anyway," Dashee said. "We do it the traditional way."

"Which is beside the point. On the roof, he's going to

notice me," Chee had said. "Sitting up here waving my arms and pointing at him. He can't help noticing me." And so would everyone else—a Navajo making an ass of himself at a Tano ceremonial.

Through all this Davis Asher had been looking up at the roof ledge, uneasily. Asher's sunburned neck bulged from the eighteen inch neck of his sport shirt and his back strained its triple X width. "Reckon it'll hold me?" Asher asked, his voice filled with doubt.

"Sure," Dashee said. He motioned around the plaza. "Look at all the people up there. Those roofs are built to hold full sized people. Like us. Or," (he paused and inspected Chee and Janet Pete) "twice as many skinny ones."

"Not me, they're not," Asher said. "But I need to be seeing some folks anyway. I've got to be going about my business. Helping the Tano economy. Buying up some goodies."

Janet Pete had settled it. "Let's sit on the roof," she said. "Come on, Asher. Don't be lazy. You can do your business later."

"Hey," Davis said. "I see another excuse. There's ole' Roger." He looked at Janet. "I'll bet you know him. He's a fellow lawyer. Works the Indian territory out of Santa Fe and for years he's been big in saving the planet."

"Roger who?" Janet asked, scanning the crowd.

"Applebee," Davis said. "The big gun in Nature First."

"Oh, yeah," Janet said. "I see him now. He talked to me about that Continental toxic waste dump proposal last year."

Davis laughed. "And he probably got you into some sort of trouble. He's been doing that to me for years. Rog and I go all the way back to Santa Fe High School. Santa Fe Demons. He was quarterback, I was fullback. He got me suspended when we were sophomores. He's the kind of friend everybody needs to keep life from being boring."

Chee had been just standing there, looking at the house top, trying to think of an argument against climbing up there. But this aroused his interest.

"How'd that happen? The suspension?"

"Well, we were having an algebra test, as I remember it, and Roger had custody of his uncle's car. I think he was supposed to get it greased or something. We'd been driving around instead of studying. So Rog says not to worry. We'll postpone the test. We call the principal, tell him we're the gas company and there's a leak in the line to the temporary building where the math class met." Davis was grinning at the memory. "It worked."

"It worked, but you get suspended?" Chee asked.

"Well, that's the way it is with the Davis/Applebee projects. Roger dreams 'em up and they sound fine and then it turns out there's something he didn't think of. This one just worked for a day or so. I made the call, because I had the deep voice. And when it turned out no gas leak, the secretary had had enough dealings with me to remember what I sounded like."

"I'd like to meet Applebee," Chee said. "I wonder if I could help him stop that waste dump project."

But then Davis had shouted: "Hey, Rog," and waved and was plowing through the crowd.

So, reduced to a party of three, they climbed the ladder behind the house of a plump middle-aged woman who Cowboy Dashee seemed to know. They sat on the packed earth of the roof with their feet dangling over the parapet—looking directly down on the pueblo's central plaza with Chee feeling disgruntled.

Chee-like, he analyzed why. It was partly because Lieutenant Leaphorn had sent him here on this trivial assignment. True, he had only been second man in the two-man Special Investigations Office for three days, but there were already signs it wasn't going to work out. The Lieutenant wasn't taking him seriously. It wasn't just not

being shifted over to the homicide, it was Leaphorn's attitude. They should be investigating Continental Collectors,
and Tribal Councilman Jimmy Chester, and those people
in the Bureau of Land Management, and the whole conspiracy to make the Checkerboard Reservation a national
garbage pit. That's what he should be doing—not chasing
after a runaway schoolboy who wasn't even a Navajo. Or
was just barely a Navajo. And hunting him just because
his aunt was a big shot on the Navajo Tribal Council.

So he was in a down mood today partly because of
the sense of having his time wasted. But, to be honest with
himself, it was mostly because the way this had all worked
out.

When Leaphorn had given him his orders, Chee had
decided to make the best of it. Janet Pete's legal aid office
was closed on Saturday. He'd called her at home and
invited her to come and watch the ceremonial. She'd said
fine. She'd meet him in front of the Navajo Nation Inn.
And she was standing there when he drove up. But, alas,
she was talking to Cowboy and Asher Davis, and a lot of
the glitter quickly vanished from what had been a very
good idea.

"Do you know this fellow, here?" Cowboy had asked
Chee. "He's Asher Davis and he is what you college educated people would call an oxymoron. He's an Honest
Indian Trader." While they shook hands, Dashee was looking at Davis, reconsidering the compliment.

"Well, let's make that read FAIRLY HONEST INDIAN
TRADER. We've been out to Hopi Mesas and I've got to
admit that Asher did try to cheat some of my kinfolks."

Davis was obviously used to this. "As a matter of fact,"
he told Chee, his expression somber, "cheating Cowboy's
kinfolks is something I haven't been able to pull off. His
uncle there at Mishongnovi sold me a nineteenth century
Owl Kachina and when it got it home and looked under
the feathers I found one of those 'Made in Taiwan' labels.'"

Dashee was grinning. "Actually, it said 'Made in Taiwan in 1889 by Hopis.' So at least it was ancient."

"Good to meet you, Mr. Davis," Chee said. "We've got to be shoving off."

And Cowboy had said where you going and, alas, Chee had admitted they were going to Tano to see the ceremonial, and Cowboy had said he hadn't seen that one and had heard it was interesting and Davis had said it was, indeed, and Tano had an unusually good market and he sometimes picked up some old pots there, and the Jicarilla's brought in their baskets for sale and, alas again, Janet had then said we have plenty of room. Why don't you come along.

Thus what Chee had planned as a quiet duet with plenty of time to talk and explore their relationship, had deteriorated into a noisy quartet. And here now was Janet's grinning when Cowboy needled him, and siding with Cowboy on whether they should sit on the roof. Worse, now they were up here on the roof, it was obvious that Cowboy was right. But, to hell with it.

Chee extracted the photograph of Delmar Kanitewa from his jacket pocket and re-memorized it. The grainy copy had come from the boy's portrait in last year's Crownpoint High School yearbook. It showed a wide grin, white but slightly crooked teeth, high cheekbones, slightly cleft chin, and a bad haircut. Clearly, the genes of Delmar's Tano mother had overridden those of his Navajo father. He would look like scores of other Tano Pueblo teenagers, and a lot like hundreds of other teenagers from the other pueblo tribes, and a lot like a Hopi, for that matter. But Chee would recognize him. He was good at faces when he tried to be.

"His mother's house is one street south of the plaza," Leaphorn had told him. "But don't go there. We got the B.I.A. who covers Tano to check with Kanitewa's mama and she said she hadn't seen him. She's probably hiding him, or something. So don't tip your hand."

"It's funny, though," Chee had said. "Didn't she send him to the school in the first place? You'd think she'd want him back in his classes."

Lieutenant Leaphorn had not thought that worthy of comment, or even looking up from his note pad.

"When you find him, here's what you do. Ask him why he ran away from school and where he's staying. Make sure he knows you're not after him so he won't take off again. Then call me and tell me where he is. Nothing else."

"I don't pick him up? Take him back to school?"

The Lieutenant had looked up at Chee's question, wearing the expression that always made Chee feel like he'd said something stupid.

"You're off the Navajo reservation. The boy hasn't broken any law. We're just doing a little courtesy work for the Councilwoman. His grandmama. I suspect this is part of a

family fuss over who has custody of the kid." Leaphorn had recited this patiently, and then patiently had added more explanation.

Kanitewa's mother, a Tanoan, had divorced the boy's Navajo father without, apparently, much hard feelings. The boy had lived with his mother and kept his Tanoan name. But when time for high school came, and he was almost a man, he decided to live with his father.

"And, unfortunately, his father is the son of Bertha Roanhorse who is on the Tribal Council Budget Committee which decides how well we eat. And she's worried. The boy hadn't told any of his friends he was running off. To the contrary. He was part of a intertribal dance group and they had a performance coming up at a rodeo in Durango. So that makes it a funny time to disappear from school."

"Maybe he wanted to go to the Tano ceremonial,"

Chee said. "If he's in high school, he's probably been initiated into one of the Tano kivas."

"Grandma said no. He'd made arrangements. He had her working to get his costume ready for Durango performance. She said he was all excited about it."

"You'd think she'd go find him herself," Chee said.

"No, you wouldn't. Not if you knew the Councilwoman. She'd get us to do it for her." And that had ended the discussion.

It was irritating. What he was doing was one level under being a truant officer. Having Leaphorn as a boss was going to be a genuine pain. Just like people had warned him.

He felt Janet Pete's elbow in his ribs. "Why so grouchy looking? You want to get down?"

"Sorry," Chee said. "No. Cowboy was right."

"Cowboy is often right," Cowboy said. "Just learn to count on it."

The double-line of Kachinas had completed the circle of the plaza now and moved almost directly below their housetop. Chee looked at figures foreshortened by perspective, seeing the tops of the tubular leather masks which converted farmers, truck drivers, loggers, policemen, accountants, drunks, fathers, sons and grandfathers into the benign spirits who linked the people of Tano to God. He could see very human sweat glistening on their shoulders, a very ordinary Marine Corps anchor tattoo on the arm of the seventh Kachina, the very natural dust stirred by the rhythmic shuffling of their moccasins. Even so, even for an unbelieving Navajo outsider, the dancing figures seem more than human. Perhaps it was the pattern of sound the drums made, perhaps the effect of the perspective. He glanced up from the dancers. The audience was silent, even the children almost motionless.

Then across the plaza laughter erupted.

"Here come the Koshares," Cowboy said.

Four figures had emerged on a roof across the plaza. They wore breech cloths and their bodies were zebra striped in black and white, their faces daubed white with a huge black smile painted around their mouths, their hair jutting upward in two long conical horns, each horn surmounted with a brush of what seemed to be corn shucks. Koshare. The Sacred Clowns of Pueblo people. Chee had first seen similar clowns perform at a Hopi ceremonial at Moenkopi when he was a child, and since then at other Hopi dances. These seemed to be much the same.

Two of them now stood at the parapet of the building, pointing downward at the line of kachinas, gesturing wildly. The other two, a fat man and a youth with a weight-lifter's body, were carrying a ladder, They swung it recklessly, knocking first one, and then the other, of their partners head over heels to the delight of the audience. They managed to get the ladder over the side, wrong side down. A mock battle ensued, with much falling and general clumsiness, to determine who would go down the ladder first. The fat man won. He started down head first. One of the others, a skinny fellow, climbed over him, also head first. Their legs entangled. They started to fall, were caught by one of the two partners still on the roof. The weight lifter had managed to get off the roof and below the ladder. He was climbing down under the tangle—also upside down.

The crowd was laughing, shouting encouragement. The drums kept their steady rhythm. The kachinas danced on, sublime spirits oblivious of such human imperfection.

"Somebody's going to get killed," Janet Pete said. "They'll break their necks."

A fall probably would break something, Chee thought. It would be a two story drop onto earth packed as hard as concrete.

"They've been doing that a thousand years," Cowboy

said. "Nobody ever gets hurt." But he was frowning. "These guys are just fair," he said. "You ought to see em at Shongopovi, or Hotevilla, or Walpi, or . . . "

"On any Hopi village," Chee said. "That's Cowboy's slogan. Hopis do it better."

Cowboy was shaking his head. "Chee always get that wrong." he said. "It's Hopis do it best."

"Do they always do it like that?" Janet sounded both disbelieving and disapproving. "'They're disrupting the ceremonial?"

"Not disrupting. It's part of the ritual. It's all symbolic. They represent humanity. Clowns. Doing everything wrong while the spirits do everything right."

Janet Pete looked unimpressed. The Koshare made it down the ladder to ground level. They stood, pointing excitedly at the Kachinas, talking stage-loud in a language Chee couldn't understand. The Tanoans, he thought, spoke Tewa. Or maybe it was Keresan. One of the Koshare ran to the line of kachina dancers, threw his arms around one of the masked men and pulled him out of the formation. He was shouting something to the other Koshare. Janet glanced at Cowboy, an inquiring look.

"He's saying: 'This one is mine. This one is mine.' Or something like that." Cowboy said.

"You understand Tewa?"

"No," Cowboy said. "But the ceremony is pretty much the same as one we do. The idea is to make fun of how humans try to possess everything."

The crowd seemed to be enjoying it. An unmasked man in ceremonial kirtle and moccasins (Cowboy had said he was the "Father of the Kachinas") grabbed the koshare's arm, freed the Kachina, and provoked an exchange which produced a burst of laughter. Three boys, teenagers, emerged from between two houses and skirted behind a row of Tano women in chairs at the edge of the dance ground. The tallest one was Delmar Kanitewa. At least he looked like Kanitewa.

Chee touched Janet's knee.

"Look," he said. "See those three boys almost directly across the plaza. Behind the women. Notice the one in the red shirt."

"Yeah," Janet said. "It looks like him. But isn't he too tall."

"The description said five foot eight," Chee said. "That's pretty tall for a Pueblo kid."

"I'll go get him," Cowboy said, pushing himself up from the roof. "Keep an eye on him."

That was easy enough. Red Shirt and his two friends had found a wall to lean against. Chee watched. Red Shirt said something to his companions and pointed up the dance ground. He was pointing at a man, half-hidden from Chee's perspective by a huge cowboy hat, who trotted out of an alley onto the dance ground riding a stick horse. Behind him came another man, this one wearing a black Homberg hat. Homberg was pedalling a toy car so small that his bobbing knees were as high as his hunched shoulders. White dollar signs were painted on the red toy and it dragged a flat black object also decorated with dollar signs. Behind the car came a third man. straw-hatted and dressed in a blue three piece business suit. He was pulling a toy wagon loaded with assorted objects and with signboards attached to its sides. The three paraded past the audience. There was laughter, then silence, then a buzz of talk.

"Now what?" Janet Pete said. "You understand what's going on?"

"A little," Chee said. "The koshare team at a ceremonial usually has some other guys working with them. They come in like that and put on little skits. Sort of call attention to things that are wrong in the pueblo. Make fun of it."

"The cowboy's pretending to take pictures of everybody," Janet said. "See. He's acting like he has the camera hidden in his hat." She laughed. The top of the cowboy's hat was hinged. The cowboy pointed the crown of the hat at a cluster of girls, pulled it open, and flashed a flash bulb. The girls dissolved into giggles.

"Did you see that?" she said. "That's pretty clever."

"I missed it," Chee said. He was watching another part of the skit. The driver of the toy car had climbed out of it and picked up the object he'd been towing. It proved to be an grotesquely oversized wallet, and from it he extracted a sheaf of oversized copies of dollars. He was waving these at the puller of the wagon. Now Chee could read one of the signs.

"Sacred Objects For Sale"

Not much laughter now. Not among the Tanoans anyway. This seemed to be serious business. It provoked a nervous murmur.

The wagon puller sold something that looked like an over- sized wooden doll, poorly made, and then engaged in exaggerated

haggling over what seemed to be a black stick, perhaps a walking stick—finally accepting a paper bag full of the pseudo dollars. Next he extracted from the wagon bed what appeared to be a oval slab of stone. The buyer jumped up and down in mock excitement. The audience had fallen so silent that Chee could hear the dialogue of the clown. Even the children and the visitors were simply listening now—sensing the tension.

Janet was wearing a broad grin. "I hope ole Asher is seeing this," she said. "That's him they've got in mind."

"Money! Money! More Money!" Wagon Puller shouted.

Buyer had opened his purse, dumping out more green paper on the packed earth. Both of the clowns, on hands and knees now, scrambled for it.

"Oops," Janet said. "I'm wrong."

"You sure are," Chee said. "Can you imagine Asher pouring out his money like–." He stopped. Cowboy was standing just below, looking up at him, signaling a question.

Chee glanced across the plaza, pointed to where the three boys were standing. Had been standing. Two of them were still there, watching the clowns. Red Shirt had disappeared.

"Aaaah," Chee said.

"What's wrong?" Janet said.

Chee cupped his hands, shouted to Cowboy. "I lost him."

Cowboy shrugged, trotted down the row of spectators, hunting the boy.

Janet Pete was looking at him. "I screwed up," Chee said. "Took my eyes off the little bastard. I gotta go help Cowboy hunt him."

"I'll go with you," Janet said. "Look over there. By the mouth of the alley. Applebee. The Nature First lobbyist Davis was telling us about. You ought to meet him."

"Maybe later," Chee said, and scrambled down the ladder.

They scouted the plaza, the sales booths along the side streets, the rows of vehicles, mostly pickups, jamming every possible parking space. At the house of the Kanitewa family, they peered through the open doorway and into windows. The long table in the kitchen-dining room was loaded with food but no one seemed to be home. Back at the dance ground, they saw Cowboy, his eyebrows raised with a question.

"No luck," Chee said.

"Which direction was he headed?" Cowboy asked. "Last time you saw him."

"I took my eyes off him." Chee admitted. "I glanced at the clown show and he just vanished."

"Yeah," Cowboy said, his expression skeptical. "Well,

he'll be back."

Behind Cowboy, there was an outbreak of laughter. A kachina figure wearing a mask with oversized eyes and feathered tufts for ears was threatening one of the koshares with a whip of yucca. The koshare offered the big eyed kachina a bowl. The other koshares came running up, making pugnacious gestures.

"Now what?" Janet Pete asked.

"That's what Hopis call the Owl Kachina," Cowboy said. "Or sometimes 'The Punisher.' If it was Mafia, you'd call him the 'enforcer.' And if what's going on is like in the Hopi villages, he's warning the Koshare to behave themselves, and the Koshare Chief is trying to bribe him, and the other koshare are suspecting their chief of selling them out."

Cowboy laughed, punched Janet Pete lightly on the shoulder. "We pueblo people have always had a realistic view of the human nature."

"Original sin," Janet said. "Fallen man."

Chee had been ignoring the clowns, scanning the crowd, hoping that Kanitewa's red shirt would reappear. He was imagining himself in Leaphorn's office. Leaphorn would be sitting behind his desk, face blank. Chee would be explaining how he'd let Kanitewa slip away. Long moment of silence while Leaphorn digested this, then Leaphorn asking what the devil he was doing up on the roof, and that leading into some sort of explanation of how he'd turned this assignment into a Sunday outing with friends.

"Look," Chee said. "Forget the theology for now. Let's find that kid."

So they looked again, splitting up, canvassing the crowd, checking the sales booths, watching Kanitewa's home, peering through the windows of countless pickups, even checking the hay sheds and sheep pens between the village and the fields.

At three p.m., as arranged, Chee reclimbed the ladder to the roof. Cowboy and Janet there, eating snowcones while they waited for him. They didn't have to tell him they'd had no better luck than his own.

"I found the two boys who were with him," Janet said. "They didn't know where he was. Anyway they claimed they didn't. But they did confirm that their friend was our missing elusive Delmar."

"I found what the little boy shot his arrow at," Cowboy said. "Nothing."

The Kachinas were gone now and much of the crowd had shifted from the plaza to the sales area. Chee spotted one of the boys who had been with Kanitewa, paper cup in one hand and a slab of fry bread in the other, leaning against a wall. He saw Davis Asher leaning over a table where a Navajo was selling sand cast silver belt buckles, laughing about something. He saw a Bureau of Indian Affairs cop he'd met once at a briefing in Albuquerque worked with–a Cheyenne named something-or-other Blizzard—inspecting a basket at an Apache woman's booth. He saw two red shirts, but a young woman was wearing one and an old man the other.

Chee climbed down the ladder again. He patrolled the narrow streets, took a look through the sheep pens, horse corrals and hay storage area, prowled through the ranks of parked vehicles peering through windows. He didn't see Kanitewa, but he ran into Cowboy, who was buying a snow cone..

"The Kachinas will be back in thirty minutes of so, and there'll be more dancing," Cowboy said. "Probably the kid'll come back then for the second act. Or after the dance, he'll go home and we can catch him there."

"Maybe," Chee said, trying not to sound skeptical. "But his mother is probably hiding him out. She told the B.I.A he hadn't come home." This was not proving to be a good day and Chee was not optimistic about it getting better.

"There's Applebee again," Janet said. "The guy with the hotdog in his hand, buying something at that booth. You want to meet him?"

To their left at the mouth of an alleyway from which the Kachinas had emerged, there was a sudden flurry of sound and excitement. The clown who had ridden the stick horse emerged, running frantically, hat missing now but still wearing the costume chaps. He was shouting something. It sounded like "get the ambulance." It was "get the ambulance."

"Somebody must be hurt," Cowboy said.

Two men and a woman emerged from the alley, the woman sobbing.

"They killed him," she was saying. "They killed him."

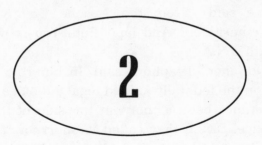

2

"YOU WERE SITTING on the roof?" Lieutenant Joe Leaphorn kept the tone of the question neutral.

"Yessir," Jim Chee said. "You can see the whole plaza from up there."

That was the advantage, of course. The disadvantage being that you couldn't catch the kid once you saw him. But Leaphorn didn't press that point. It was obvious from Chee's slightly abashed expression that he was aware of it. Instead Leaphorn put the first page of Chee's report face down on his desk and re-read the second and terminal page. It was neatly typed but—by Leaphorn's standards—sadly incomplete.

"When you heard the woman shouting you say here that you presumed the person killed was the Kanitewa boy? Why did you presume that?"

"Well, I had him on my mind. We were looking for him. Trying to figure out where he had gone."

Leaphorn looked up from the report over his horn-rimmed glasses. "We?"

Chee hesitated. "I had Deputy Sheriff Dashee with me," Chee said. "From the Apache County Sheriff's Office." He hesitated. "And Janet Pete. You know her. The lawyer with D.N.A."

"I know her," Leaphorn said. In her role as public defender in the federally funded legal aid office, Ms. Pete had sometimes been a thorn in the side of the Navajo Tribal Police. D.N.A. they called it, short for *"Dine'Biina neel Nahiilna be Agadithe,"* which translated to English as something like "People who talk fast to help people out." But it seemed to Leaphorn that the people being helped out were usually the people the Tribal Police were chasing, and never the Tribal Police.

"You made a sort of outing out of it, then," Leaphorn said. "Sort of a picnic. The three of you?"

"Four," Chee said. "Asher Davis went along. You know, the big—"

Leaphorn violated his own custom and Navajo tradition by interrupting. This day wasn't starting well. "The trader? Great big guy from Santa Fe?"

Chee nodded. His week was off to a terrible start. The first week on this new job, and maybe it would be the last week, too. And what if it was? He'd go back to being a patrolman. He never had been confident he could work with this guy. This super cop.

"Sounds like you sort of formed a posse? To catch the kid?" Leaphorn's expression was totally bland.

Chee tried to match that, but he could feel his face flushing. Cops who had worked under Leaphorn before the Lieutenant had been shifted into this new Special Investigations office had warned Chee that the man could be an arrogant son of a bitch.

"No sir," Chee said. "It just happened that way. You told me to find him. I was going to start by seeing if he'd show up at his home. For the ceremonial. If he did, I'd catch him and talk to him, and find out where he was staying, and tell him to call his grandma. As instructed. Miss Pete wanted to see the kachina dance, and she asked Dashee if he wanted to ride along, and then . . . " He let the explanation trail off.

"It violates a rule," Leaphorn said.

"Yes sir," Chee said.

"You understand the reason for the rule?"

"Sure," Chee said.

Leaphorn pushed himself out of his chair and walked to the window. He stood with his back to the window, looking out.

Thinking how he's going to tell me he's suspending me, Chee thought. *Thinking how to put it.*

"It's clouding up," Leaphorn said. "Looks like they might be getting a rain over on the Hopi Reservation."

Chee let that pass. The silence stretched.

"Or maybe some snow. I've gotten out of the habit of working with anyone since they put me in this office," Leaphorn said, still talking to the window. "One man operation, until now. Now there's two of us. I guess we're going to have to have some rules." He sat behind the desk again. "Or call them policies."

"In addition to department policies?"

"Just our own. Sort of above and beyond," Leaphorn said. "Like now. You did a job. I want a full report. To do that for me, you have to tell me some things you wouldn't normally tell your district captain."

Leaphorn paused, studying Chee. "Like you'd just as soon not tell the boss that you made a social event out of an assignment," he continued. "That get's you, maybe, in a jam. Trouble. Some days off without pay. Easy enough to just sort of forget some of the details. Maybe you remember it a little different. Like you met Miss Pete, and Dashee and Asher Davis there at the kachina dance. That would have sounded perfectly plausible. I'm glad you decided not to handle it that way." He studied Chee. "You must have thought about it."

Leaphorn paused, waited for a response.

Chee, who hadn't thought about it, just shrugged. He was guessing what the Lieutenant was driving at. He was pretty sure he knew what was coming next.

"My point is that when we're working on something, I want you to tell me everything. Everything. Don't leave out stuff you think is trivial, or doesn't seem to bear on what we're interested in. I want it all."

Chee nodded, thinking: *Right. Officer Chee as eyes, ears and nose. Collector of data. The Lieutenant as brain, doing the thinking. Well, I have my application filed with the B.I.A law and order people and with the Apache County Sheriff's Office and the Arizona State Police. Good resume. Good record. Well, pretty good.*

Leaphorn was studying his expression. "Now," he said. "Tell me everything Sayesva did?"

It took a moment for Chee to connect the name with the plump man he had watched yesterday clowning on the roof. The man with his body painted with the stripes of the Koshare clown. The man who somebody had clubbed to death just about 40 yards from where Chee had been sitting. "Everything?" Chee said. And he began describing everything he could remember.

Leaphorn digested it.

"Same with the boy," Leaphorn said, "Everything you can remember from where he was when you first saw him to the last glimpse."

That didn't take long.

"Anything to connect the boy and Sayesva? Anything like a signal. Anything like that?"

Chee thought. "Nothing," he said. "The boy, he seemed to be just another spectator."

"Sayesva was his uncle," Leaphorn said. "Maternal uncle." "Oh," Chee said. "I didn't know that." *Maternal uncle meant a special closeness. At least to Navajos. Would it be the same for the Tano people?*

"I just found out a minute ago," Leaphorn said.

Which means on the telephone. On the call he took just as I came in. But who would be calling to tell him something like that? Who else but somebody Leaphorn had called to get just that information for him. Why would he do that?

"You thought they might be kinfolks?" Chee asked.

"You look for connections," Leaphorn said. "Two homicides." He reached behind him and tapped the big map on the wall behind him. "One out at Thoreau on the Checkerboard Reservation and one way over at Tano Pueblo. Nothing to link them, right?

Chee could think of nothing, and said so. "To tell the truth, about all I know about that Thoreau homicide is what I heard on the radio."

Leaphorn detected something that might have been resentment in the voice.

"Yeah," he said. "I'm sorry about that. I'll get you the file. We'll be running errands for the FBI on it."

The file so far included only two sheets of paper—the report from the investigating officer at the Navajo Tribal Police office in Crownpoint. It didn't tell Chee much he hadn't already heard. Eric Dorsey, aged 37, wood and metalwork teacher, school bus driver and maintenance man at Saint Bonaventure Indian Mission. Found dead on the floor of his shop by students arriving for their after-noon class. Apparent cause of death: a blow on the back of the head. Apparent motive: theft. The door of a supply cabinet usually locked was found open. An unknown quantity of silver ingots believed missing. No witnesses. No suspects.

"I can't see anything to connect them," Chee said.

"Sayesva was a Koshare? That right?"

"Right," Chee said, baffled.

"Do you see anything in that Dorsey homicide report about a Koshare?"

Chee picked up the folder, re-read it. "Nothing."

"There's no reason there should be," Leaphorn said. "All sorts of stuff was stacked in the shop where Dorsey taught. The sort of things his students were making. Some sandcast silver, leather work, wood work projects, and two or three half-finished kachina dolls. One of them was a Koshare. About a foot tall. It still needed some work. No mention of it in the report."

"Well, hell," Chee said. "The Tano homicide hadn't happened yet. The investigator couldn't know and you wouldn't want to list all that . . . " Chee let it trail off. He saw the point Leaphorn was making. Unreasonable, but a point. Put everything in even if it seemed irrelevant.

"You could think of ten thousand explanations for the koshare," Leaphorn said. "Kids in an arts and craft shop trying to make stuff they could sell. The koshare's an interesting figure. Easy to paint. And so forth."

"Pretty weak link." Chee agreed. "I can't see it,"

Leaphorn rubbed the back of his hand across his eyes. He looked glum. "I can't either, but I always look. It's an old habit. Wastes time, usually. All we have here is two men hit on the head. Same method. The kid runs away a little bit after the Thoreau killing. If he had been a student of Dorsey's we would be very, very interested. But he went to school over at Crownpoint. Thirty miles away. Nothing there."

"Nothing," Chee said. *But you are thinking that if I hadn't let the kid get away maybe he could explain all this.*

"I don't like coincidences," Leaphorn said. "Even if this isn't much of one. I guess I'll find out which student was making the Koshare."

"I have a thought about the Sayesva thing," Chee said. "I hear he was a Certified Public Accountant. I heard he worked for that savings and loan outfit in Phoenix that went belly up. I heard that maybe a grand jury down there was interested in something or other. Maybe Sayesva knew something damaging."

For the first time, Leaphorn's expression shifted into something close to a smile.

"You get a 'he is', and a 'he was', and a 'I hear that too,' and a 'maybe so' on all that," Leaphorn said. "But the trouble is, Sayesteva is none of our business. That case is way out of our jurisdiction. It's strictly Bureau of Indian Affairs and FBI work. The late Eric Dorsey was our business because he was killed on the reservation."

Leaphorn swivelled in his chair, stared at his map. It was freckled with clusters of pins in a variety of colors. Some day, Chee thought, he'd learn what they signified. If he stuck around long enough. Now he was only conscious that Leaphorn hadn't been interested enough in his Sayesva theory to pursue it. He wasn't going to enjoy this job.

"Like what?" Leaphorn said. "What do think he might have known? About what?"

"I don't know. Nothing specific. It's just that an accountant, you know, would know things. Like maybe somebody's stealing. Or cheating on taxes. Things like that. So you'd want to know who he was working for. The people he was auditing."

Leaphorn was behind his desk again, studying Chee.

"We wouldn't want to know that," Leaphorn said. "The FBI might. Or the Sheriff's Office. But you and I wouldn't have any interest in that at all."

"Not unless it tied in with something that was our business," Chee said.

Leaphorn scratched his ear, studying Chee. "If, for example, he'd been auditing the Thoreau school, for example," he said finally. "It that was true we'll find out because the feds will tell us. Meanwhile, I want you to find the Kanitewa boy,"

The tone of that said this conversation was ended, but Chee stopped at the door.

"Lieutenant. You know that business with Continental Collectors wanting to establish the waste dump out in the Checkerboard. I've been hearing some things about that."

Leaphorn was shuffling through his file cabinet. He didn't look up. "You mentioned that before," he said. "And I told you our business in this office is crime, not politics."

"Sometimes they mix."

Leaphorn still didn't look up.

"What have you been hearing? It better be more than some old gossip about somebody from Continental bribing Tribal Councilmen. There's always gossip about somebody bribing somebody."

"I guess that all I know."

"Do you know which councilmen. Or where you can get a witness? Or any kind of evidence at all?

"No sir."

"Then we've got plenty of other stuff to work on," Leaphorn said. "Find the kid. That's the thing that's pressing on us right now." He got up and stood looking out the window, hands clasped behind him.

"When we get that out of the way," he said, talking to the glass, "I'd like to see what you can do with a vehicular homicide case. I'll give you the file on it and you're going to see it looks pretty hopeless."

"Which one?" Tribal law prohibited sale or possession of alcohol on the reservation but bars flourished in the border towns and deaths caused by drunk drivers was common fare for the NPD.

"The victim was an old man named Victor Todachene. Lived near Crystal. Details are in the file," Leaphorn said.

"Okay," Chee said.

"What isn't in the file is the Chief's interested in this

one." Leaphorn still seemed to be looking at something through the glass. "He was out at the Shiprock office when it got reported and he went out with the investigating officer. It was an usually bad case."

"How?" In his relatively short tenure as a Navajo Tribal Policeman Chee has seen an infinite variety of vehicular homicide. All ugly. All bad. Badness was measured by the number of bodies.

"Well," Leaphorn said, "Bad in a sense. The victim was a pedestrian. The vehicle sort of sideswiped him and then backed up—apparently to see what had happened—and then drove away and Mr. Todachene spent about two hours bleeding to death before the next driver came along."

"Oh," Chee said.

"I don't think the Chief has done a lot of work out on the road. I think it sort of shocked him."

It shocked Chee too. Driving away turned an accident into murder. The worst sort of murder. Murder with no motive except keeping one's self out of trouble.

"The Shiprock office has done all the regular stuff," Leaphorn said. Checking car repairs places, sale of car paint, that sort of thing. It dead ended. But the Chief thinks we ought to solve it."

"So do I," Chee said. "But we probably can't."

"I guess you know that I think this job you got deserves the rank of sergeant," Leaphorn said. "I haven't been able to sell that yet. But the way the Chief feels, if you solve this hit-and-run problem making sergeant is a dead cinch."

Chee had no comment to that. He had been a sergeant once. Acting sergeant. But he hadn't liked it much and it hadn't lasted. He and the Captain at Crownpoint hadn't agreed on how an investigation should be handled.

"Yes sir," Chee said.

"But first find the Kanitewa boy."

"Yes sir."

"Remember the Sayesva homicide is absolutely none of our business."

Chee nodded and headed for the door, which in Lieutenant Leaphorn's office, was always open.

"One more thing," the Lieutenant said. "Stay off of roofs."

3

"THE FACT IS," said Sergeant Harold Blizzard, "this Sayesva thing is none of your business. Your business ends at the Navajo Reservation boundary."

Blizzard was wearing his Bureau of Indian Affairs Law and Order Uniform with a New York Yankee cap. He was talking slowly and looking straight over the steering wheel and out the windshield. Jim Chee had been reading a book of Margaret Atwood's short stories he'd borrowed from Janet Pete, thinking it might impress her. He decided Miss Atwood would call Blizzard's expression either bleak or stolid. Or maybe "wintry." That fit the weather, too. It was cold for November, but Robin Marchment had assured them on her KRQE weathercast last night that the snowstorm hitting Utah would stay a little to the North.

"I know the Sayesva thing is none of my business," Chee said. "In fact my Lieutenant just told me that. He said to find the Kanitewa kid. Nothing else. He's the grandson a member of our Tribal Council. A woman. The lieutenant said get that woman off his back. Told me to keep my nose out of everything else and just find the kid."

Blizzard devoted his attention for a while to guiding the patrol car into that section of the gravel road in which the washboarding was the least severe. Even so, the jolting rattled his clip board, and the radio mike, and everything not fastened down. "The thing is," Blizzard said, "The feds want to talk to the kid, too. So your nose is right in the middle of it. Both nostrils." This caused Blizzard to chuckle.

Chee had lost patience with Blizzard about fifty miles ago—maybe even before they'd left the parking lot at Blizzard's B.I.A office in Albuquerque. There was no reason for Blizzard to act like this. He knew how the feds worked. The kid's name was on the F.B.I. list along with everybody known to have talked to Sayesva in the day or so before he was killed. That included just about everybody at Tano Pueblo and a lot of other people. There was no reason for Blizzard to be such a hardass over this, and Chee was tempted to tell him so. But he didn't. He was in Blizzard's jurisdiction, but that wasn't what inhibited him. Blizzard was a Cheyenne. And even with the Yankee cap on, he looked like a Cheyenne. He had that hard, bony face. Profile like a hatchet. Chee had grown up seeing the Cheyennes and the Sioux with their war bonnets and lances, fighting the cavalry in the drive-in movie at Shiprock. Even when the movie had been made south of Gallup and you knew the Cheyennes were actually Navajos making some beer money as extras, they took on the aura of warriors under those war bonnets. When Chee and his friends at boarding school played Cowboy and Indian, the Indians were always Cheyenne. It wasn't a hangup Chee had quite grown out of. To Jim Chee man, as Jim Chee, boy, the Cheyenne was the Indians' Indian.

"I'm not going to cause anybody any trouble," Chee

said. "Your F.B.I wants to you to find the kid. My boss has ordered me to find Delmar Kanitewa. I'm just supposed to give his bigshot grandma a chance to talk to him about running away from school. So, like I said, if I can find him, I'll tell you first, and then I'll tell my boss. You tell the FBI in Albuquerque, and my boss tells the tribal council-woman. Then I get to go back to doing something useful. Everybody's happy."

Harold Blizzard didn't look happy. He said "Uh huh," filling the sound with skepticism, and turned the car onto the road into the Tano Pueblo. He didn't hear a word I said, Chee thought. What a jerk. But he was wrong about the first part. Blizzard had been listening.

"Trouble with all that is this boy is about name number sixty on the list the feds gave me," Blizzard said, "and the list looks to me like they copied the son-of a bitch out of the Tano Pueblo census report. I think it's everybody who's been around Sayesva for the last month or so, plus his kinfolks. And I think everybody out here is kinfolks. And having a Navajo cop under foot, and having to squire you around is trouble. It's both a pain in the butt and a time waster. You find the kid, and tell me and I tell the feds and by then they forgot what they wanted to ask him. So don't try to tell me you're going to make me happy."

Mrs Kanitewa didn't look happy either. She was standing in the door of a fairly new frame and plaster house—one of twenty or thirty such houses built on the fringes of the pueblo to the meet the specifications of Indian Service housing. She was holding a box of frozen green beans and a butcher-paper package which Chee guessed would be ground beef to be thawed for supper. Through the doorway behind her, Chee could see a great pile of shucked corn filling a corner of the room. Mrs. Kanitewa gave them the smile made mandatory by tradi-tions of hospitality. She didn't look like she meant it.

"Well, come on in then," she said. "Delmar's not home

yet but if you want me to tell you about it again, then come in."

"In" did not prove to be the frame and stucco Indian Service house. She led them across the hard packed yard toward an adobe. It slouched under an immense cotton-wood which looked almost as old as the building. A fringe of ragweeds and Russian thistle growing in its dirt roof gave it a disreputable, unshaven look. But paint on the window frames was a fresh turquoise blue and geraniums were blooming in boxes beside the door. Mrs. Kanitewa seated them in the front room, which served as parlor, living room and dining room. They sat side-by-side on a sofa whose plastic upholstery creaked and crackled under their weight.

"I guess you haven't found him yet, either," she said. She looked worried now, as if maybe they had found him and were bringing sorrowful news.

"No mam," Chee said.

Blizzard had been looking around the room. Its brick floor was uneven in places, but mostly covered with cheap made-in-Mexico throw rugs and one pretty good Navajo horse blanket. It's ceiling was that criss-cross pattern of willow branches supported by Ponderosa poles which New Mexicans call "latilla." Its corners were obviously off-square by three or four degrees and the white plaster covering its walls wavered with the irregular shape of the adobe blocks behind it. Blizzard cleared his throat.

"That other house," he said. "The new one. Does that belong to you?"

The question surprised Chee, and Mrs. Kanitewa too.

"Yeah. The government built it. We use it to store stuff. They put a big refrigerator over there." She laughed. "They wanted us to live in it."

Blizzard opened his mouth, and closed it, leaving the question unasked. Chee answered it for him. After all, this Cheyenne was new to adobe country.

"This one's warm in the winter, and cool in the summer," he said.

"This one's home," Mrs. Kanitewa added.

Chee waited a moment in deference to Blizzard. But Blizzard seemed to have assumed the role of spectator. After all, he had already gone through questioning of Mrs. Kanitewa once before.

"When Sergeant Blizzard was here," Chee began. "Before the ceremonial, Delmar had just got home then? Is that right?"

Mrs. Kanitewa hesitated. "That's right," she said, looking embarrassed. "I didn't say that when he first asked me because I thought it was just about his running away from school. I wanted to talk to Delmar before they took him back to his dad." Clearly Mrs. Kanitewa lied reluctantly, even for her son.

"That day at the ceremonial, I saw Delmar at the kachina dance," Chee continued. "Mr. Blizzard said he understood that Delmar had come back to the pueblo but he hadn't had time to come by the house."

Mrs. Kanitewa looked uneasy. She glanced at Blizzard. "It wasn't quite like I told him," she said. She sighed, the weight of motherhood heavy. "He got home the day before. And he told me he was going back to school right after the ceremonial. Robert Sakani was going to drive him back. That's his cousin."

Sergeant Blizzard was trying not to look impatient. He failed.

"But after what happened to Mr. Sayesva, you didn't see him any more after that? He didn't come home to get his extra clothes or anything like that?"

Mrs. Kanitewa had raised her defenses. Her expression was blank. "No," she said, "He didn't."

Chee was looking past the woman into the kitchen, letting some time pass. He heard Blizzard shifting uneasily on the sofa. Blizzard, he thought, must be a city

Cheyenne. With a clock for a his brain. What the hell was the hurry?

"I ran away from boarding school myself once," Chee said. "The man was waiting for me to take me back when I got home. But it worried my mother."

"It does," Mrs. Kanitewa said. "It worries you."

"I guess you thought maybe he'd gone on back to school with his cousin. But that would worry you, too. Because why wouldn't he come home and say goodby? It doesn't make much sense to me."

"That's what I was thinking," she said. "Where was he? He wouldn't just go like that. He would stay for the funeral."

"You would want to bury Mr. Sayesva right away," Chee said. "Isn't that the rule of the pueblo. You want to do the burial before sundown."

"That's the way it is supposed to be. But they wouldn't let us do it. There was a deputy sheriff here when it happened, and Mr. Blizzard was here. And the police said they had to take him into Albuquerque to get an autopsy done to find out what killed him. " Mrs. Kanitewa's expression suggested she considered this hard to understand. "He'd been hit on the head and his head broke, but they said they had to let the doctor see him anyway, to get it all down on paper, and they would try to get him back in time."

"They didn't, though," Chee said, making it a statement rather that a question. It would have been clearly impossible. Chee had seen a funeral at Zuni Pueblo. The body would have be washed and dressed, the hair combed out, everything made ready for Sayesva's four day journey through the darkness toward his eternal joy. A Tano child of God going home. And he was probably a Roman Catholic as well. The parish priest would also send him on his way with another blessing.

"It was two days before we got the body back," she

said. "Then his wife and some of his people had to go there and get him. To make sure they didn't embalm him. They do that if you're not careful. The undertaker gets a lot of money for it."

"We Navajos have that trouble, too," Chee said. "If you're not there to stop it, the funeral home people will get the body and mutilate it and charge you a lot of money for doing it. Like they do with white people."

"They charge you a lot of money," Mrs. Kanitewa agreed. "I read in the papers that the funeral home people even got a law passed so you can't have the corpse incinerated. Even if you say so yourself, you got to get all the kinfolks to sign papers." She rubbed her fingers together—society's universal metaphor for the greed of its predator class. "They want to squeeze that money out of the widow."

Blizzard shifted his weight on the plastic sofa, creating a round of crackling and signaling his impatience with this philosophizing. "Well," he said. "You got about all you want?"

Chee ignored him.

"I'm not supposed to be asking anything about Mr. Sayesva because they handle that out of Albuquerque," he told Mrs. Kanitewa. "I'm just interested in talking with Delmar. Do you know why he came home?"

"Yes," she said. "He said he had to talk to his Uncle."

Ahh, Chee thought. He glanced at Blizzard to see if he'd noticed this, if he was aware that Sayesva was the kid's uncle. Blizzard was. Too late now.

"With your brother?" Chee asked.

She nodded. "Yes. With my brother."

"He came to tell your brother something?"

She nodded.

Blizzard ceased being the stoic Cheyenne sitting motionless on the couch waiting for Chee to finish wasting his time. He cleared his throat and leaned forward.

"We're talking about Mr. Sayesva now," he said. "What did your boy tell him? What did he want to see him about?"

"It was religious business," she said. "He didn't tell me." Sergeant Blizzard looked skeptical. "So how did you know it was religious? If he didn't tell you?"

The question surprised Mrs. Kanitewa. "Because he didn't tell me," she explained. "If it wasn't religious, he would have told me."

Blizzard's expression changed from skeptical to blank. He said: "I don't quite . . . ," and then stopped. Chee considered interrupting to explain things. To give Blizzard a little lecture on how the Tano people, and most of the other Pueblos, kept their religious duties very much to themselves. Neither the boy, nor any other citizen of the pueblo, would discuss the business of their particular religious society with anyone not initiated into its kiva. Not even with his mother. Nor would she ask him to. If Delmar's discussion with his uncle was religious, only his uncle would know about it. Chee respected that. To hell with Blizzard. Let the Sergeant handle this himself.

It took a little longer that way, but Blizzard eventually got it straightened out. Delmar had arrived at the Pueblo the afternoon before the ceremony. He had dropped off his back pack and gone to the house of Sayesva. Then he had come home, eaten supper, talked to his mother about school. He had told her he would go back after the ceremony. Then, before he went to bed, he'd gone to see his uncle again.

"Saw him again?" Blizzard asked. "Why?"

Mrs. Kanitewa considered. "I don't know. He didn't say. But I think now that it might have been something he heard on the radio."

Blizzard's expression suggested this conversation was full of surprises. "Like what? What did he say?"

"Well, he said he had to see Mr. Sayesva again. And

he ran out of the house."

Blizzard was leaning forward now. "I mean, what did he say he'd heard on the radio? Was it a news program or what?"

"He just said he had to go see his uncle. I didn't hear what he was listening to."

"What did he tell you when he came back?"

"I was asleep when he came back. It was late. Here we get up early so we go to bed early."

Blizzard leaned back, looking thoughtful. Digesting all this. Chee formed a question. What station was the radio tuned to? What time was it when Delmar heard whatever he'd heard? He stirred, took a deep breath.

"Could you estimate what time it was when you were out in the kitchen. When Delmar. . . ."

Blizzard held up his hand. "Officer Chee," he said. "Hey, now."

"Supper time," Mrs. Kanitewa said. "Just getting dark."

Blizzard was glaring at him. Chee swallowed the next question. The radio was on the end table beside his chair. He looked at the dial. Now it was tuned to KNDN. "Kay-Indun." The fifty thousand watt Farmington voice of the Big Rez. KNDN AM was all-Navajo, but the FM version was mostly English. The Kanitewa radio was tuned to FM.

"Sayesva had a telephone," Blizzard said. "At his office in Albuquerque and in his house here. The boy could have called him from school."

"He was bringing him something," Mrs. Kanitewa said.

Another surprise. "What?"

She shrugged. "He didn't tell me. Something for Mr. Sayesva. Not my business."

"Something he wouldn't tell his mother about?" Blizzard asked.

"Not my business."

"Didn't you ask? Weren't you curious?"

"Not my business."

"Did you see it?"

"I saw a package."

"What did it look like."

"Like a package," said Mrs. Kanitewa, whose expression suggested to Chee that what little patience she once had for police had worn thin. But she shrugged, and described it. "Sort of long." She held her hands about three feet apart. "Not big around. I thought maybe it was a poster or a picture or something like that. It was round, like one of those cardboard tubes people get to mail big pictures in."

"You didn't ask him what was in it?" Blizzard's tone made it clear that he knew she had asked him.

"No," she said. Her expression made it clear to Chee that she was surprised Blizzard would even think such a thing.

"Where's the package?"

"He took it with him. I didn't see it no more."

"Took it when he went to see Sayesva?"

She nodded.

"And he didn't bring it back?"

Another nod.

And that was about it. There were a few of details which Chee gingerly collected to keep Lieutenant Leaphorn happy. For example, the object was wrapped in a newspaper, but Mrs. Kanitewa didn't notice which one. For example, she had no idea where her son might be staying because he'd never done this before. For example, she asked them to promise to let her know as soon as soon as they found the boy. She didn't have a telephone but they could call the Senas just three houses down.

Blizzard drove directly back to the access road and headed the patrol car back toward the highway.

"You think we ought to go to Sayesva's place?" Chee

suggested. "See if we can find whatever it was the kid brought for him?"

Blizzard steered around the worst of the bumps. "Tell me how that helps you find the kid," he said, staring straight ahead. "It won't, so I'll take care of finding the package."

Chee considered that answer.

"But not now?"

"Later," Blizzard said.

"When I'm not around?"

"Like you explained to me. Sayesva's not Navajo Police business. It wouldn't be nice to get you in trouble with your lieutenant."

Chee let it ride. Leaphorn would ask him what was in the package and he would tell the Lieutenant why he didn't know, and about Blizzard. Maybe that would spare him working with Blizzard in the future.

"Wonder why the lady wouldn't tell us what the kid brought home?" Blizzard asked. The tone, for Blizzard, was friendly. "Did that strike you as funny?"

"No," Chee said. "She didn't tell us because she didn't know."

Blizzard gave him a sideways glance. "Man, what are you talking about? You don't know women, if you say that. Or you don't know Mamas."

Chee said, "Well . . . " and then dropped it. Why try to instruct this knucklehead in the Pueblo culture. The patrol car rattled off the gravel road, onto the asphalt toward Albuquerque. Chee let his imagination wander. He saw himself scouting for the Seventh Cavalry, shooting Cheyennes. The satisfaction in that fantasy lasted a few miles. He rehearsed his report to Leaphorn. He thought about Janet Pete. He thought about how the tip of her short-cut hair curled against her neck. He thought about the funny way she had of letting a smile start, letting him get a glimpse of it, and then suppressing it—pretending she hadn't appreciated his humor. He thought about her legs and hips in those tight jeans on the ladder above him at the Tano ceremonial. He thought about her kissing him, enthusiastically, and then catching his hand when . . .

"Why do you say she didn't know?" Blizzard asked, frowning at the windshield. "You know these people better than I do. I'm a city boy. My daddy worked for the post office in Chicago. I don't know a damn thing about this kind of Indians."

"There's a lot I don't know, too," Chee said. "Haven't been around Tanos much."

"Come on." Blizzard was grinning at him. "I been here just two months. I need help."

So do I, Chee thought, and you've been a pain in the butt. But, brother cop, brother Indian.

Well," Chee said. "In most pueblos Delmar would be old enough to be initiated. He'd belong to one of the religious fraternities and he'd have religious duties. The way I understand it, you keep the secrets of your fraternity—your kiva—because just the people who have to know these secrets to perform their duties are supposed to know them. If uninitiated people know them, it dilutes the power. Waters it down. So I guess Delmar was probably a member of Sayesva's kiva. And whatever he brought his uncle was in some way religious. His mother wouldn't ask about it because you just don't ask about such things. And he wouldn't tell her if she did ask. And if he had told her, she damn sure wouldn't tell us."

"Interesting," Blizzard said. "Is it that way with you Navajos."

"No," Chee said. "Our religion is family business. Traditionally the more who show up at a curing ceremonial and take part the better. Except for some of the clans that live next to Pueblo tribes. Some of them picked up the Pueblo idea."

But even as he said it, he knew it wasn't totally true.

The *hataali* kept their secrets. He had been a student of Frank Sam Nakai since his middle teens, but he knew that Nakai—his uncle, his "little father"—still withheld something from him. That, too, was traditional. The *hataali* didn't reveal the final secret of the ceremonial he was teaching until–. Until what? Chee had never been quite sure of that. Probably until the *hataali* knew the student was worthy.

"Interesting," Blizzard said, and starting telling Chee something about the Cheyenne religion. It was something to do with how–a long, long time ago, a delegation of Comanches had come north and brought a string of horses with them as gifts to the Cheyenne. But the Comanches had told the Cheyennes that if they accepted the horses, they would have to change their religion because the horses would totally change their lives. Blizzard was saying something about following the migrating buffalos. But Chee had stopped listening. It occurred to him just then that he was going to marry Janet Pete. Or try to marry her. And he was thinking about that.

4

LEAPHORN AND DAVID W. STREIB took the short way
from Window Rock to Crownpoint, following old Navajo
Route Nine past the Nazhoni Trading Post, Coyote Wash,
and Standing Rock and crossing that invisible line that
separated the Big Rez from the Checkerboard. Special
Agent Streib worked out of the Farmington office of the
Federal Bureau of Investigation. Since the wrongful death
of Eric Dorsey was clearly a felony committed on a federal
reservation and therefore a federal offense he was
responsible for the investigation. But that didn't make it
particularly interesting to him. Streib could be described
as a Bureau old timer. He should have been in an assignment much loftier than a tiny office in Northwestern New
Mexico from which he dealt mostly with Indian reservation business. But the whimsical sense of humor which
had earned Streib his nickname of Dilly had not earned
him the confidence of those selected by J.Edgar Hoover to
run his F.B.I. And while Hoover was now long gone,

43

Hoover's reign had lasted longer than Streib's ambitions. Special Agent Streib had evolved into a laid-back, contented man with lots of friends in Indian Country.

One of them was Joe Leaphorn, which was fortunate on this day because even the short way from Window Rock to Crownpoint involved some eighty miles of mostly empty road. Plenty of time for conversation. They covered Streib's plans for building a greenhouse behind his home when he retired from the Bureau.

They rehashed cases they had worked together, skirted around the sensitive subject of what Leaphorn intended to do with his accumulated leave time, and covered an assortment of gossip about the small world of Indian Country law enforcement. Just as they passed the turnoff to the Nahodshosh Chapter House, they got to the question of why anyone would want to kill a Saint Bonaventure Mission School arts and crafts teacher. Theft was clearly the number one choice, since some silver ingots and other materials seemed to be missing from Dorsey's shop. Trouble over a girl friend made number two as the motive. Trouble with a student made number three. No number four suggested itself.

Finally, Streib brought up the sensitive subject.

"You going with the professor?"

Leaphorn was sure he didn't want to open this subject to discussion. Not even with Dilly.

"Where? What do you mean?"

"To China with that Professor from Northern Arizona University, goddamit," Streib said. "Bourbonnette the name. I heard that's the plan. What are you being so goddam coy about?"

Leaphorn had never, ever discussed going to China with Bourbonnette with Dilly or with anyone else that he could think of. It wasn't the sort of thing he would discuss. But it didn't occur to him to be surprised that Dilly knew. In empty country everybody knew everything about everybody. One's inner thoughts seem to transmit themselves through the clear dry air without need for verbalizing.

"Yeah," Leaphorn said. "That's the plan."

"That's what I heard." Streib said.

Leaphorn looked at his watch, a $13.99 Casio digital. He pushed the proper buttons and adjusted the seconds.

"I checked it when they gave the time on the radio," he said. "It's a little slow. Or maybe the radio is a little fast. Probably it was exactly right. Makes you wonder why anyone would pay a hundred bucks for a watch. Or one of those five thousand dollar jobs."

Streib ignored this signal to change the subject.

"That's a hell of a long ways to go," Streib said. "All the way to China. If you got something going with the lady, why not just stay here. Nobody would care. You're a widower. I think she's single. That's what I heard."

"I always wanted to go to China."

"Yeah," Streib said. "Really. I'll bet you did."

The skepticism provoked Leaphorn. "I used to talk about it with Emma," he said, irritated with himself for explaining this to Streib. "But she didn't like to travel. She went to New York with me once. And once to Washington. But it was really just to keep me company. It made her nervous, being away from the reservation. Even when we just went to Albuquerque. Or Phoenix, she'd be anxious to get home."

"I heard the lady was doing a research project in China. Quite a coincidence." The tone remained skeptical. "Good thing she wasn't doing research on Antarctica or you'd be telling me of your lifelong fascination with penguins."

"Back when I was a grad student at Arizona State I got interested," Leaphorn said. "We had an anthro professor who was into linguistics. The evolution of languages, that sort of thing. He'd ask me how my grandfather said

45

things, and my relatives. And he'd show me the charts he'd accumulated about the Athabascan languages up and down the Pacific Coast, Canada, Alaska and across the straits among some of the Siberian tribes. It got me interested."

Leaphorn looked up, made a depreciative gesture. "You know," he said. "Where's my homeland? Where'd the Dineh come from? Where are my roots."

"You Navajos came up from the underworld," Streib said. "Up from the fourth world into the fifth world. Through a hollow reed, wasn't it?"

"Flooded out, just like you belagaani." Leaphorn said. "You guys made yourself an ark out of gopher wood. Hauled out the animals. We had to climb through a hole in the ceiling and the animals had to climb out, too."

"I guess my ancestors—the German ones—came out of Alsace. That part that switches back to France depending on who won the last war. But I never much wanted to go see it."

Streib uncapped his thermos, poured coffee into cup marked AUSTIN SAM FOR TRIBAL COUNCIL, NEW LANDS CHAPTER, and handed it to Leaphorn. He poured coffee into the thermos cap for himself. "Maybe if I had a good looking woman as a travelling companion I'd find Alsace more interesting."

Leaphorn let it pass. Sipped coffee.

Streib grinned at him. "Admit it." he said. "Knock off the bullshit about tracking down your roots. I've met the prof a couple of times. At cultural doings there at the University. She's a nice looking woman."

Leaphorn finished his coffee slowly.

"Don't tell me you hadn't noticed," Streib said.

"See if you can pour me some more coffee," Leaphorn said, passing the cup. "Without talking."

"I'm not knocking it," Streib said. "I think its a good idea. Why not? You've been alone now for too damn long.

It's making you cranky. The old testosterone must still be working. Young man like you. You better find yourself a permanent lady or you'll be hanging around the squaw dances and getting yourself into trouble."

Leaphorn thought: A year and eight months and eleven days since the nurse had awakened him in the chair in Emma's room. She slipped away, the nurse had said. Emma had died while both of them were sleeping. Six hundred and twenty two days. A lot longer if you counted the days before the operation, the days when the tumor had pressed against Emma's brain and cost her ability to think clearly. It had robbed her of her memory, her happiness, her humor, and her personality, and even—on some terrible days—of her knowledge of who she was, and who he was. He remembered those nights when she would awaken beside him confused and terrified. When . . .

"Change the subject," Leaphorn said, and Streib instantly detected the anger in his voice.

That took them back to the killing of Eric Dorsey, routine as it seemed. A bit odd, perhaps, with no motive apparent immediately, and no promising suspects. But such things took time to develop and the case was less than a week old.

"One oddity though," Leaphorn said. He told Streib about Delmar Kanitewa running away the day Dorsey was killed, the bludgeon murder of his uncle, and the koshare effigy in Dorsey's shop.

"So," Streib said. "What's the connection?"

"Sounds unlikely," Leaphorn said. "But maybe."

"Or maybe not," Dilly said. "Maybe the kid just happened to take off the same day."

"And the boy's uncle being killed there at Tano. How about that?"

"I know you don't believe in coincidences," Streib said. "But they do happen. For example, you and the lady both wanting to go take a look at China. And this looks like another one. Unless you can see some possible link."

"I can't," Leaphorn said. "But I'd like it better if we had a suspect in custody."

Which, as it happened, they did.

5

"HIS NAME'S Eugene Ahkeah," said Lieutenant Toddy. "The family lives out toward Coyote Canyon but he's got a place in Thoreau. He works out at the Saint Bonaventure Mission. Sort of a handyman job."

The Lieutenant had spread an array of items on his desktop. "When he's sober," he added. He handed Strieb an inventory sheet.

Strieb glanced at it and passed it to Leaphorn.

1. Cardboard grocery carton in which the following items were found:

2. Plastic bread wrapper containing two ingots of silver.

3. Plastic grocery bag containing following items:

    a. Sandcast silver bracelet

    b. Sandcast silver concha belt

    c. Hammered silver ornamental pin

    d. seven silver belt buckles

    e. four ingots of silver.

4. Ballpeen hammer with blood stains on hammer head and on handle.

Leaphorn looked from the list at the array on the table, making an unnecessary check of the inventory, Unneeded but not useless. It kept him from thinking his dreary thoughts. About the wages of avarice. About, almost certainly, the bloody cost of alcohol. Among The People, whose hunger was rarely for money. It was for oblivion bought by the bottle.

"Did You sent a blood sample off to the lab?" Streib was asking.

"It's ready to go," Toddy said. "We just found this stuff this morning."

"It was under his house?" Strieb asked. "That what you said?"

"Actually, it's a mobile home."

"Did you get a search warrant?"

Lieutenant Toddy gave Leaphorn an uneasy sidelong glance.

"We told him we gotten this call. A man called— wouldn't give his name—and reported some things taken from Dorsey's shop were under Ahkeah's place We told him we'd get a search warrant if he wanted us to," Toddy said. " And he said there wasn't anything under there. And I told him we'd have to find out for ourselves, one way of the other, and he said, 'Well, let's go see, then.' And he came out and pulled away the plywood he had there to keep the animals out, and there was the box. In plain view. Just pushed back in there."

Lieutenant Toddy paused, wrinkled his forehead at the weirdness of human behavior, shook his head.

"He pulled the box out himself," Toddy added.

"How did he act then?" Leaphorn asked.

"What'd he say? Any explanation?

Toddy shrugged. "He acted like he'd been drinking. He said how'd that get under there?"

"Was he drunk?"

"About two thirds. Maybe four fifths."

"Any idea at all who the was call from? Did Ahkeah have any idea?"

"The dispatcher took it," Toddy said. "A man. He wouldn't give a name. She said he sounded like an Anglo. And Ahkeah. He acted like he didn't have any idea."

"I'll handle the blood sample," Streib said. "Get it to the lab for you. Did you get a statement from Ahkean?"

"He said he didn't know anything about it." Toddy extracted a clip board from his In basket and handed it to Toddy. "He said Dorsey was a friend of his. That he didn't kill him."

Streib read, lips pursed. He handed the clipboard to Leaphorn. It was a brief statement and Toddy had summarized it well. He'd only left out that Ahkeah wasn't going to talk to anyone anymore until he got a lawyer. Everybody was watching television these days. Doing it like the did it on TV.

"Did he call a lawyer?" Leaphorn asked.

"He said he didn't have any money so we called D.N.A. for him. He said they were going to send somebody out from Window Rock."

Leaphorn felt one of those uneasy premonitions, The supply of legal aid people at Window Rock was small. Those competent to defend criminal cases even smaller.

"Did they say who they're sending."

"That woman," Toddy said. "Janet Pete."

"Oh, shit," Leaphorn said.

Streib noticed the tone.

"She's trouble?"

"She's the lady friend of my new assistant," Leaphorn said. "At least I think he wants her to be. That's what I hear."

"That could be trouble," Streib said.

"Yes, indeed."

51

Back in the lockup section, they found Ahkeah doz-
ing on his bunk under the window. He was slightly overweight and slightly gone-to-seed. Leaphorn guessed his
age in the late forties. He sat up clumsily into the sunlight,
facing them first with the apologetic confusion of one
emerging from alcoholic sleep, and then with the defiant,
tense look of a worried man. Seeing him now in the bright
sunlight, Leaphorn reconsidered his judgement of
Ahkeah's age. Maybe early thirties, with fifteen years of
subtracted from his prime by whisky.

"I don't want to talk to you," Ahkeah said.

"You don't have to if you don't want to," Streib told
him. "We just wondered how that silver, and jewelry, and
all that other stuff got under your place. If you could help
us with that maybe we could get you out of here."

"I got a lawyer coming," Ahkeah said. "Talk to the
lawyer."

"You don't have to talk to us if you don't want. It just
saves everybody some time. Maybe it would fix it so you
could go on home."

"Or maybe not," Ahkeah said. "I just tell you one
thing, though." He wiped his hand across his face and
then stared directly into Streib's eyes. "There's no way I'd
ever hurt Eric. He was a friend to me. There's no goddam
way I'd ever hurt him," he said, and his voice was shaking
as he said it. Then Eugene Ahkeah slumped back on his
bunk, turned to the wall and put his pillow over his head.

The twenty seven twisting miles up and over Borrego Pass
to Thoreau gave them time to talk about Ahkeah.

"He'd be pretty dumb to do it that way, or pretty
drunk," Streib said.

"You know," Leaphorn said. "If I had just one single
wish what I think it would be. It would be get rid of booze.
No more beer. No more wine. No more bourbon, or
Scotch, or any other damn thing that causes a man to hit

his friend on the head with a hammer."

"You think he did it?" Streib's sideways glance showed surprise. "That anonymous telephone tip. I'll bet that makes you uneasy?"

"It makes me uneasy some. But that little speech me made there at the end was sort of like a confession."

Streib looked surprised again. "You mean, where he was telling us he'd never hurt Dorsey?"

Leaphorn sighed. "Sounded to me like a drunk trying to convince himself that it all a bad dream."

The acting assistant director of Saint Bonaventure Indian Mission was named Montoya but she was clearly a Pueblo Indian and she looked to Leaphorn like a Zuni. She said she didn't know for sure why all that silver hadn't been reported missing from the craft shop inventory but she said she could make an educated guess.

"I'll bet it was because Eric didn't put it down in the first place."

"Why not?" Streib asked.

"Because he was always buying stuff out of his own money. Buying stuff we couldn't afford. Tools. Turquoise. Special fancy woods. " She shrugged. "Everything. Eric wasn't very practical."

"So he didn't log it in when it was delivered. Is that what you mean?"

The conversation was getting more specific than the acting assistant director enjoyed. She looked slightly flustered.

"You should be asking Father Haines. He'll be back next Tuesday."

"We'll ask him," Streib said. "We just wanted to hurry things along a little. How about the jewelry. The concha belt. The bracelet?"

"I saw something about the belt here on the desk," she said, and fished a piece of salmon-colored note paper out of the in basket and read from it. "'Tom Tso wants to pick up the concha belt he was finishing in Eric's class. How does he get it? And some other students want to get their projects. Let me know what to tell them.' That's from Mister Denny. He helps Eric with driving the school buses." She made an odd face, and Leaphorn guessed it was to keep from crying. "Helped, Eric, I meant. No more Eric now."

"Mrs. Montoya," Streib said. "I want to ask you to get us a list of everything students had in that craft shop that's missing now. We particularly wanted to know who was making one of the kachina dolls in there. The koshare. And then could you shed any light on a sort of funny-looking wood and cloth contraption we found on Dorsey's shelf. Looked like it might have been a hand-puppet." Streib demonstrated with his own hand. "It looked like a duck."

But Mrs. Montoya was focused on the koshare doll. "Oh that koshare," she said. "That's my son doing that one." she said. The thought startled her. "Why you want to know about that."

Streib glanced at Leaphorn. "See," he said. "It's a class project?"

"Mr. Dorsey always wanted them to make something they thought they could sell. Allen thought he could see one of those. Why?"

"We thought it might be significant," Leaphorn said. "But it probably isn't if it's a student project. Do you know about the hand puppet duck?" He gave Streib a glance. Dilly hadn't told him about this duck.

Mrs. Montoya seemed relieved. She laughed. "Mr. Dorsey was our school comedian," she said. "When the kids put on programs they'd get him to be the master of ceremonies. He was a ventriloquist. He wasn't very good at it, but the children thought he was great."

"A funny man, then?" Streib said.

"He was our school clown," she said, looking sad at the thought. "He could always make other people laugh, but I don't think he laughed much himself."

This aroused Streib's interest. "Why not?"

"I don't know," she said. "Maybe Father Haines would know. Maybe he was lonely." She made a wry face and changed the subject. "I'll be glad to get that information for you," and while she was writing a reminder on her note pad, she added: "Eric Dorsey was a good man." She looked up, at Streib and then at Leaphorn, as if challenging them to deny it. "A kind man. And gentle. And talented, too."

"The students liked him?" Leaphorn asked.

She nodded. "Everybody liked him. He wasn't a Catholic you know, but I think he was a saint. Everybody loved him."

"Not quite everybody," Streib said. "Do you have any idea who didn't?"

"I really don't," she said. "And I've thought about it, and thought about it, but I just don't." She tapped the list Lieutenant Toddy had given them with a plump finger. "I thought you thought somebody killed him to steal this stuff."

"Maybe that was it," Leaphorn said. "But we used to think maybe he was killed over a woman."

"Well," Mrs Montoya said. "It wouldn't be that."

"You sound sure of that," Leaphorn said.

Mrs. Montoya looked flustered.

"Could you tell us something that might bear on who killed Eric Dorsey?" Streib asked. "If you can, it's your duty to tell us."

"I talk too much," Mrs. Montoya said. "I gossip. I shouldn't gossip about the dead."

"My mother used to say the only thing gossip can't hurt is live sheep or dead people," Leaphorn said. "Maybe it would help us find who killed the man."

"You sounded awful sure no woman was involved. Is there some reason for that?" Streib asked.

"Well," Mrs. Montoya. She moved a letter from the out basket back into the in basket, and then reversed the process. She looked around the tiny, cluttered office, searching for something to guide her. "Well," she repeated, "I think maybe Mr. Dorsey was gay."

Dilly Streib, who had been looking only moderately interested, now looked extremely interested.

"Homosexual?"

She shrugged. "That what people thought."

"Was Eugene Ahkeah his boy friend?"

Mrs. Montoya looked shocked. "Of course not," she said.

"You sound like you know," Streib said.

"Well, Gene had a wife." She laughed. "Once, anyway. And maybe a couple of girl friends, too. I know Eugene wasn't gay."

Leaphorn became aware that he was tired. Streib had occupied the only visitor chair. Leaphorn leaned a hip against Mrs. Montoya's filing cabinet. It had been a long day. He was weary. He cleared his throat.

"Do you know if Mr. Dorsey had a boyfriend?"

'No. I don't think so. Not here, anyway. Maybe back where he came from."

Back where he came from, if the report Streib had showed him was correct, was Fort Worth, Texas. ERIC DORSEY, laboratory equipment maintenance technician, Texas Christian University, single, next of kin: Mr. and Mrs. Delbert Dorsey, Springfield, Illinois. Cause of death. Blow to base of the skull followed by blow to the left temple.

"Maybe you could help with something that puzzled me," Leaphorn said. "The investigating officer's report showed he had an envelope full of gasoline credit card receipts in his room. Several hundred gallons. All bought at the station here at Thoreau so he wasn't going very far. You have any ideas where he was going?"

Mrs. Montoya looked surprised. "No," she said. "He was usually around here. He has an old Chevy but . . . " A sudden thought interrupted the sentence. "Oh," she said. "You know what I'll bet. I'll bet he paid for the gas for the water truck. He drove that on weekends. That's when we did the deliveries. That would be just like him. Father Haines would know."

"Water truck?" Streib asked.

"He taught during the weekdays, and drove the bus. But on weekends and some evenings he drove the water truck. Took water and food out to the hogans. Hard to get water a lot of places out here so people haul it in. But people get old, or they get sick, or their pickup breaks down and they don't have any way."

"That sure made for a long work week," Streib said.

Mrs. Montoya thought she detected skepticism. Her smile went away.

"Yes," she said. "You don't leave your job and come out here and live in an old mobile home for that three hundred dollars a month Father pays you if you don't want to work.

"Is that what Dorsey was making? " Leaphorn asked. " Three hundred a month?"

"And he brought his own truck. And you have to pay for your own food out of it, of course." She stared at Streib. "And he paid for the gas, too, I guess. Out of his own pocket."

"Sounds like a rich guy," Streib said. "You know anything about his family."

"I don't think he was rich. He told me once that his dad had retired from the fire department."

"Couple more questions," Streib said. "The first one is why do you think he was homosexual if he didn't have any boy friends.

"I think he told Father Haines he was," she said. "Ask Father."

Streib frowned. "I want to come back to that, but the second question is why don't you think he had a boy friend?"

Mrs. Montoya shrugged her plump shoulders. "How big is Thoreau?" she asked. "If anybody has a boyfriend on Tuesday, or a girl friend, or anything else, then everybody knows it by Wednesday."

Streib nodded. "If Father Haines knew, wouldn't he have a problem having a homosexual teaching these kids."

Mrs. Montoya's expression, which had shifted from friendly to bleak a few moments earlier, now turned wintry.

"I can't speak for the Father," she said. "But I know him pretty well. I'd say he'd have exactly the same problem with a gay fooling around with the students as he'd have with a heterosexual fooling with the students. He keeps an eye on that sort of thing."

"It wasn't happening?" Streib asked.

"It was not," she said.

Back in the car, Streib summed up their progress for the day. "Nothing," he said. "Nada. Except maybe we can rule out an indignant husband. We seem to be dealing here with a man beloved by all—the wrongful death of a chaste and saintly homosexual clown."

Leaphorn didn't comment on that. He was thinking that Francis Sayesva, in his role as a koshare for his people, was also a sacred clown.

6

JANET WAS WEARING a blue skirt, a white shirt which looked to Jim Chee's unpracticed eye like some sort of silk, and a little jacket which matched the skirt. The total effect was to make Miss Pete look chic, sophisticated and beautiful. All of this caused in Chee strong but ambiguous feelings—on one hand a soaring joy at the beauty of this young woman and on the other a leaden sense of doubt that she would ever, ever, ever settle for him. She slid into the booth with the autumn sunlight reflecting through glossy black hair.

"Sorry I'm late," she said, dazzling him with a rueful smile. She looked at her watch. So did Chee. It looked expensive. A gift, he guessed, from the lawyer she had worked with in Washington. And lived with and, presumably, had loved. Being the token redskin, as she had told him herself, in the Washington, D.C. firm of Dolman, MacArthur, White and Hertzog.

"Eight minutes late," she said. "In Washington, I could

blame it on the traffic. In Window Rock, no traffic to blame it on so that won't work."

"Eight minutes you don't mention," Chee said. "You have to be a lot later than that to claim you're working on Navajo Time." He noticed that his voice sounded perfectly natural.

"I have an excuse, though. The phone rang just as I was leaving. It was Roger Applelbee. He's staying at the Inn here. You remember me telling you about him."

"Sure," Chee said. "The Nature First guy. I'd like to talk to him. We got a glimpse of him there at Tano. What's he doing in Window Rock."

"What everybody's doing in Window Rock," she said. "He's lobbying." She gestured around the room. The tables in the coffee shop of the Navajo Nation Inn were crowded with Navajos in their best boots and silver and with white men in dark business suits. "When the tribal council's in session it draws the lawyers like, like–." She searched for the proper simile.

"I'd say like a dead sheep draws crows," Chee said. "But since you're a lawyer yourself, I guess I won't."

"How about like honey draws bears," she said. "That sounds nicer. By the way, Roger told me he saw your letter in the Times. He liked it. He said he thought it was the best way to attack it."

Chee found himself reacting as he did too often to praise from Janet Pete. Embarrassment. "Did you do some of that when you worked in Washington? Lobby, I mean."

"Not much," Janet said. "One branch of the firm sort of specialized in representing tribes, and fights over tribal water rights. That sort of thing. All sorts of disagreements involving Indian affairs." She laughed. "Need I say we were on whatever side of the affair had the money to spend. But mostly I just did research and paperwork. They only sent me over to lobby for something when they

needed a real Indian to look good for a liberal Congress-
man."

"You would have looked good to me," Chee said. "I
like real Indian ladies."

She smiled at him. "I try to look good," she said. "How
do you like this new shirt?"

Chee inspected it, trying not to stare at the curve of
her breasts too obviously and to think of exactly the right
thing to say. He rejected two ideas as inappropriate, and
decided on "wonderful." But before he could say it, a big
voice just behind him said:

"Hey, Janet. I wondered if I'd run into you. Someone
said you'd come back out here."

"Hello, Ed," Janet said, in a carefully neutral voice.
"How are you?"

Ed was standing beside their table now, looking down
at them. "Just fine," he said. "Maybe getting a little old for
all this travelling. How about you, though? You're looking
good?"

"Jim," Janet said. "This is Ed Zeck. Ed Zeck, Jim
Chee. Ed's one of the associates in Dolman and so forth.
He runs the Santa Fe operation. He's sort of an expert on
Pueblo water rights, and lands claims and things like that.
That made him one of my multitude of bosses. And Mr.
Chee is an officer of the Navajo Tribal Police."

"Don't get up," Zeck said to Chee. He offered his
hand and Chee shook it. He was a big man, over six feet
tall, Chee guessed, and broad, with a round, friendly face
and a receding hairline. His eyes were blue, made to look
even lighter than they were by his dark, suntanned com-
plexion. Those eyes were now studying Chee, full of
thought. Chee's instant first impression was of power, self
confidence, and the easy going nature with which power
and self confidence seemed to endow some white men.

"I hope I'm not intruding here," Zeck said to Chee.
"But if you're arresting Janet, reading her rights before

you take her in, maybe I can get a job representing her."

"We're just talking," Chee said, wishing he had said something witty and hoping that Janet wouldn't invite this man to join them. It was nothing against Zeck. It was just that he didn't want Janet distracted.

"Jim Chee," Zeck said. "I seem to connect that name to a letter in the Navajo Times. Am I right? Same Jim Chee?"

"Same Chee."

Zeck's expression was less friendly. "I didn't realize the writer was a Tribal Policeman," Zeck said. "Wasn't that pretty political for a policeman?"

"We don't sign away our First Amendment rights," Chee said. He wasn't quite sure how to handle this so he laughed and said: "It was just another way to defend the people from the bad guys."

And then he sat there feeling foolish, conscious of how pompous that must have sounded.

"The bad guys in this case being Ed's client," Janet said. "Is that correct, Ed? Is the firm handling Continental Collectors these days?"

"That's us," Zeck said. "Working as always to bring a little economic development where it's needed."

"Are you staying at the Navajo Inn?" Janet asked, obviously eager to change the subject. "I'd like to call you and catch up on old times. What's the Conventional Wisdom on the Hill. Who is double-crossing whom in the regime of Bill Clinton. All the gossip."

"Wonderful," Zeck said. "Even though all the gossip doesn't leak down to Santa Fe." He fished his room key from his pocket, inspected it. "Two seventeen," he said. "I'm having dinner with a couple of council members tonight, but I'll be in after that."

"What else are you pushing with the tribe?" Janet said. "Does the firm still represent Peabody Coal?"

"We lost 'em," Zeck said. "I'm here this time solely as

counsel for Continental Collections Corporation. They're lining up the paperwork to use an old strip mine over in New Mexico as a waste disposal site. Hire a hundred or so local folks at about eighteen dollars an hour to handle the machinery. Cause a big reduction in the unemployment rate. Put a big influx of property tax money into the school funds. Take a big bite out of the unemployment rate. And, as if fills up in about a hundred years, get that old hole in the ground reclaimed under a thick layer of topsoil so grass will grow on it. Mr. Chee here can tell you all about it."

"Yes," Janet said. "It sounds great if you like a garbage landfill in your backyard."

"You know anything that could be helpful?" Zeck asked. He glanced down at Chee and then back at Janet. "I think we might need a legal consultant here."

"I'm working for the Navajo Nation," Janet said. "I'm not for—." She paused, picking the word. "—for hire," she concluded.

"It would be a great way to represent the tribe," Zeck said. "I know it's mostly on Tano land, not on the Reservation, but the the rail spurs cross some Checkerboard land so it'd be worth something to have the council for it."

"I've heard it would be toxic waste dump," Chee said. "Chemicals. Maybe radioactive stuff. Why don't you store it there at Santa Fe. Or in Connecticut. Or Maryland. Someplace near your own back yard?"

Zeck smiled down at him. "I bet you know the answer to that. It would cost too much money. They don't have a big, empty open pit mine back there in Connecticut with the roads and railroad tracks already built."

"And non-union labor," Janet said.

Zeck transferred his smile to her. "That, too," he said. "Labor is cheaper out here. I'll bet you've noticed that yourself."

"I took a pay cut," she said. "But it costs a person less

to live out here. Cost less than Washington I mean. And I'm not talking about money."

Zeck's smile widened. "Janet," he said, "you haven't lost your sting, have you? But have you become a tree hugger? Or, as we call them in dilettante Santa Fe, a fern fondler?"

She didn't answer because another voice from behind Chee was saying. "Ah ha, Miss Pete. I have caught you consorting with the enemy."

"Here comes the man from Nature First," Zeck said. "Hello, Roger. How are you?"

"Fine," the man said. "How about you?"

"I think Janet and I are both losing it. We're arguing, and we're both lawyers, and lawyers don't argue without getting paid for it. With that I have to leave you."

So did the man from Nature First. "I'll be right back," he said to Janet. "I want to tell the waitress not to hold that table for me."

Zeck looked after him, then down at Janet: "Well," he said, "I think you already have a luncheon conference. Or is it a consultancy?" He chuckled. "I'll see you later."

"He's not joining us, is he?" Chee asked. "That second guy?"

"That's Applebee. I guess he's out here working the other side—trying to stop the waste dump. You said you'd like to talk to him," Janet said. "Here's your chance. He wanted to see me, so I asked him to join us."

"Oh." He'd intended it to sound neutral, but it came out disappointed.

Janet looked up at him. "I guess I could have gotten out of it. I could still meet him later. But he'll want to talk about the waste dump and you're interested in that. Or I thought you were."

"That's OK," Chee said. "Sure I am."

"Did you want to talk to me privately? You know. Not just for a chat?"

Chee managed a grin. "Always," he said. "I want your undivided attention. Just you and me. We just shut out the world."

She grinned back at him. "Getting romantic? You must be running out of girl friends. Or is it just the season. That time of year?"

"You're thinking of Spring," Chee said. "This is autumn. That's the time to be serious."

Janet's small grin developed into a laugh. Clearly she didn't think Chee was serious. "So, go ahead," she said. "Be serious. And with this buildup, it better be good."

Chee, who had sipped two thirds of his coffee while waiting, finished the rest of it. *What did he want to say? Come live with me and be my love, he'd say. I think of you when I'm trying to go to sleep. I think of you when I awake. I dream of you. I—*And thinking of nothing appropriate to say, he just looked at her.

"Go ahead," she said. "I know what you're after. You want to pump me about Eugene Ahkeah."

"No I don't," Chee said.

"Yes you do. Any time I'm representing anyone in a case you're involved with, you always push me right to the edge of violating professional ethics."

"I don't care anything about Ahkeah," Chee insisted. "I've never seen him. Never talked to him. Don't have anything to do with that. That's Lieutenant Leaphorn's baby."

"You work for Leaphorn."

"Okay," Chee said. "If you insist, what should I ask you about Ahkeah?"

"He didn't do it."

"Well, that's a relief," Chee said. "I'll tell the Lieutenant to turn him loose."

Janet looked surprised. "Really," she said. "You don't want to ask me about Ahkeah."

"I want to ask you to go to Gallup with me. Have dinner. Go to a movie. So forth. How about it?"

65

Now she looked skeptical. "You could have asked me that on the telephone."

"What would you have said?"

But Janet was looking past his shoulder. "Here he comes," she said. And Roger Applebee was at their booth, smiling and nodding.

He was not quite as young as he looked at first glance, perhaps fifty five or so, small, slender, blond hair worn long, and in the proper garb for an autumn morning in Window Rock, Arizona, the desert West. His boots had been polished a few days ago, his jeans were faded, his bolo tie was loose and decorated with a silver bear claw and his pale blue shirt hung open the standard two buttons. Taken all together, Applebee was a handsome man. He looked totally healthy. Outdoorsy, Chee thought. But shining through the good looks was a fierce intensity which made short work of the usual small talk. Applebee was the sort who got to the heart of the matter. And the first matter was Jim Chee.

"I liked your letter," he said. "The one in the newspaper the other day." And while he was saying it, he was looking past Chee at Janet Pete, expression quizzical, asking the wordless question. Can this man be trusted to hear what we say? Will he be discrete?

"Mr. Chee is with the Navajo Tribal Police," she said, motioning Applebee into the booth. "As you know, he doesn't like seeing our part of the world made a dumping ground any better than we do. And he is used to listening, and keeping what he hears to himself."

That produced from Applebee a smile. "Is he assigned to this business?"

"No," Chee said. "No. Just interested."

The Applebee smile disappeared. "Well," he said, and hesitated, caught his lip between his teeth, released it, exhaled. "I'll give you a rundown first. The bad, and then the good. From what we hear in Washington, everything is go in the Interior Department. Continental has its well-placed buddies and your friend Zeck went back there last week to join in the lobbying. We're told that the Bureau of Land Management has agreed to withdraw the acreage they hold from grazing—with a payoff to the lease holders of course. That's bad, but it's what we expected. That leaves the Navajo Nation and Tano."

He paused, acknowledged the waitress standing beside him, and ordered a hamburger.

"Coffee?"

"What kind of tea do you have?"

The waitress was a plump Navajo teenager from Two Grey Hills who often waited on Chee since his transfer to Window Rock. She raised her eyebrows, puzzled. "Iced," she said. "Iced tea."

"No. No. I mean what kind of herb tea. Do you have Lemon Zinger? Almond Sunset. Or any of those Celestial flavors? And hot tea. Just bring me a cup of hot water and the tea bag." Applebee looked back at Janet. "We also think we have some hope in Tano. Governor Penitewa is still favoring the idea as far as we can tell but they have their election coming up in January and a lot of people in that Pueblo don't want that dump on pueblo land. The Governor can be beaten. There's way we can beat him."

Applebee paused. The waitress was still standing there, looking indecisive. "Just bring me a cup, and a pot of hot water and any tea bag you can find in the kitchen," he said.

"How about here?" Chee asked. "Will the tribal council approve moving that toxic stuff across our land?"

"Not so good, here, by the looks of it," Applebee said.

Councilman Chester is working hard for the dump. We're worried about that."

Chee was watching Janet. She said nothing, which pleased him. That was properly polite Navajo. Like Blizzard, she was an urban product. City bred, city raised,

Navajo only by her father's blood. She had to learn what it was like to be one of The Dineh. He would help teach her. Happily. Lovingly. If she would let him.

Applebee decided he wasn't getting the expected sounds of support and approval. "Well," he said, "Let's talk about Mr. Chester." He looked at Chee. "Do you know him?"

"From Horse Mesa Chapter?" Chee asked. "Jimmy Chester? I know him a little."

"What do you think of him?"

Chee shrugged. "I'm a policeman," he said. "We don't have opinions about politicians."

"How about your aunt?" Janet asked. "The councilwoman."

"She's a former councilwoman now," Chee corrected. "It's allowed to have opinions about kinfolks."

"I just didn't want to say the wrong thing if Chester was a friend. Or something." Applebee said.

"Nope," Chee said. "I can say I know he's a big operator in the cattle business out in the Checkerboard. And the people I know when I was working out of Crownpoint thought Chester was a jerk."

Applebee seemed relieved to hear this.

"Well," he began, voice lowered, "We hear ... " He stopped, waited silently while the waitress deposited cup, saucer, tea bag a large coffee thermos from which steam was rising, and a slice of lemon. He read the label on the tea bag, frowned, and made tea. "We hear that Councilman Chester is a consultant for Continental."

He looked at Janet and then at Chee. Clearly this was the reason for this meeting, the message to be delivered. It seemed to Chee more of a firecracker than a bombshell. But Applebee was checking their faces, looking for reaction. "Taking money," he explained.

"It's probably legal enough," Janet said. "But it can be bad politics and he's up for reelection in the spring."

Applebee looked surprised. "Really. You think it's legal?"

"I'd have to check the tribal code. It prohibits council members from voting on anything in which they have a personal financial interest. I doubt if it goes beyond that, but I'll check."

Applebee looked disappointed. "So it would just mean Chester couldn't vote on the dump issue. I was hoping we could put the son-of-a-bitch in jail."

"You have some evidence?" Janet asked. "Do you know how much they're paying him? Any details? He'll be trying to get the Horse Mesa chapter to pass a resolution backing the dump. The Tribal Council usually goes along with whatever the local chapters want in their own district. And if the people out at Horse Mesa know he's being paid to sell them on the dump–. Well, it makes them suspicious."

"I don't have anything on paper," Applebee said. He gestured disappointment with his hands. "Nothing you'd call concrete evidence."

"Nothing he can't deny?" Janet asked. "What's your source of information?"

Applebee examined his tea cup and ignored both questions. "I think I can get something," he said. He sipped, thoughtful.

Something?" Janet asked.

Applebee smiled. "Something useful," he said. "I think I know how I can get something he can't deny."

7

THE WAITER IN THE Dowager Empress had long since abandoned hope of freeing his best table for another set of diners. He was outside the kitchen door, leaning on the wall, sneaking a smoke and enjoying Flagstaff's cold autumn air and the dazzle of stars overhead. At the table inside, Joe Leaphorn and Professor Louisa Bourbonnette sat side-by-side. The assorted dishes of Chinese food on which they had dined were gone, replaced by a clutter of maps.

"How about this," Bourbonnette was saying. "We take the American flight to Hong Kong, transfer to Air China to Shanghai. I want to do some work in the library there. About two days, maybe. Or three. You could either do the tourist thing, sort of get used to China, and Chinese food and their way of doing things, or you could take a flight on up to Beijing and see what you could find out about contacts in Outer Mongolia. And I could join you because I have some stuff I want to get copies of there. Now these

Chinese airline schedules are from when I was there three years old but it looks like . . . "

Leaphorn found himself only half listening to Bourbonnette's recitation of flight schedules to places which sounded totally unreal. He was looking at the top of her head, bent over the schedules. He was thinking that the hair was gray but looked alive. Clean and healthy. (Emma's hair to the very end remained a glossy black.) He was thinking Louisa needs to get her bifocal prescription changed. She is bending too low over the maps. Emma always balked at getting her eyes examined. He was thinking of how being alone in the interior China held no terrors for him. It would be strange. Speaking not a word of Chinese would be a problem. But it would be exciting. Louisa had said arranging an interpreter would be no problem. Easy but expensive. So what? What did he have to spend his savings on?

Professor Bourbonnette looked up at him and smiled. "That sound all right? We can always change it."

"Sounds fine," Leaphorn said, thinking *Dilly Streib was right. She is a lovely lady.*

Thinking of what Dilly had implied about sex with her. Thinking of all the things she was doing for him—taking him along as dead weight on this trip. What did he owe her for that? What would she expect?

The waiter appeared at Leaphorn's shoulder, smelling of cigarette smoke. "Anything else I can get you? Refill on the coffee?"

"Not for me," Leaphorn said. "Louisa?"

Professor Bourbonnette gathered up her maps. "I think we'd better go," she said. "If you're driving back tonight. Do you have to?"

"I have a lot of work to do," Leaphorn said. Actually, he didn't intend to go home. He'd spent four hour on the highway this afternoon. That was enough. He was tired. There was a Motel Six on the way out that always had a vacancy once the tourist rush was over.

"I have a guest room," Bourbonnette said. She laughed. "Or something I call a guest room. Anyway, you're welcome to use it. You're tired. That's almost two hundred miles from here to Window Rock."

"Two hundred and eighteen," Leaphorn said.

She was studying his expression. Her own was whimsical. "I guess—," she began, then shook her head. "Think how badly I'll feel if you go to sleep on the interstate and run into somebody and kill yourself."

"I could get a motel room," Leaphorn said. "I don't want to be any trouble."

"Thirty five bucks. Or probably forty five these days. Just think how much that money would buy out there in Outer Mongolia."

And so Joe Leaphorn's GMC Jimmy followed Professor Louisa Bourbonnette's little Honda Civic to her house.

It stood on a narrow street only four blocks from the campus of Northern Arizona University, a brick bungalow, aged and small. The guest room was also small—very small, and crowded with a small couch, a work table, chair, computer, printer, supplies, books, odds and ends. Everything, it seemed to Leaphorn, except a bed.

"The couch folds out. Just grab those tabs at the bottom and pull. I think its already made up," she said, disappearing back into the hall. "But I'll have to get you a pillow."

Leaphorn pulled. The couch converted itself into a thin, narrow bed. It looked lumpy and uncomfortable under a fresh white sheet.

Professor Bourbonnette's voice came through the doorway. "How about a glass of wine first? Make you sleep." There was the sound of things being moved. "Sorry. I forgot. How about a cup of tea then? I have a box here of something called 'Sleepytime."

"Fine," Leaphorn said. "Although I don't think I'll

need it."

He sat in a well-worn recliner in the living room and looked at a framed print of a Georgia O'Keefe landscape on the wall across from him—a landscape of red and black erosion. Probably near Abiquiu, he thought, but it could have been done a thousand places on the Big Rez. He shifted in the recliner, relaxing, comfortable, glad he hadn't gone to a motel. What would be would be. In the kitchen, a tea kettle began to whistle. Cups clattered. Leaphorn found his mind settling into an old, old groove. This was when he did his best thinking—just before sleep. He would review whatever puzzle was bothering him, turn the facts over and over, look at all sides of them, knock them together, and then explain it all to Emma–as much to organize it in his own mind as to ask her opinion. But her opinion was often wise.

Louisa Bourbonnette appeared carrying a tray. Two saucered cups, a steaming tea pot, a little pitcher of cream. She put the tray on the table beside Leaphorn's recliner, handed him his cup, dropped a tea bag into it, poured in hot water.

"I would have offered you coffee, but I'm out of decaf. And you shouldn't be drinking the high octane stuff this late."

"This is fine," Leaphorn said. "Better for me."

"It really is," she said, perching on the sofa across from him with her own cup. "Especially this herbal stuff."

"How are you with puzzles," Leaphorn said, and found himself surprised as he said it.

"Puzzles?"

"I'm working with an officer named Jim Chee," Leaphorn said. "You met him last summer."

"I remember Jim." she said.

"He's my assistant now. Brand new. Just started. When I came into my office to check on things before I left for Flag this afternoon, he'd left me a memo. A kind of report."

He paused, watching her expression. "About a homicide I've been working on. Somebody killed a teacher out at an mission school on the Checkerboard Reservation." He paused again.

"Go on," she said. "I'm waiting for the puzzle."

"It may not really be one," he said. "Just a little oddity, probably. But, being a Navajo—" He grinned at her. "I have to start at the beginning."

"The perfect place," she said.

"Two cases," he said. "Two incidents. Unconnected. But are they?"

He told her first of the death of Eric Dorsey, the telephone tip, the circumstances which had led to the arrest of Eugene Ahkeah, and his denial of the crime.

"Sounds like no mystery there," she said.

"Exactly," Leaphorn said. "It sounds typical of the homicides we work on the reservation. Too much whiskey."

"And that, I've guessed, is why you don't drink wine," she said.

Leaphorn sipped his tea. "Then, four days later and a long ways off at the Tano Pueblo we have another homicide."

"I read about that one," she said. "The Koshare killed at his kiva right in the middle of a kachina ceremonial. Created quite a sensation. Nothing like that had ever happened before."

"That one's not our case and I don't know everything about it. But from what I do know, they don't have a suspect, or a motive or anything much to go one. Just somebody showed up at the little building off the plaza where the koshares dress, and rest and so forth. He hit this guy on the head and nobody saw a thing." Leaphorn paused again, watching her.

She sipped her tea, looked at him over the rim, put

down the cup. "Go on," she said. "If the story stopped there you wouldn't be telling me."

"It just happened that Jim Chee was there when the homicide took place," he said. He told her about the effort to find the Kanitewa boy to keep his Navajo grandmother happy, and what had happened, and about Chee going back with Sergeant Blizzard, the cop from the BIA. Finally, he told her about the memo, reciting it to her almost word for word.

Bourbonnette picked up her cup again and sipped.

"What do you think?" Leaphorn asked.

"Don't rush me," she said. "You've had all day to think about it."

"Take your time."

"Right off the cuff, I'd say you picked a smart assistant. Pretty smart, Chee. Good thinking. Making the connection with the radio broadcast." She paused, thinking. "Or was it hearing the broadcast that caused the boy—what was his name—caused him to run back to see his uncle again."

"Kanitewa," Leaphorn said. "Tomorrow, when I get back on the job, we'll see if we can find out."

"He'll tell you?"

"Why not? Unless it has something to do with his religion."

"I was thinking that. He's a teenager. Old enough to be initiated I'd think. I don't know much about Tano specifically. But I'd think they'd be like the other pueblos."

"So would I," Leaphorn said. "But how do you think the two things connect? Kanitewa was going to school at Crownpoint. That's maybe thirty five, forty miles from Thoreau."

"What do you think could have been in that package. The one Chee mentioned, wrapped in the newspaper?"

"We'll find out tomorrow," Leaphorn said.

"If it's not something religious."

"Yeah," Leaphorn said. He felt an intense urge to yawn, stretch. Instead, he settled deeper into the chair. "The trouble is, we don't have enough details to speculate."

"We can speculate anyway," Professor Bourbonnette said. "Maybe the boy had some way of knowing what's-his-name. The teacher who got killed. Maybe there was some connection between Kanitewa's dad and the teacher. What's your theory?"

Lieutenant Joe Leaphorn didn't answer, having gone soundly to sleep in the recliner.

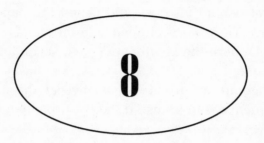

8

JIM CHEE NOTICED a neat stack of papers in his In basket when he walked into his office. He ignored them for a moment to stand staring out his window. The window was why he'd picked the office over a slightly larger one when he was transferred from Shiprock to Windowrock. From it he could look eastward at the ragtag southern end of the Chuska range, the long wall of sandstone along which Windowrock had been built and which, because of the great hole eroded through it, gave the capitol of the Navajo Nation its name.

He looked out today into a windless autumn afternoon. No traffic was moving on Navajo route 3 and a single pickup truck was ambling northward up Route 12 past the Navajo Veterans Cemetery. The trees at Tse Bonito park were yellow, the roadsides were streaked with the purple of the last surviving October asters, and overhead the sky was the dark, blank blue. Chee exhaled a great sigh. Would she go to Gallup with him tonight? She had neglected to answer that question. Or, worse, avoided it. Or, worse still, forgotten it.

He sat behind his desk and fished the papers out of the basket. They were clipped together under a memo sheet which bore the Lieutenant's neat script and the initials, J.L.

"I'm going on an extended leave at the end of the week. Attached find items I'd like you to clean up before then."

The first item was the file on Todachene hit-and-run case. It was relatively old now, old enough normally to be dumped into suspense file. This one was alive twenty five per cent because of the inhuman callousness involved and seventy five per cent because it had caught the Chief's eye. Chee remembered most of it but he flipped glumly through the attached reports to see if the patrol officers had found anything new. Nothing had been added to what Leaphorn had told him.

He put that aside and picked up the next one. Offering sergeant stripes for solving that one was sort of like the offers you heard about in fairy stories. You can marry the princess if you do something impossible—like putting a mountain in a pea pod. How in hell could you solve a hit-and-runner with no clues, no broken headlight glass, no scraped paint, no witnesses, no nothing. He thought of another parallel. How in hell could he expect to win the princess, a full scale city girl lawyer, if you couldn't make sergeant.

He'd heard of the second case, too. Theft of an antique saddle and other artifacts from the Greasy Water Trading Post. Under that was one he hadn't heard of—a series of fence cuttings and cattle thefts around Nakaibito. He flipped through the rest hoping for something unique or interesting. No such luck.

The final item in the stack was another memo sheet, initialed J.L.

"Don't forget to find the Kanitewa boy."

Chee made a rude noise and dropped the memo back on the stack. Trying to find Kanitewa was typical of the whole list. What do you do? First, you let everybody you can think of know you want a call if they see the kid. If he shows up at school, they call you. Well, he'd done that. What else can you do? The same with the vehicular homicide. It was just drone work. Call every place that fixes cars and tell 'em to tip you if somebody comes in for body work. Stake out the auto supply stores for somebody buying the right kind of right front headlight. Then for the cow stealing, you do about a thousand miles of back road driving around Nakaibito finding out who saw what and when, and who was eating fresh beef or drying cowhides, and –

The telephone rang.

"Jim Chee," Chee said.

"This is Blizzard," the voice said. "You still interested in that kid?"

"Kanitewa? Sure." Chee felt a mixture of surprise and pleasure. Blizzard wasn't quite as hardassed as he'd thought. "What do you hear?"

"He's back at school," Blizzard said.

Chee let that sink in for an unhappy moment. So much for promises. That principal said he'd call just as soon as the boy showed up. Chee could still see the man, shaking his hand, saying: "Yes sir. I sure will. I've got your number right here on the blotter." The secretary had promised, too. So much for promises.

"How'd you know?" Chee asked, trying not to sound bitter.

"I'm calling from the school," Blizzard said. "Just dropped the little bastard off there. I found him near the bus station at Grants and I gave him a ride."

Chee didn't ask how Blizzard knew Kanitewa would be at the bus station at Grants. The Cheyenne had staked out all the bus stations where the kid might show up. Chee hadn't thought of doing that. Maybe that's why the Cheyennes beat Custer.

"He was headed back to school?"

"He said he was," Blizzard said, sounding sour. "That's about all he did say."

Chee looked at his watch. "So he was going back to live with the Navajo side of his family. With his father? That what he said?"

"Yep."

"Well, thanks," Chee said. "Appreciate the call. I owe you one. Anytime I can be helpful." He picked up the memo, wadded it, flipped it toward the wastebasket. It hit the rim and dropped on the floor.

"Yeah," Blizzard said. "How about right now."

"Like what?" Chee said.

"I'm city In-dun," Blizzard said, picking up the Navajo pronunciation. "I don't understand these sheep camp Ind-uns yet. Polite as I am known to be, I think I must say the wrong things some times. Not come on just right." Blizzard paused, awaiting a comment, and getting none, went on.

"Back at the Kanitewa house at the pueblo, you got his mama to talking. You think you could get the boy to talk?"

"I don't know," Chee said. "Not if its anything to do with his religion."

"I don't care about his damn religion," Blizzard said. "What I want to know about is what his mama told us. About why he was in such a sweat to see his uncle, and why he had to go back and see him the second time, and what he had in that package he brought for him."

"It must have been something long and narrow. Maybe something rolled up in a tube. Didn't you guys find anything like that in Sayesva's place."

"Nothing," Blizzard said. He paused. "Well, hell, there

was plenty of long narrow stuff in his house, you know. It could have been anything."

"And the boy wouldn't tell you?"

"Just shut totally up," Blizzard said.

"You asked him specifically. About what he'd brought for his uncle in the newspaper?"

"He said it had to do with his kiva. His religious outfit. Said he couldn't talk about it."

"He won't tell me, either, then," Chee said. "I don't think you Cheyennes have that philosophy. We don't either. Our religion is family and the more that take part in a ceremony the better it is. But the pueblo people, it diminishes the power if people who shouldn't be involved in a ritual are told about it. Or see what they shouldn't. Or photograph it. He's not going to tell me."

There was a long silence. Then Blizzard said: "Uh-huh," in tone which said a lot more than that. "Well, then, thanks a lot and to hell with it."

"Wait a minute," Chee said. "I'll have to get out there anyway." He delivered to Blizzard a self-depreciatory laugh. "I'm supposed to get him to call his grandmother. So when I get out there, I'll see if I can get anything out of him. If I do, I'll call you."

"Yeah," Blizzard said. "Good." A long pause followed.

"Anything I can provide you?" Blizzard asked.

"I don't think so," Chee said, sounding puzzled.

"You got my phone number?"

"Oh," Chee said. "No."

"I didn't think so," Blizzard said, and gave it to him.

Chee copied it, read it back. "I'll call," he said.

"Like about when, you think?" Blizzard said. "Maybe today."

"What's the hurry?"

"The hurry is my Agent-In-Charge. I told him about the two visits, and the package. And that got him all heated up. He hasn't got another damn thing to work on

83

in this case. So then when I found the boy and let him off at the school, I called the son-of-a-bitch. And I told him what the boy said. About it just being religious business. The package and all. And he wants to know exactly what was in the package."

"Oh," Chee said.

"Or bring the kid back to Albuquerque for him to question him."

"Fat lot of good that will do," Chee said. He was thinking of the Grandmother Councilwoman, who would be plenty pissed off, and would pass it along to Leaphorn who would– Would what? He had just worked for the man a few days. How would Leaphorn react? "But I guess you don't have much choice," Chee concluded.

"Well, some," Blizzard said. "While I was talking to the feds in Albuquerque, the kid took off again."

"Oh," Chee said. "Not again." He was silent a moment, absorbing the disappointment. Back to square one. It didn't surprise him much. But it was interesting. So was Blizzard. Chee found himself thinking of the man not as a Cheyenne but as a cop new to the territory, not knowing the people, lost. For Chee that was a familiar role.

"Tell you what," he said. "You get yourself something to eat in that diner by the gas station, and then get over to the Crownpoint police station. I'll meet you there. The Lieutenant in charge is a man named Toddy. Try to be nice to him. It'll take me maybe two hours and if anything hangs me up, I'll call you there."

"Done," Blizzard said, and hung up.

Chee put on his cap, his gunbelt, and his jacket. He called the dispatcher and told her he would be driving to the subagency office at Crownpoint. He sat for a moment, thinking, then picked up the phone book and extracted the number of Radio Station KNDN.

The woman who took the call was cooperative. She put him on hold for few moments, and then read him the transcript on the six p.m news of three nights ago. It included six items: the change in schedule of a rodeo at Tuba City, a plan to improve the runway of the landing strip at Kayenta, the death in the hospital at Gallup of the former chairwoman of the Coyote Pass Chapter, the replacement of the retired principal of the Toadlena school, and the murder of Eric Dorsey at the St. Bonaventure Navajo Mission.

Chee took two steps toward the door. Then he turned and sat, cap, jacket and gunbelt on, typing a memo for Lieutenant Leaphorn. He had worked for the Lieutenant long enough now to make it a long one.

9

"HE SHOULD BE IN just about any time," said Virginia Toledo, examining Chee over her glasses. "He went to Flagstaff yesterday and he called a little while ago and said he'd be late."

"Called from here?" Chee asked. "Or called from Flag? Or radioed in from somewhere?" He was holding a folder in his right hand and his uniform cap in his left.

Virginia Toledo had not yet decided what her relationship would be with Officer Jim Chee and did not like the sound of this abrupt questioning. For the past twenty three years her job title had been administrative assistant, Navajo Department of Public Safety, and she was, in fact, the work-a-day nerve center of the Window Rock operation. What's going on? Ask Virgie. Why's Desbah not in his office? Virgie will know. What happened at that meeting last night? Get Virgie to tell you. Virgie knew exactly how to deal with everybody in the building, including Joe Leaphorn, Chee's boss. But now this young Jim

Chee was holding down that little office upstairs. She didn't know him. She'd heard he was sometimes something of a screwup. She inspected him over her glasses. His tone had struck her as unduly demanding. He was a college man. Maybe he'd been around white men so long he'd lost his good manners. Maybe he'd picked up the belagaana attitude about women. She checked his expression, looking for some sign of irritation or arrogance. She saw only excitement. That was all right. He was young. If you're going to get excited, that was the age for it.

"He called from his house," she said. "Just about ten minutes ago."

"If he calls again," Chee said, heading for the stairs, "would you tell him I'll be waiting in my office. And I need to see him." He stopped, turned and smiled at Administrative Assistant Virginia Toledo. "Please," he said. "And thank you."

The door to Leaphorn's office was about 15 feet from Chee's door. He tapped on it on his way past, got no response, tapped again and turned the knob. Of course it wasn't locked. He'd heard it wouldn't be—that one of the Lieutenant's several idiosyncracies was a refusal to lock his office. "If you have to lock your door in the police station," Leaphorn would say, "then it's time to get new policemen." But that attitude seemed to be common in the department. Nobody locked doors at the Tuba City station either. Nor, come to think of it, at Crownpoint when he'd worked out of there.

Chee said "Lieutenant?" in a loud voice, and looked around. Neat, tidy, the desktop clear. No sign of dust. Dust wouldn't dare.

In his own office, Chee re-read his report.

Blizzard had been waiting in the parking lot outside the Crownpoint station—sprawled across the front seat of his patrol car, long legs dangling out the open door, head resting on his jacket folded against the passenger door, reading a book. The book, Chee noticed, had a dust jacket which looked science fictionish and bore the name Roger Zelazny.

He had put it on the dashboard, pushed himself erect, looked at Chee and then at his watch. "I see you're operating on Navajo time," he said.

Chee had let it pass and let Blizzard tell him what had happened. That hadn't taken long. Blizzard had told the boy to wait at his car while he made his telephone call to Albuquerque. When he finished talking to his Agent-In-Charge and came back to the car, the boy was gone.

"The school buses were loading up and leaving when I went in to use the phone. So I found out which one'd he'd take to get home, and chased it down but he wasn't on it. Then I found out where he lived and went out to his daddy's place. His step- mother was there but she said she hadn't seen him since he took off the first time."

"So he didn't go home," Chee said. "That's funny."

"Maybe not," Blizzard said. "When I picked him up there at Grants he was walking out toward the Interstate. I didn't ask him where he was going. I just let him in the car, and he was in before he knew I was a cop, and then I told him I'd give him a ride back to his school."

"So maybe he was actually headed somewhere else."

"I should have found out," Blizzard said, sounding repentant. "He told me he'd gone in the bus station to buy a ticket but he didn't have enough money. I figured the ticket was just to Thoreau."

"Probably right," Chee said.

"Maybe," Blizzard agreed. "He acted nervous. I think I told you that."

"His step-mother. Did she give you any guesses about where he might be staying? Kinfolks? Friends?"

"She said she had no idea. Didn't have a clue. She wasn't very talkative."

That hadn't surprised Chee. He had stopped thinking of Blizzard as a Cheyenne and was thinking of him as a city man. Chee had concluded years ago that not many city people knew how to talk to country people. Delmar Kanitewa's Navajo step-mother would definitely be country people. Blizzard had probably offended her.

"Let's go find the school bus driver," Chee said.

That had proved easy. His name was Platero, he lived less than a mile from the school and, yes indeed, he could tell them who was Delmar's best friend. It was a boy named Felix Bluehorse. "Sometimes Felix gets off at his place, and sometime vice versa," Platero said. "Good buddies."

Even better, Felix Bluehorse's mother worked for the Navajo Communications Company and lived in Crownpoint. Better yet, Felix was home when they got there and was anxious to talk to somebody. But first, he wanted to see their police identification. Felix was small and about sixteen, with enough white blood mixed with his Navajo genes to make him vulnerable to acne. He stood in the doorway of his mother's mobile home looking down on them. Obviously, he was enjoying this.

"I've got to be careful who I talk too," Felix said. "Somebody's after Delmar." He looked at Blizzard, then at Chee, savoring their reaction.

Chee waited. They were in Navajo country, but it was Blizzard's case.

"Who?" Blizzard asked. "Why?"

"The man who killed Mr. Dorsey," Felix said.

Abruptly, it wasn't Blizzard's case. Now it was Chee's case.

"You know what," Chee said. "I think you have some very important information. Can we come in and sit down and talk about it?"

In the crowded Bluehorse living room it proved that Felix Bluehorse did have quite a bit of information, if one could only calculate what it meant.

Chee was thinking of that now, going over it in his mind, reading through the report he'd typed for Lieutenant Leaphorn, wondering if he'd left anything out. If he had, it was too late to do anything about it. There was a tap on the door, it opened and the Lieutenant looked in at him. The Lieutenant looked old and tired.

"Virginia said you were looking for me."

"Yes sir," Chee said. He stood, handed Leaphorn the file folder.

"You find him?"

"No sir," Chee said. "Well, not exactly. Blizzard found him hitchhiking. . . "

Leaphorn expression stopped Chee. It was a broad, happy grin.

Chee hurried on. ". . . near Grants, and he picked him up and took him to Crownpoint." Chee swallowed. "But he got away again."

Leaphorn's grin disappeared. He tapped the folder. "It all in here?"

"Yes sir."

"I'll read it," Leaphorn said. His tone suggested to Chee that reading it would not have high priority.

"It connects the Kanitewa boy to the homicide at Thoreau," Chee said.

Leaphorn took his hand off the door knob, flipped the report open, scanned it, looked up at Chee. "Let's talk in my office," he said.

But before they talked, Leaphorn eased himself into the chair behind his desk, put on his glasses, slowly re-read Chee's report, placed it on the desk top, restored his glasses to their case, put the case in his shirt pocket, and looked at Chee for a long moment.

"What'd did you think of the Bluehorse boy?"

"He seemed like a nice kid," Chee said. "He wanted to cooperate. Enjoying the excitement, somebody paying attention to him, Liking being important."

"He said he had no idea where Kanitewa was hiding out. You think that's true?."

"Maybe," Chee said. "I doubt it. I'd bet he could give us two or three guesses if he wanted to."

Leaphorn nodded. "He told you that Kanitewa thought the man killed Dorsey would be after him?"

"Right," Chee said.

"And the man was a Navajo?"

"Oh," Chee said, embarrassed. "I think he actually said Kanitewa told him it was a man he'd seen around the Saint Bonaventure Mission. You know, you're dealing with a hearsay, secondhand description. He said Kanitewa said this man was kind of old, and had dark, dark hair. I think we just took for granted we were talking about a Navajo because he didn't says "white," or "Chinese," or "Hispanic."

Leaphorn produced an affirmative grunt. He extracted his glasses, re-read part of the report.

"You say here Bluehorse said he didn't know whether Kanitewa had actually witnessed the crime."

"We pressed him on that. He said he wasn't sure. Maybe Kanitewa had actually seen it. But he didn't tell him he had. I'd say if Delmar had seen it, he have said so. And he would have yelled. Reported it."

"Yeah," Leaphorn said.

"I'd guess that when he heard the radio broadcast about Dorsey being killed, he remembered seeing this guy coming out of the shop and put two and two together."

Leaphorn nodded.

"Could it be Eugene Ahkeah?"

Leaphorn said: "Dark. Big. Kind of old. That could be just about anybody. Could be Ahkeah. He's not much older than you. But for a teenager, kind of old is anybody over twenty."

"And Ahkeah was there that day," Chee said. "Other

people saw him?"

"Yep," Leaphorn said. He sighed, got up and walked to the window and stood, hands in his pockets, looking out. "We've got our man in jail," he said, finally. "We've got him at the scene. There's no question he had the opportunity. We've good motive—theft plus drunkenness. And we have physical evidence tied to him. All that stolen stuff. Now it seems as if we have another witness who must have seen something incriminating." He turned and looked at Chee. "The trouble is, I was thinking we had the wrong man."

"Why?"

Leaphorn shook his head Laughed. "Be damned if I know why. I used to think I was logical. Usually I am. It's just that this Ahkeah seemed wrong for it." He walked around behind the desk, rummaged in the drawer and took out a box of pins. "Ever have that happen to you. Your brain tells you one thing. Your instinct another."

"Sure," Chee said. "I guess so."

"And which one is right?" In the map on the wall behind his desk he put a pin at Tano Pueblo, and another between Crownpoint and Thoreau, about where Kanitewa had stayed with his father. Chee noticed they had pink heads, the same color as the pins already stuck in the map at Thoreau, and at the place in Coyote Canyon where Ahkeah lived. Leaphorn dropped the surplus pins back into the box. "Did you ever wonder why I fool with those pins?"

"Yeah," Chee said. He'd heard of Leaphorn's pin-littered map ever since he'd joined the force. Captain Largo, his boss when he worked the Tuba City district, told him Leaphorn used them to work out mathematical solutions to crimes that puzzled him. Largo couldn't explain how that worked. Neither could Chee.

"I don't know myself, exactly," Leaphorn said. "I got into the habit years ago. It seems like sometimes it helps me think. It puts things in perspective." He tapped the pin at Tano with a finger. "For example, we seem to have a connection now between two crimes. Or do we? About seventy miles apart on the map. Does the Kanitewa boy connect them? It sure as hell looks like it now."

"It does to me. I'd bet a year's pay on it," Chee said.

Leaphorn made a tent of his hands and looked at Chee over it. "Why?" he asked. "Why are you so certain?"

"Because–" Chee began.

The telephone on Leaphorn's desk interrupted him. Leaphorn picked it up, said: "Call me back in ten minutes," and hung up.

He looked at Chee, motioned for him to continue.

"Because of the package, mostly," Chee said. "Because of the chronology."

Leaphorn nodded. "Yes. I think so too. But what was in that package?" He was asking both of them the question. He looked at Chee. "Any ideas?"

"None," Chee said. "Except Kanitewa must have thought it was in some way connected with his religion. That's what he told Blizzard. And he took it to his uncle. To the Koshare. We know that. And we think we know that he picked it up in Eric Dorsey's shop."

Leaphorn swiveled in his chair, looked at the map a moment and then back at Chee.

"The way your report reads, Kanitewa's dad was driving in to Gallup. The boy had his dad drop him off at Thoreau because Bluehorse had been making a silver bracelet in Dorsey's class. Bluehorse wanted to give it to his girl friend that night and he'd asked Kanitewa to pick it up for him. We don't know when his dad dropped him off. Probably mid-morning and probably it doesn't matter. The next thing we have an approximate time on is when Kanitewa called Bluehorse and asked him to come and get him. That was late in the noonhour because Bluehorse remember's he'd just finished eating lunch. Am I getting this right?"

"So far," Chee said.

"Kanitewa told Bluehorse he was calling from the pay phone out in front of the mission. He said he had Bluehorse's bracelet, he couldn't wait for his dad to come back from Gallup and could Bluehorse come and get him. Pick him up, but not at the school or the mission but at that little place by the highway where they rent videotapes. Kanitewa was very excited. It was very important. Don't let me down friend. That sort of thing. So Bluehorse borrowed his mother's pickup truck and drove over to Thoreau and pulled up at the video place. But Kanitewa wasn't just sitting their waiting for him. So Bluehorse went inside to look for him, and when he came out, Kanitewa was sitting in the cab of his pickup."

Leaphorn paused, studying Chee.

"You remember what I was saying the other day about putting in the details. Your report reads: 'When Bluehorse came out Kanitewa was sitting in his pickup.' But was he crouched down out of sight, or sitting up? That's an example. If we knew that it would tell us something about how scared the boy was at that point."

Chee allowed himself to make a minuscule nod. He was not in the mood for a lesson in report writing.

"Kanitewa gives Bluehorse the bracelet," Leaphorn continued. That seems to mean that he had to have seen Dorsey. He must have given Dorsey the note from Bluehorse–the receipt for the bracelet. Otherwise Dorsey wouldn't have turned it loose. Right?"

"I'd think so. As far as we know, Dorsey had never met Kanitewa."

"Now you need to know some things," Leaphorn said. "That bracelet was probably in a cabinet in a little storeroom between the shop and Dorsey's office. That's where Dorsey kept his supply of silver ingots, and turquoise and the more valuable stuff the kids were working on. To get it for Kanitewa he'd have to leave the shop, or his office if the boy had found him in his office."

Leaphorn paused, checked Chee's expression to determine if he understood the implication of this. Chee understood. It meant Kanitewa would have had an opportunity to steal something. Perhaps to steal something to be taken away, wrapped in a newspaper and delivered to his uncle, the Koshare.

"Was the cabinet unlocked when they found Dorsey's body?" Chee asked.

"Unlocked," Leaphorn said, looking thoughtful. "And a lot of stuff that had been in it was missing. The silver and the other stuff found in the box under Ahkeah's place, all of that came out of the cabinet."

"All of it?" Chee asked.

"That's a good question," Leaphorn said. "I think Toddy was jumping to that conclusion. But I don't know for sure."

"It probably doesn't matter," Chee said.

"No. But how do we know whether it does or not?"

They thought about that for a moment. For the first time, Chee found himself feeling comfortable with the Lieutenant. Leaphorn had swivelled again and seemed to be looking at the map. Now he made a dismissive gesture, and turned back.

"Bluehorse told Kanitewa he didn't have enough gas to take him all the way to Tano, but he could take him down to the Giant Truck Stop on Interstate 25 and he could get a ride there," Leaphorn said. "That correct? And Bluehorse didn't see the package until Kanitewa got out?"

"Right."

"But it was already wrapped in the newspaper? Whatever it was?"

Chee nodded.

"And Bluehorse asked what it was and Kanitewa said he couldn't tell him. It was religious."

"Something from Dorsey's office?" Leaphorn said.

"Probably."

They thought about that.

The telephone rang. Leaphorn lifted one end of the receiver with a finger to break the connection. "You see any other possibility? You think maybe he brought it with him when he came from his home?"

"He could have," Chee said. "But I think somehow that whatever it was, it was the object that caused all the excitement. The big excited call to Bluehorse. That 'can't wait for dad' business. All the game playing."

Leaphorn considered that. The telephone rang again. He picked up the receiver, broke the connection with his forefinger, laid the receiver on the desk. "Yes," he said. "I think you're right. And how about chronology now. Was Dorsey alive and well when Kanitewa left him?"

"I'd say yes."

"Yeah," Leaphorn said. nodding. "But when Kanitewa was leaving, he saw somebody coming in. I'm guessing now but am I right? Maybe Ahkeah. Maybe somebody else."

"I think you're right. And they saw him. And he knew it," Chee said.

Leaphorn considered that, nodded.

"So when the boy heard the radio broadcast, when he heard Dorsey had been killed, then everything clicked. He rushed off to warn his uncle about it."

"Maybe," Chee said. "At least I can't think of anything better."

"So what did the Koshare do then? As far as we know, he ignored the warning. Did nothing."

Chee was remembering the Kachina dance, the koshare performance. "He did his duty," Chee said. "From what little I heard at Tano, and mostly from what Blizzard picked up and passed along, I think he was that kind of a man. Blizzard said everybody he interviewed liked him.

He said it was more than just 'don't speak bad of the dead,' more than just the usual everybody being nice you get when somebody gets killed. Blizzard said they really respected him. Admired him. He must have been a good man."

"The kind they'd call a "valuable man," Leaphorn said. He stood up, put the telephone receiver back on the hook, looked at the map again. "You know," he said. "Maybe we've got another connection here. This Dorsey was also a valuable man." He smiled at Chee. "How do you like the idea of a serial killer who hates valuable men."

"Bluehorse told us Dorsey's gay," Chee said. "Or supposed to be gay. He said he drove the water truck. The one the mission runs to refill water barrels for old people who can't get around. He took them meals. All that."

"That's right. You better read the file on it," Leaphorn said. He dug it out of the basket on his desk handed it to Chee. "See if what you know about the Sayesva case connects with anything at Thoreau."

"Okay."

"And one more thing. I still want you to find the Delmar Kanitewa."

10

THE TROUBLE WAS Chee couldn't find the Kanitewa boy. Neither could Harold Blizzard. Now both the Albuquerque and Gallup offices of the Federal Bureau of Investigation, each with its own separate and individual federal reservation homicide case, decided it was important to have a chat with Delmar. Gallup was wondering how in God's green earth Chee had let him slip away and Albuquerque was asking the same question of Officer Blizzard.

Blizzard resented this. "The son of a bitch looks right at me and says: 'You just walked into the school and made the telephone call and left him sitting there?" Blizzard had raised his voice two notches to represent the voice of the Agent In Charge at Albuquerque. "And I say, 'That's because there's no telephone in the patrol car.' And he says, 'You didn't think about taking him into the school with you?' and I say:" If I had of known he was going to slip away we wouldn't be having this stupid conversation."

Chee laughed." Did you really say that?"

They had met at the Gallup police station and decided to leave Blizzard's car there and take Chee's pickup to begin another phase of what Blizzard called The Great Delmar Hunt. Now they were jolting down Navajo Road 7028 about fifteen miles west of the Torreon Trading Post, looking for a dirt road which would, if they could only find it, lead them across the South Fork of Chico Arroyo and thence to the place of Grey Woman Benally, who was some sort of paternal clan relative of Delmar's. Blizzard was driving, giving Chee a rest. It was early afternoon, and both were tired of driving down bumpy dirt roads, tired of searching for people who weren't at home, of asking questions of people who didn't know the answer—and maybe wouldn't have told them if they did know. Besides, Chee's back hurt. His lower back, about where the hips connect.

"Well," Blizzard said. He had been silent so long that Chee had forgotten what they were talking about," Maybe not exactly those words, but he got the idea." He gestured out the windshield." Look at that," he said." Those colors. In the clouds and in the sky and in the grass. I think I could get used to this. Nothing much to do out here in the boonies, but lots to look at."

Chee shifted his thoughts from back pain to landscape. Indeed it was beautiful. The sun was in its autumn mode, low in the southwest, and shadows slanted away from every juniper. They formed zebra stripes where the slopes ran north and a polkadot pattern where they slanted southward. The grass was never really green in this land of little rain. Now it was a golden autumn tan with streaks of silver and white where the sickle-shaped seeds of gramma were waving, tinted blue here and there by distance and shadow. Miles away, beyond the hills, the vertical slopes of Chivato Mesa formed a wall. Above the mesa stood the serene blue shape of Tsodzil, the Turquoise Mountain which First Man had built as one of the four sacred corner posts of Navajo Country. And over all that, the great, arching, multilayered sky—the thin, translucent fan of ice crystals still glittering in the full sun. Thousands of feet lower, a scattering of puffy gray-white cumulus clouds–outriders of the storm the weatherman had been predicting—marched eastward ahead of the wind.

It's beautiful. I'll give you that." Blizzard said." But you need some way to pull it together a lot better. Everything is too damn far apart."

"You get used to that, too," Chee said." Somebody once wrote a book about it. They called it" The Land of Room Enough, and Time."

"We're sure wasting enough of that today," Blizzard said." You keeping track of the mileage."

"The man said it was sixteen point three miles from the gas pump at the trading post," Chee said." That ought to be it up ahead."

Up ahead, tracks led from the gravel into the roadside borrow ditch, climbed out of it, crossed a cattle guard between two fence posts and wandered erratically through the grass toward the horizon, disappearing on downslopes and reappearing on ridges.

"Not exactly the Pennsylvania Turnpike," Blizzard said." And when we get down it, Gray Lady what's her name won't be home."

"She's home," Chee said." But it'll turn out she's the wrong Mrs. Benally."

"She won't be home. I'll bet you," Blizzard said. He reached for his billfold.

"You lose," Chee said. He pointed." See the old boot stuck on the fence post. The toe's pointed in. If it's pointed out, they're gone to town and you save yourself the drive."

Blizzard stared at him, impressed." My God," he said." That's pretty damn clever. Wonder if us Cheyennes figured out anything like that."

"You've really never been to your reservation? Never lived out there with your people at all?"

"Just once," Blizzard said." When my dad's mother died, we went out for the funeral. I think we just stayed a couple of days. I remember the night. I was little and about all I could think of was how cold it was in my uncle's shack. And I remember the other kids didn't seem friendly."

"You were a town boy," Chee said." They were country kids. Bashful. They figured you'd be stuck up." He grinned, trying to imagine this hardassed cop as a boy." I bet you were, too."

The dirt track to the Benally place proved to be smoother than the washboard gravel of Route 7028. It led a mile and a half to an expanse of packed dirt on which stood a log hogan with a dirt roof and one of those small frame houses which, before the era of aluminum mobile homes, were hauled around on flatbed oil company trucks to shelter crews of drilling rigs. It had been painted white once but not much paint had survived the winters. Two standard 55 gallon oil drums stood on a platform beside the door. An empty corral was behind it, with too many poles missing to make it useful, and behind the corral, a brush arbor sagged.

A woman with a shawl over her head leaned in the open doorway, watching while Chee parked. To Chee, she looked about eighty, or a little older, with a once-round face now shrunken by the years.

"I hope you are well, grandmother," he said. He told her his mother's clan, and his father's, and that he was a tribal policeman." And this man beside me is a Cheyenne Indian. His people were part of those who beat General Custer. And we have come to find out if you can help us with a problem."

Gray Old Lady recited her clans, including being born to the Bitter Water People of Delmar Kanitewa's father. She invited them in, and signalled them to seat themselves on a bench beside the table, and offered them coffee. While the pot& heated on the wood stove against the wall, Chee made his pitch. It was the fifth time he'd made it since morning and he hurried through it, making sure the old woman knew they didn't want to arrest the boy—only to talk to him.

She poured the coffee into two tin cups. The pot held only enough for a half-cup for Chee and Blizzard. None for her. She put it back on the shelf.

"I know the boy," she said." My grandson's son. We called him Sheep Chaser. But I haven't seen him this year. Not for a long time."

Chee sipped the coffee. It was strong and stale. Through the doorway into the other room he could see a form laying motionless under a blanket." Does Sheep Chaser have any good friends around here. Somebody he might be visiting?"

"I don't think so," she said." He goes to live with his mother's people. The Tano People. I don't know anything about him any more."

Which was exactly what Chee had expected to hear. He translated the gist of it to Blizzard. Blizzard nodded and grunted." Tell her I said thank you very much for all the assistance," Blizzard said.

"We thank you," Chee said. He nodded toward the doorway." Is someone in your family ill?"

She turned and looked into the bedroom." That is my husband," she said." He is so old that he does not know who he is any more. He has even forgotten how to walk and how to say words."

"Is there anyone helping you," Chee said." Taking care of things?"

"There is the belagaana from the mission at Thoreau," she said." He comes in his truck and keeps our water barrel filled and twice a week he brings us food. But this week he hasn't come."

Chee felt sick." Is his name Eric Dorsey?"

Gray Old Lady produced an ancient-sounding chuckle." We call him our *begadoche*. Our water sprinkler. Because he brings our water. And because he makes us laugh." She memory of laughter produced a small, toothless smile." He has this thing, like a duck and he pretends to make it talk." But the smile went away and she drew her hands up to her chest, looking worried." Except this week, he didn't come."

"How much water do you have," Chee asked.

"One barrel is empty," she said." The other one, maybe about this much." She demonstrated six inches of water with her hands." When he comes he always looks into the barrels, and last week he said he would fill them when he came this time. But he didn't come."

Blizzard had said polite words to the old woman in English and was walking back to the car. She kept her eyes on Chee, looking worried.

"Do you think he will come next week," she said." If he doesn't come next week I will have to use less water."

"I will send someone out here to fill your water barrels, Grandmother," Chee said." I will send somebody from the mission at Thoreau or somebody from the tribal office at Crownpoint. And when they come you must tell them that you need help."

"But the belagaana has helped us," she said, looking puzzled." In many ways." She pointed into the room, at the rocking chair. It was beautifully made with simple lines and looked new." He made that for us, at the school I think. He said that chair would be better for my back when I sit beside the bed. And with the duck he would make my husband laugh."

"Grandmother," Chee said." I think the belagaana who helped you is dead."

She seemed not to hear him." He brings us food and

he fills our water barrels and he took my man in to see the belagaana doctors. And he helped us when my daughter had rugs to sell. He told us the man at the trading post was not paying enough. And he sold them for us and got a lot more money."

"Grandmother," Chee said." Listen to me."

But she didn't want to listen." The trader had been giving us fifty dollars but Begadoche got three hundred dollars once, and once it was more than six hundred. And when I had to sell my necklace and my bracelets because we didn't have any money he told me the pawn place in Gallup didn't give us enough, and he knew someone who would pay a lot more because they were old and he got them out of pawn and the man he knew gave us a lot more money."

Chee held up his hand." Grandmother. Listen. The belagaana won't come any more because he is dead. I will have to send someone else. Do you understand?"

Gray Woman Benally understood. She must have understood all along because even while she was talking her cheeks were wet with tears.

11

LOOKING BACK ON IT, trying to analyze how it came to be, Chee finally decided it was partly bad luck and mostly his own fault. They had left Blizzard's car at Gallup. Bad luck. It meant they had to head back in the direction of Chee's place to get it. Bad luck, again. It happened that way because the very last people they'd wasted their time checking lived over by the Standing Rock Chapter House. So they drifted homeward past Coyote Canyon on Navajo Route Nine. That took them right past the Ya-Ta-Hay intersection, which put them closer to Chee's trailer in Window Rock than to Blizzard's car in Gallup. And somewhere before then Blizzard had said he was just too damned tired of driving to drive home. That brought them to the part which was Chee's own fault.

"Why don't you get a motel in Gallup?" Chee said. "Then you can just call your office tomorrow. Find out if they're ready to let us give up on this one."

"I'll just sleep in my car," Blizzard had said.

It was at that point Chee had screwed himself up once again. Maybe it was being tired himself—not wanting to drive into Gallup and then back to Window Rock—or maybe it was feeling sort of guilty for thinking Blizzard was such a hardass when actually he was just new and green. Or maybe it was sympathy for Blizzard—a lonesome stranger in a strange land—or maybe he was feeling a little lonely himself. Whatever the motive, Chee had said:

"Why don't you just bed down at my place? It's better than the back seat of a car?"

And Blizzard, of course, said: "Good idea."

And so there they were, Blizzard deciding he'd sleep on the couch and saying he'd volunteer to cook supper unless Chee wanted to go back into Window Rock and eat some place there. Then the telephone rang.

"It's Janet," the caller said. "I got the impression the other day at the Navajo Inn that you wanted to talk to me about something? Was I right?"

"Absolutely," Chee said.

"So I have an idea. Remember you telling me about that old movie that used Navajos as extras, and they were supposed to be Cheyennes but they were talking Navajo, and saying all the wrong things? The one that they always bring back to that drive-in movie at Gallup. Sort of a campy deal, like the ROCKY HORROR SHOW?"

"Yeah," Chee said. "Cheyenne Autumn. A couple of my relatives are extras in it."

"Well, its back again and I thought—"

But Blizzard was eavesdropping. He overheard. He entered the conversation. "Cheyenne Autumn," he said. "Yeh!"

"Who was that?" Janet said. "You have company?"

"A B.I.A. Policeman. Harold Blizzard."

"You told me about him," Janet said. "He's a Cheyenne, himself, isn't he? I bet he'd like to see that movie. Why don't you ask him to come along."

"I'm sure he's already seen it."

"No, I haven't seen it." Blizzard said, in a voice which Chee felt was inappropriately loud. "I've heard about it, but I never have seen it."

"He hasn't seen it," Janet said. "I heard him. Why don't you bring him along. Don't you think it would be fun to get a Cheyenne's reaction?"

Chee didn't think so. Janet didn't know this Cheyenne. He glanced at Blizzard, sitting on the edge of his couch, looking expectant. "You wanna go?"

"Sure," Blizzard said. "I'd love to go. If I won't be in the way."

"We can talk after the movie," Janet said.

Of course. But they could have also talked during the movie. And talking about the movie during the movie–celebrating the small victory of The People over the white man which this John Ford classic represented—was the reason Navajos still came to see it, and the reason the owner of the Gallup Drive-in still brought it back. And besides talking during the movie, if things developed as Chee had hoped, there were things to do besides talk.

So here they were in Janet Pete's Ford Escort, parked fifth row from the screen with pickup trucks on both sides of them, with Janet sitting beside him and Officer Harold Blizzard hulking over them in the back seat. But one might as well make the best of whatever fate was offering.

"Right in here," Chee said. "Just a minute now. She'll be first girl you see doing the drumming. There she is. That's Irma. My oldest sister."

The scene was solemn. Three Navajos playing the roles of three Cheyenne shamans were about to pray to God that the U.S. Government would keep its treaty promises—a naive concept which had drawn derisive hoots and horn honkings from the rows of pickup trucks and cars. A row of Cheyenne maidens were tapping methodically at drums accompanying the chanted prayers.

"How about the song?" Blizzard asked. "Is that Navajo, too."

Blizzard was leaning forward, chin on the seatback, his big ugly face between Janet and Chee.

"Sort of," Chee said. "It's a kind of modification of a song they sing at Girl Dances, but they slowed it down to make it sound solemn." This was not the way Chee had intended this date with Janet Pete to turn out.

Richard Widmark, commanding the cavalry detachment in charge of keeping order at this powwow between government bureaucrats and the Cheyenne, was now establishing himself as pro-Indian by making derogatory remarks about the reservation where the government was penning the tribe. Since the landscape at which Widmark was pointing was actually the long line of salmon colored cliffs behind the Iyanbito Chapter House just south of Gallup, this produced more horn honking and a derisive shout from somewhere.

And so it went. Scenes came in which somber-looking Cheyenne leaders responded to serious questions in somber-sounding Navajo. When converted back into English by the translator the answers made somber sense. But they produced more happy bedlam among the audience and the "What did he really say?" question from either Janet or Blizzard—and often both. What he really said tended to have something to do with the size of the Colonel's penis, or some other earthy and humorous irrelevancy. Chee would sanitize this a bit or put the humor in the context of Navajo customs or taboos, or explain that the celebratory honking was merely noting the screen appearance on somebody's kinfolks.

It was a long movie, but not long enough for Chee to come up with a plan which would have disposed of Blizzard. The most obvious solution was to simply drive by the Navajo Nation Inn, drop him off and tell him you'd pick him up in the morning. But that was blown by the fact that Blizzard had left his briefcase at Chee's place and the briefcase contained (as Blizzard had proudly told him) "everything you have to have if you get caught somewhere overnight." Coming up with something better, such as sending Blizzard off to the snack bar at the projection center to buy another bucket of popcorn and driving off without him, was ruled out by Janet's unexpected behavior. She seemed to have developed a liking for the man, laughing at his jokes, engaging him in discussions of their mutual childhoods as a city Indians, and quizzing him about what he knew about his tribe, and so forth.

And so, movie finally over, Janet drove them home. And there, with the car still rolling to a stop, Harold Blizzard did something to reestablish himself in Jim Chee's esteem.

"Janet," Blizzard said, "this has been a lot of fun, and I hope to see you again, but now I'm going to rush right in and get some sleep." And he had the door open and was out even before he finished the sentence.

Janet turned off the engine. And the lights. Without a word they watched Blizzard disappear into Chee's trailer.

"I like him," Janet said.

Chee considered what had just happened. "Me, too," he said. "And he was right. It was fun."

"It was," Janet said. "And it was sweet of you to bring him along."

"It was, wasn't it." Chee said. "But why do you think so?"

"Because you wanted to talk to me."

"Yep," Chee said.

"About what?"

"Us."

"Us?" Light from the autumn moon lit her face. She

was smiling at him.

"We've been friends a long time," Chee said.

"Two years, I guess. More than that. Ever since you were trying to nail that old man I was representing up at Farmington. Almost three years if you add in that time I was away at Washington."

"I wasn't trying to nail him," Chee said. "I was looking for information."

"And you tried to trick me?"

"I did trick you," Chee said. "Remember? I found out what I needed to know."

"I remember," she said. "But now I think I'm ready to forgive you."

And with that, Janet Pete leaned across, put her hand behind Chee's head, pulled his face down and kissed him, and sighed, and kissed him again.

It was quite a while later, although the moon was still illuminating Janet's face, when she said:

"No, Jim. No. Time to stop."

"What?" he said. "Why?"

"Because," she said. "I think we sort of stopped being just friends. So now we have to get better acquainted."

"That's just what we were doing," Chee said.

"No," Janet said, sitting up straight, buttoning buttons. "I tried that way once. It doesn't work. It hurts too much if you're wrong."

"In Washington?"

"In Washington, and in law school."

"Not this time," Chee said. "This time you're not wrong. It's me. And you're right."

Janet looked at him, and then out the windshield, thinking. "When you're a certain age," she said. "When you're young, and you fall in love—or think you have—then you think that sex is the way you prove it. Prove that you're in love." She was still staring straight ahead, out the windshield, straight ahead. "But it doesn't prove a damned thing."

Chee thought about that. "What you're saying–."

"What I'm saying is I know I like you. Maybe I like you a lot. Even an awful lot. But it doesn't have anything at all to do with–" She paused. Looked at him. Grinning at him now. "To be exactly correct, it doesn't have MUCH to do with your pearly white teeth, and your long, lean lanky frame, and all those muscles. I started liking you because you're kind to people."

"If I had known that, I would have been even kinder," Chee said.

"But I'm not going to be just another of Jim Chee's girl friends."

"Hey," Chee said. "What do you mean by that."

"I mean we hear about things. We women."

"No truth to it," Chee said. "I'm too busy."

Janet laughed. "Exactly what I hear," she said. "Very busy. A girl at every chapter house."

"Come on, Janet," Chee said. "Knock it off."

"Remember," she said. "You told me about the school teacher at Crownpoint. The one you were in love with."

"A long time ago," Chee said.

Janet was silent for a moment. "How about her? Are you still in touch?"

"She sent me a Christmas card," Chee said. "Wrote "Happy Holidays" on it.

Janet smiled at him, her face illuminated by the moon. "That sounds safe enough," she said.

"Now its your turn. How about The Professor of Law?"

It took her a while to answer. And while he waited, Chee felt his stomach tighten. What would she say? How would she say it?

She said, in a small voice: "I don't like to think about him.

And Chee, who really wanted to drop it, knew that he couldn't. He said: "Tell me why not."

113

"Because it makes me feel so totally stupid. Naive. Dumb." She slammed her fist against the dashboard. "What the hell was I thinking of. I get so angry I want to cry."

"You don't love him any more?"

"I don't think I ever did. I'm sure I didn't. I thought he was sophisticated. And glamorous. He made me feel important, or something to have a REAL PROFESSOR interested in me. But, actually, I don't even like him."

He put his arm around her, pulled her against him and talked into her hair. "I can understand that," he said. "I'll tell you why. Because way back when you and I got acquainted, fairly early on, I got to thinking sort of like that. I'd think I'm a kid out of a sheep camp. Janet's beautiful. She's a sophisticated city girl. A lawyer. All that. Yet I think she likes me. It made me feel great. Made me feel about nine feet tall."

Janet snuggled against him. "Ummmmm," she said. "You know how to make me feel good. My mother's a Scot, but if she was Irish, she'd say you were full of blarney."

"Blarney?"

Janet laughed. "I don't know if the Navajos, if we Navajos, have a word for it. But we certainly should. Sort of like baloney. Or maybe bull."

"No I'm not," Chee said. But if REAL PROFESSORS impress you, I should tell you I might get made into a REAL SERGEANT."

"Well, I think its high time that happened. But weren't you already a sergeant once?"

"Acting sergeant," Chee said. "But that only lasted a few months."

"I remember. It was when you worked at Crownpoint. Before you burned your hand so terribly. Trying to open the door on that burning car." She snuggled against him again. "But tell me about getting promoted."

Chee found himself wishing he hadn't brought it up.

It wasn't likely to happen.

"I probably won't," he said. "It's really more like a joke. But the Lieutenant told me that the Chief himself is personally interested in nailing the guy in that Toadach-ene hit-and-run thing I told you about. The one where the driver backed up and took a look at the pedestrian he'd hit and then drove away and let the man bleed to death." Chee produced a mirthless chuckle. "The Lieutenant says that if I can find the guy, I'll get promoted."

"Oh," Janet said.

"The catch being that there isn't a clue. Everything you can check out in a case like that has already been checked. The garages, paint shops, people who might have seen something. There's nothing to go on."

"That's not fair," Janet said. "You should have been promoted a long time ago anyway. But so what?"

"But what you said about burning my hand reminds me," Chee said. "I'll tell you what made me really feel great about you. I'll never forget it."

He waited. She snuggled again. "Okay," she said. "Go ahead and tell."

"They let me out of the hospital at Albuquerque with that hand all wrapped up so I couldn't use it, and when I got home I found you'd gotten into my trailer and washed all the dishes, and swept,and got the windows all shiny, and cleaned out the refrigerator, and put in some fresh milk and eggs and things like that, and did the laundry, and–"

"Women lawyers like to play housekeeper now and then," she said. "And you had the blues, too. Remember that? You were really down. I didn't want you to come home to a dirty house. All alone, and everything's a mess. I've done that often enough to know it's awfully depress-ing."

"Anyway, I loved you for it. And I still do."

And having said that, he put his hand under her chin,

and treasured the silky feel of her skin, and raised her face and kissed her. And she kissed him. And this went on for quite a while.

And having done that he knew it was time—in fact it was way past time—to pose the question he had been dreading to ask.

"You remember when I asked you about your dad. About where he was from. What part of the reservation. And what his clans were. And you said he was just little when his parents were relocated to Chicago and he never talked about it, and you said you really didn't know. You remember that?"

Janet's head moved against his face, her hair incredibly soft, smelling clean, smelling beautiful, looking beautiful in the moonlight. It was an affirmative nod.

"And you said you'd ask him next time you talked to him? Get him to be more specific."

Another nod.

Chee took a deep breath. He should have handled this a long time ago. But he was afraid to press it because it seemed presumptuous. After all, they were only friends. Now he was afraid of what the answer might be. Chee mother's clan was the Slow Talking People, and his father was born to the Bitter Water Clan. If Janet Pete's father belonged to either of those on either side of his family, then what he and Janet had been doing here was wrong. It violated one of the most stringent taboos of the Navajos—the rigid and complex rules by which The People prohibited incest. Probably Mr. Pete didn't belong to either of them, There were about 65 other clans he could belong to. But then there was Janet's paternal grandmother's paternal clan, and his own family's linked clans. They, too, would make any sexual relationship between Janet and him taboo. He had to find out.

But Janet wasn't saying anything.

"Did he tell you?"

"He wasn't sure," Janet said.

Chee wanted to think about that. He had never known a reservation-born Navajo who didn't know his clans. It was almost like not knowing whether you were man or woman. But perhaps this man's parents—living in a white man's city a thousand miles from the sacred mountains—had wanted to make a white man out of their son. That sometimes happened. Or maybe Janet's father simply didn't want to tell her. Or was kidding her for some reason. Chee couldn't imagine why he'd do that.

"Did he have any idea? Could he tell you anything helpful?"

"He was sure he didn't know about my grandfather's clans, because grandfather had died before they moved. When dad was a just a little boy. But he said he thought his mother might have belonged to the Hunger People. He said he remembered her joking about that. Saying it was appropriate for their family."

Chee probed through his memory. "Hunger People," he said. "That's the Dichin Dine'e."

Janet sensed his mood.

"Why all the questions?" she said. There was no snuggling now. "As if I hadn't been out here long enough to know the answer to that one." She pushed herself away from him. "Well," she said. "How did I do. Am I eligible?" She laughed as she said it.

"I'm like your dad," Chee said. "I'm not sure. Maybe I'm poison for you." He tried to make it sound like a joke.

They sat in the cold moonlight. Janet sighed. "You know what?" she said. "I have a long day tomorrow. And you have to do whatever you policemen do on Tuesdays. So, if I can think of a way to get you out of the car, I'll go on home and get some sleep."

This was not the way Chee wanted this evening to end. He wasn't ready to step out into the cold night.

"I want to ask you about something," he said. "Did you notice when we were—"

"No more questions, Jim. I don't feel like any more questions."

"This one's about Blizzard," he said. "Did you notice how different his reaction was to some of the scenes in that movie? We Navajos would be laughing and honking our horns at our private joke, and he would be looking sad. Same scene, exactly. He'd be watching the destruction of his culture. We'd be watching our kinfolks making fun of the white folks in the movie."

"Different for me, too," Janet said. "My Navajos wasn't good enough to get the joke most of the time." She frowned at him. "How do you know how Blizzard was taking it? You were watching him in the rearview mirror, weren't you."

"Yeah," Chee said.

"And me too, I bet."

"Mostly you," Chee admitted.

"Sneaky," Janet said. "Why watch us?"

He wanted to say *Because you're beautiful. Because it makes me feel good to look at you. Because I have stupidly, hopelessly, allowed myself to fall in love with you.* But he didn't say it. There was the problem of the Dichin Dine'e. Was his memory correct? Was there some linkage of that little clan and one of his own? A long time ago, on a winter night when such teaching is appropriate, Hosteen Frank Sam Nakai, his mother's elder brother and thus his "little father", had given him the history of his Slow Talking People—tracing it all way back to the mythic times just after Changing Woman had left The People to rejoin her lover, the Sun. He had been a boy then, and some of the clan connections had seemed vague and unimportant. But now the name of The Hunger People stirred something in his memory. And now it had become terribly important. It determined whether Jim Chee and Janet

Pete were permissible as friends but taboo as lovers.

So instead of saying what he wanted to say, he said:

"I was thinking about you and me and Cowboy sitting on the roof at Tano—watching the kachina dance. Cowboy's Hopi, and he's in one of the Hopi kachina societies himself, so he saw a lot that we missed. But not as much as the Tano People. All of us up there on the roof were outsiders, I mean. Like the Cheyenne watching the Navajos pretending to be Cheyennes. He missed a lot. We missed a lot, too. I wonder what."

"Me, too," Janet said, voice glum. "I mean, me and Blizzard, too. There was a lot I didn't understand at the movie. Not understanding Navajo very well. And to tell the truth, not understanding about being a Navajo."

Chee studied her profile. He realized, abruptly and with shock, that she was trying not to cry. He experienced a sudden jarring enlightenment. He was seeing a Janet Pete he had even dreamed existed. He was seeing a lonely girl. He, who had been a sheep camp boy surrounded by the town kids in boarding school; he, who had been the country bumpkin among the sophisticates at the University of New Mexico; he, of all people should have recognized what Janet would have encountered on this Big- Reservation-Full-Of-Strangers. But he hadn't. He had seen only the shrewd attorney who looked great in expensive clothing, wore the armor of wit, humor, education, intelligence. He hadn't seen the girl who was trying to find a home. He felt an almost overpowering urge to pull Janet Pete to him, wrap his arms around her, comfort her, warm her against this cold moonlight, tell her he understood, tell her that he loved her and would care for her forever, and would die to make her happy.

Almost overpowering. He could have done it a week ago when they were friends. Now there was the question of the Hunger People. They had moved into that territory beyond friendship and Chee didn't know the way back. If there was a way . . . Perhaps. Chee couldn't think of it. So he simply looked at her profile, as she sat, forlorn, shoulders slumped, staring out the windshield. And he said:

"Remember at Tano? The koshare had come tumbling down off their roof and a couple of them had grabbed one of the kachinas. They were doing a lot of loud talking, gesturing, that sort of thing. And the crowd was laughing. Good natured. Everybody was having fun. Getting into what was going on. And then the clown came in dressed up like a cowboy, riding the stick horse. And two or three clowns with the little toy wagon, selling their stuff to the guy dressed up like he was supposed to be a tourist, or a trader. And remember, sort of suddenly the laughing stopped there for a moment. Everything got quiet."

"Okay," Janet said. "Okay. I remember."

"I wonder what we missed." Chee said. "I wonder what that meant."

"I don't know what that meant," Janet said. "I have no idea. But I guess this conversation we're having right now means we have reverted back to our traditional status."

"Traditional status?"

"Back to being old friends," Janet said. "Good buddies. Remember? Back to telling each other our troubles. Giving each other all sorts of bad advice. About our love affairs with other people."

"I wouldn't say that," Chee said. He couldn't think of anything more sensible to say. "But don't you have any ideas about what might have been going on there at Tano. Any—"

Janet leaned across him and opened his door. "Out," she said. "Go to bed. Be a cop tomorrow."

In the trailer, Chee dropped on his bunk still in his jacket and boots and managed not to think of Janet Pete. He thought of the Todachene case. The case without leads. He considered where it had happened—on a light traffic byway used mostly by reservation locals. That meant the driver was probably a Navajo. No matter how drunk he'd been, he must be aware by now of the nature of his crime. He would feel the guilt. It would force him out of *hozho,* out of that state of harmony which is goal of Navajo metaphysics. If he was a traditional, he would be calling on a shaman for help. Tomorrow, Chee thought, he would begin putting out the word to the medicine people in the Checkerboard and on the Northeast side of the Big Rez. If he was patient, maybe some information would come drifting back. A ceremonial cure for a man who had been involved with death. The man was probably a drunk, someone who had left the Navajo Way. But it was worth a try.

The second thing he would do tomorrow would be provide the Lieutenant with a memo about the Sayesva homicide. Leaphorn had made it clear he didn't want Chee intruding in that very-federal, very off-reservation affair. But rigid as he was, Leaphorn was also smart. He'd earned his reputation. The memo would inform the Lieutenant that something odd seemed to have transpired at the Tano ceremonial, something involving the performance of the clowns. Leaphorn could take it from there.

And with that thought, Chee sat up, undressed and got under his blanket. He listened to the night sounds, which on this night included the heavy breathing of a sleeping Cheyenne. And he thought about the choice he might have to make between Janet Pete and the religion which had always given his life its purpose.

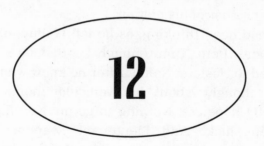

12

TOMORROW WAS A DAY off for Officer Jim Chee. He drove Blizzard to Gallup to pick up his car and the police station. He went to the office on the chance he might catch Leaphorn and didn't. He typed up the intended memo and put it in the in basket on the Lieutenant's tidy desk. He spent a moment examining the oversized map which decorated the wall behind Leaphorn's desk. He noticed that the symbolic pins with which the man marked locations now connected the Tano Pueblo homicide with the one at Thoreau. He nodded to Virginia on the way out and spent the rest of the morning at Gallup Quality Electronics getting the Citizen Band radio in his pickup truck back in working order. That done, he drove north on U.S.666, along the east flank of the Chuska Mountains, past Tohatchi, and the Naschiti Boarding School, and the Sheep Springs chapter house, to the New-comb turnoff—and then climbing westward, past the little cluster of buildings that was Two Grey Hills, past the old

Toadlena boarding school, and onto the old rutted road that led to the sheep camp of Hosteen Frank Sam Nakai, the elder brother of his mother.

He had been thinking, as he left Gallup, of anything except Janet Pete. Time enough for that later. After he had talked to Hosteen Nakai. After he knew what to think. Now he thought about his vehicular homicide case. Apparently hopeless. Nothing to go on. Nothing to hope for except luck. And Lieutenant Leaphorn did not approve of luck. He thought about why Leaphorn, in the face of fairly solid evidence, didn't seem to believe that Eugene Ahkeah had killed Eric Dorsey, or anyone else. He thought about where he might look next for Delmar, his sneaky little problem. And about why the crowd had fallen silent when the clown's wagon appeared in the Tano Plaza. If Leaphorn was interested how that crime connected with the Dorsey case, he would ask the right people at Tano and find out about that.

Then, as his truck jolted higher into the summer pastures of the Chuskas, and ponderosa pine replaced juniper and pinon and the air was colder in his nostrils, and brought the old high country smells back to him, he thought of Hosteen Nakai, the Little Father of his boyhood.

Nobody was home at the summer shack of Hosteen Nakai. Chee found Nakai's mixed flock of sheep and goats in a meadow a mile away, and his uncle sitting on a rotted log with his horse grazing under the aspens. A transistor ghetto blaster sat on the log beside him, apparently tuned to KNDN. From it from it came the impassioned voice of D.J. Nez singing: "My Heroes have always been Indians."

"*Dichin Dine'e*" said Hosteen Nakai. "That would have been way back, a long time ago when we got mixed up with them. Let me think about that a little bit." While he thought he extracted a package of cigarette papers and a sack of Bull Durham from the pocket of his shirt, offered both to Chee, and made himself a cigarette. "It would have been back when the Army made us prisoners and herded us off to Bosque Redondo. Back when we made the Long Walk. Everybody got mixed together then and there was some marrying back and forth. Even some marrying with the Apaches. They had a bunch of Mescalero Apaches penned up there with us."

He lit the cigarette. Exhaled. "Why you interested in the Hunger People? It sounds to me like you finally found yourself a Navajo girl."

Chee nodded.

Nakai said: "I don't know. Her father's mother was born to the *Dichin Dine'e,* you think. But what's her father's clan? What's the rest of the family connections?"

"She doesn't have a 'born to' clan," Chee said. "Her mother is a white woman. Her dad's a Navajo. But he's one of those relocation families. The government moved his family off the reservation in the 1940s. He was just a kid when it happened and I guess his family raised him white. He thinks his mother was Dichin Dine'e. Says he doesn't know about his father's clan."

Hosteen Nakai considered this, exhaled a cloud of blue smoke, muttered some imprecation under his breath.

"Tell me about this woman," he said. "And tell me about yourself. Tell me about the work you are doing."

Chee told Hosteen Nakai about Janet Pete, the city Navajo. And he told him about the driver who had hit the drunk walking beside Navajo Route 1 and left the man to die beside the highway. Could Hosteen Nakai spread the word about this man among the small fraternity of medicine people? Nakai said he would. Chee told him about the deaths of the Christian at Thoreau and the Koshare at Tano, and how nobody seemed to know why either one had died. and about his frustrating hunt for Delmar Kanitewa.

Nakai asked questions, about the Christian, about

the koshare, about the grandmother of Delmar, about the package Delmar had carried.

Five goats had separated themselves from the flock and drifted downslope. Nakai whistled to his dogs, resting in the tall grass beside the aspens. He pointed. The dogs raced down the slope, circled, brought the reluctant goats back to the fold. The autumn sun was low enough now to begin giving shape to rolling plains far below them. Chee could make up the dark line of shadows cast by Chaco Mesa forty miles to the west, North of that, the yellow-tan of the gramma grass prairie was marked by spots of darkness and color—the slate erosion of the Bisti Badlands and the De-Na-Zin Wilderness. Beautiful. Peaceful. But Chee was nervous. Pretty soon Hosteen Nakai would be finished thinking and be ready to talk. For the first time Chee noticed that his uncle had become an old man. Now, what would he say?

"The man who hit the drunk, and left him to die," Nakai said. "I will ask the right people. You are right, if he is following the Beauty Way of the Navajos he would want to cure of that. But why do you want to find him? What good does it do for the man he killed? What good does it do him?. I think you would put him in jail. That won't help him." Nakai shrugged, dismissing it. He allowed the silence to take over, giving Chee time to frame his response. Chee simply nodded.

"The Christian and the Koshare. Two good men, you tell me. Valuable men. But somebody killed them. Usually the people who get killed like this have worked at it themselves." He puffed on the cigarette, exhaled. "You know what I mean. They fooled with somebody's wife. They got drunk and hit somebody. They butchered somebody's cow. Did something wrong, usually. They got out of harmony with everything so somebody might kill them. But not this time, you tell me. Two good men who helped people, hurt nobody. And they were a lot alike in other ways. The Koshare, you know about them. I used to know a Hopi man who was a Koshare at Moenkopi. He would say to me: 'Compared to what our Creator wanted us to be, all men are clowns. And that's what we Koshare do. We act funny to remind the people. To make the people laugh at themselves. We are the sacred clowns,' he said. He is dead now, a long time, but I remember that. And now you have told me that this teacher at Thoreau was funny, too. A good man and he made the children laugh."

Hosteen Nakai tapped the ash from his cigarette and looked at Chee, thoughtfully. As if wondering if Chee could extract any meaning from this. Chee gave no sign that he had.

"Two good men who made fun and helped people. Valuable men. But somebody killed them. There has to be a reason. Everything is connected. So you have to look for something outside of them. Something evil that somehow both of them touched. If you find the driver who killed the man, you do nothing for anybody. But if you find out why it was that these valuable men were killed, you do good work then."

Nakai pushed himself up from the log, stretched, looked down at Chee. "But you want to hear about the woman. That's why you came here. The incest taboo. You know about it. How it makes you sick, makes you crazy. How it hurts your family. Gets everything out of harmony. So be careful about that woman for a while." He took another drag on the cigarette.

"I know an old man who lives over near Crystal. That's where the Hunger People used to be a long time ago before the Army moved them to Bosque Redondo. He's a *hataalii*. He sings the Mountain Top Way, and the Red Ant Way, and some of the other cures. I will talk to him about this woman. I think he will know something about the Hunger People and our Slow Talking Clan. When I know, then I will tell you."

"How long will—"

"Young men are impatient when they see the woman they want," Nakai said. "I know that. I will start tonight."

"Thank you," Chee said.

"One more thing. This boy you are looking for. You think he is running away because he is afraid. Does his grandmother still call the Lieutenant to ask about him?

"Ah," Chee said. Why hadn't he thought of that. "No. Not for several days."

"Then the grandmother knows where to find him," Nakai said. He exhaled smoke and stood looking into the blue cloud hanging in the still air. "And she also knows, I think, that the boy has some reason to be afraid."

13

THE VERY FIRST THING Jim Chee intended to do when he reached his office the next morning was call Tribal Councilwoman Bertha Roanhorse. The memos Virginia had left on his blotter asked him to return calls from Lieutenant Toddy at Crownpoint and Captain Largo at Tuba City. They could wait. So could the manila envelope Virginia had dropped in his In Basket. As it turned out, so could Jim Chee. The Navajo Communications Company telephone book listed a Roanhorse number among the nineteen telephones served by the Toadlena exchange, but a stern feminine voice on an answering machine instructed Chee to leave a message. He did. Then he called the Legislative Secretary's Office. Another blank. None of the Tribal Council committees on which Mrs. Roanhorse served was meeting today, He left another message. Next he called the Navajo Nation Inn. Yes, Councilwoman Roanhorse was registered. She didn't answer the room phone. Chee left a third message.

Having exhausted all possibilities he could think of, he returned the call to Captain Largo. Largo was out, but the Tuba City dispatcher had a message for him. "Tell Chee we have drawn a blank on front end repairs here in his hit-run case."

He called for Lieutenant Toddy at Crownpoint. The Lieutenant was in&. "I just wanted you to know we didn't forget you guys in the Navajo Nation's Capitol City," Toddy said. "We haven't forgotten, but if your vehicular homicide suspect was somebody around here nobody seems to know about it."

So much for that. The day was off to a bad start. He'd call Blizzard and tell him that he'd deduced that Councilman Roanhorse was hiding Delmar. That should impress Blizzard. But naturally Blizzard wasn't in. Chee took the manila envelope out of the In Basket. He'd see what Virginia had left for him.

The envelope had "For Officer Chee" printed big across it, but nothing else. He tore it open and poured out an audio tape cassette. He turned it over. Nothing on either side to suggest what it held. He dialed Virginia to ask her who had left it. Virginia wasn't at her desk. The radio on the shelf behind Lieutenant Leaphorn's desk included a tape player. He'd borrow that.

But the Lieutenant, like Virginia, and Blizzard and Roanhorse, was not in. Chee left the door open behind him, turned on the radio and slipped in the tape.

It produced the buzzes and clicks characteristic of amateur taping, then ringing sounds, and a voice saying: 'You have reached the office of Councilman Jimmy Chester. I can't come to the phone now but leave a message after the beep and I'll call you back." A brief silence followed, then a beep, and then a second voice:

"Jimmy, this is Ed Zeck. If you're there pick it up. I need to talk to you. Otherwise, call me down at the Motor Inn. It's room 217 and I'll be there until–

"I'm here, Ed. What do you need?"

"I need your opinion. I hear some things that worry me."

"Like what?"

"Like maybe the American Indian Movement is going to mix into this. You hear that?"

"Forget it. AIM doesn't amount to anything out here. They're city Indians. Besides, far as Navajos are concerned, they always get on the wrong side of the argument."

Chee stopped the tape. What the devil was this. Obviously, a telephone conversation. He recognized the scratchy voice of Zeck. Presumably the man responding to Jimmy Chester's answering machine was as advertised, Jimmy Chester. But should he be eavesdropping? And who had sent him this? The Nature First guy? What was his name? Applebee.

On Leaphorn's telephone, he buzzed Shirley's desk on Leaphorn's telephone. Now she was there.

"What package?" Virginia asked.

"Actually a manila envelope."

"Not me," Virginia said. "Somebody must have just dropped it on your desk. None of you guys ever lock a door or anything. You don't even close them, half the time. You think nobody steals from you because you're policemen. Well, I'll tell you what. People walk right in here and steal your purse off your chair. Steal your jacket. I had that happen. I've been telling the Chief for years he should have a rule about keeping the doors locked. When you're out. Or at least closing them." Shirley paused for a breath, giving Chee an opportunity.

"It makes everything more efficient," Chee said, wondering why he was arguing about this. "When you need to talk to someone, you can look in and see if he's there, or if he's busy. That's the way they did it at Crownpoint, too. When I was stationed there. And that's the way it was at

Tuba City."

"Well, don't blame me, then," Virginia said, thereby ending the conversation and leaving Chee staring at Joe Leaphorn's radio.

Maybe the tape itself would tell him who had brought it. He pushed the PLAY button. The memo he'd written for Leaphorn yesterday was still in the Lieutenant's In Basket. Maybe Leaphorn was out working the Eric Dorsey case, or some other crime of some importance. Or maybe he had assigned himself a drive over to Flagstaff. According to the department scuttlebutt, he was supposed to have something going with a woman professor over there. The tape stopped whirring, clicked, and abruptly began speaking in a rumbling male voice with a West Texas accent.

"–what I hear. But I'll take your word for it. The other thing. You have any push with the people at the Navajo Times?"

Ed Zeck, Chee thought. The same sound he'd heard when Zeck visited their table at the Navajo Inn.

"Not much. I know the reporter who covers council meetings. He interviewed me last month. That's about it."

The voice of a councilman, then, Chee thought. He'd read an interview with Jimmy Chester.

"I didn't want to get a big argument going in the press about the dump. Silence is golden sometimes. Especially when you're dealing with tree huggers. But the paper started running letters bitching about the project. They had one in there from a tribal cop. You think we should react? You know, seeing if we can put a stop to getting politics mixed in with the Tribal Police. Lot of people would feel strongly about that, Jimmy."

Jimmy. Jimmy Chester.

"No," Chester said.

"Just hope for the best, you mean? Hope nothing gets stirred up."

"Yes," Chester said. "Let's talk about my money."

The speakers emitted the tinny sound of Zeck's laughter. "The check's in the mail," he said. "Just like I keep telling you."

"I'm not laughing," Chester said. "The bank's not laughing. I've got to pay off that note. Remember, it was me that signed the paper."

For a moment the only sound was the tape running.

"All right then," Zeck said. "Twenty two thousand something. I'll have to do some transferring around. Tell 'em you'll have it for 'em Monday."

"And none of this 'check in the mail' crap," Chester said.

"I'll make it a cashier's check," Zeck said. "And what do you hear from Tano?"

"Nothing much. I think we're all right there. Bert Penitewa's for it. He's a popular man there and Tano pretty well does what the governor wants. It's not split like your Navajo council. There, the governor's also the big man in one of the religious kivas."

"I know," Chester said.

"We should just leave that alone then, you think? Anything else going on I ought to know about?"

"Nothing," Chester said. "You go on down and get that money transferred. And it's not twenty two thousand something. It's twenty two thousand, five hundred and thirty. Maybe those banks don't charge anything to loan money to you belagaana guys, but us Navajos have to pay interest. Twenty two thousand five hundred and thirty."

"And some odd cents, which we'll round off. So Yah Tay Hay for now."

There was a click, and then only the sound of the tape running.

Chee let it run until it shut itself off. Then he rewound it, replayed the conversation, and rewound it again. He had decided where it must have come from.

Who else but Roger Applebee. The environmentalist had said he knew a way to get some evidence proving Jimmy Chester was corrupt. And he had gotten it. Probably with an illegal wiretap. Actually, not a wiretap these days. More likely one of those gadgets which pick up wireless telephone conversations. He'd seen one in an electronics supply store in Farmington. But still the tape wouldn't be usable in court or even before a grand jury. If it was illegal, and it probably was, how could it be used?

He was thinking about that, when the telephone rang.

"Joe Leaphorn's office."

"Joe? Is Jim Chee still working on that hit-and-run vehicular homicide case?" It was the voice of the Window Rock dispatcher. "The one where—"

"This is Chee," Chee said. "The Lieutenant's away from his office."

"Hey, man. You lucked out. Your suspect just confessed. Right over the radio."

"Confessed? What d'ya mean?"

"He drove up to KNDN in Farmington, and walked in where they have that open mike for the public to make announcements on, and he said he did it, and he was sorry, and he was going to make restitution. He said he was drunk. Said he didn't know he'd hit the man."

"Who was it?"

"We haven't got him yet. He walked out and drove away."

"Wonderful," Chee said. "Didn't they call the cops? The people at the station."

"I guess so. Everybody's looking for him. Farmington police, New Mexico state cops, San Juan Sheriff's department. Our people at Shiprock. Everybody."

"Well," Chee said. "I guess I'll go join 'em." It was three hours over the mountain to Farmington but the hit-and-run was his baby. Jimmy Chester would have to wait.

14

"WHERE ALL DID YOU LOOK," Dilly Streib asked. He was standing in the door of the St. Bonaventure High School shop, looking across the clutter.

"Where?" said Lieutenant Toddy. He waved his arms in a gesture which encompassed the cosmos. "I guess you'd have to say everywhere."

"So I guess that's where we have to look again," Streib said. "How about you Joe. You got any ideas about where to start?"

Leaphorn shrugged.

"It would help me if I knew what the hell we're supposed to be looking for," Toddy said. He started sorting through the array of chisels, awls, punches, hammers, nail sets, files and planes racked on the wall.

Streib maintained his position, leaning against the doorjamb. "If you ask Lieutenant Leaphorn that question, he'll tell you to look for clues. Then you ask him how you know its a clue, and he'll give you a wise look."

"I'm in favor of just looking," Leaphorn said. "You never know what you'll find."

"That's Joe's theory," Streib said. "You don't look for anything in particular. You just look and if you look long enough you reach retirement age."

"At exactly the same speed as you do leaning in doorways," Leaphorn said.

"How about this," Lieutenant Toddy asked. He showed Leaphorn a mallet. "Could that be blood?"

Leaphorn looked at it, scraped with a thumbnail, showed the result to Toddy.

"Dried paint," Toddy said.

"I'll tell you what we're looking for," said Streib. "We hope to discover a polaroid photo of Eugene Ahkeah with his bludgeon raised, about to hit Mister Dorsey on the back on the head. See if he left it in the wastebasket."

Toddy was not enjoying Streib's humor. "We went through the waste baskets. Went through everything."

"I was just kidding," Streib said. He pushed himself off from the door jam and began opening drawers. "I wonder what these things could be for?" He displayed a small, shallow wooden box.

"They're forms for sand casting metal," Toddy said. "You put wet sand in and make the shape in it that you want and then you pour in the molten silver—or whatever you're working with. That one looks like the size you'd use to cast a belt buckle."

"How about this one?" Streib handed Toddy a much deeper box, almost a cube. "Maybe some sort of jewelry?"

"No idea," Toddy said. He put it on the work bench.

Leaphorn picked it up. It was newer than the more standard casting forms and looked carefully made. The sand inside it was packed hard and crusted by the intense heat of the metal it had formed. He stared at the indentation. An odd shape What could it have been? One of those fancy desk cigarette lighters maybe. But it looked too round for the Aladdin's lamp shape favored for those. In fact, the shape pressed into the sand must have been close to a perfect hemisphere. Maybe just a wee bit ovoid. But Leaphorn now saw it had had lettering on it. He could make out the shape of what might have been a one, and a clear eight next to it. Eighteen. But what next? Beyond the eight was a mostly erased shape that might have been a six, but the sand was too disturbed to leave a legible imprint. He placed the form carefully in the drawer of the work bench. He'd waste a little time later trying to find out which student was working with it and what sort of object the box was forming.

They spent almost an hour in the shop before Toddy declared the press of duty at Crownpoint and left. Streib decided he should question Mission volunteers again. He disappeared toward the living quarters. Leaphorn remained. Except for the sand cast form, he had found nothing that provoked interest except some shavings from a wood much heavier and darker than the oak, fir and pine which almost everyone seemed to be using. Nor did it match the various half-finished tables, benches, table lamp bases, rolling pins and kitchen shelves racked in the workshop storeroom. Leaphorn put a sample of it in an envelope and into his pocket. Later he would find someone to explain it. Or perhaps he would simply forget it. It had more relevance to his personal curiosity than to this homicide investigation.

It had always seemed to Leaphorn that the question without a satisfactory answer in this affair was why it had happened. If a man was drunk enough, not much motive was required. But Ahkeah had to have some reason. Dilly suggested that he'd run out of whisky money, had come here to borrow from Dorsey, had been turned down, and had killed Dorsey in the resulting rage. And if that reason for a drunk Ahkeah had been money, why hadn't he sold the silver ingots he'd taken? It would have been easy enough to cash them in. Why stash them away in box under his house? Any pawn shop in Gallup or Grants, or any of the places that sold supplies to jewelers would buy them. Or, if he was worried about the sale being traced, Ahkean probably knew a dozen Navajos or Zunis or Acomas or Lagunas—white people, too, for that matter—who were making silver stuff and who wouldn't ask questions if the price was right.

Leaphorn still had motive on his mind as he worked his way methodically through Dorsey's grade books. He was reading the man's notes on class projects when he heard Father Haines. The priest was standing hesitantly at the door.

"Any luck?"

"None," said Leaphorn, who had never believed in luck. He motioned Haines toward the chair beside him and carefully removed the cube-shaped form from the drawer. "You have any idea what this form is for?"

Father Haines inspected it, frowned, shook his head. "It looks like there might have been some writing pressed down in there. Maybe it was some sort of medal. A trophy for something."

"It looks like the wrong shape," Leaphorn said. "I think it must have been something sort of round—like a small billiard ball."

"A silver ball," Leaphorn said.

"He always tried to get the kids to make useful things. Or things they could sell." Haines laughed. "I think Bonaventure School is flooding the market with authentic Navajo sandcast silver belt buckles, and bracelets and so forth."

"And it sounds like (Leaphorn tapped Dorsey's class notes) these kids were making pretty good stuff."

Haines laughed. "Actually some of them were. Some of these kids are really talented. But Eric had this policy of trying to make these youngsters feel a little more artistic than they actually were. I don't think he ever saw a student-made belt buckle he couldn't find something good to say about."

"There wasn't much turquoise here," Leaphorn said. "Was it all accounted for?"

"Probably. He didn't ever have much. No budget for it. If one of the boys was doing something special, he'd usually just dig up some money and buy some stones in Gallup." Haines paused. "You don't think Eugene did it, do you ?"

"I don't know. You saw the box they found under his place. It looks like he was the one."

They thought about it. Father Haines had been on the Reservation long enough to have learned from The Dine'e something that some whites never learn in a lifetime–that there's nothing wrong with mutual silence. The clock above the door made one of those sounds that old electric clocks sometimes make. The high notes of a shout and a dog barking drifted faintly through the glass. All the smells of a high school crafts shop were in the air around them—machine oil, wood shavings, resin, turpentine, wax, paint, sawdust. Healthy smells, Leaphorn thought, that covered up the smell of a good man's blood.

"Last winter Eric and some of the rest of us had gone down to that big Giant Truck Stop beside Interstate 40. We were having dinner at the coffee shop there. Eric got a phone call. Some kid —one of Eugene's nephews—was calling from here to tell him that Eugene was having car trouble. So Eric wraps his hamburger and his fries in a napkin and says he has to go. I remember I said Eugene can wait a little while. Sit down and finish your supper. And I said he's probably half drunk anyway—feeling no pain. And Eric said: 'Yeah, that's why I've got to hurry.'"

"So you don't think Eugene killed him."

"I don't know," Haines said. "With whiskey involved, you can't tell. Mothers kill their children when they're drunk. Or drink when they're pregnant, which is about as bad as killing them."

But, Leaphorn was thinking, even with whisky there has to be some sort of reason. Something to ignite the lethal rage. He extracted the envelope from his pocket, shook the shaving onto his palm and showed it to the priest. "Any idea what that's from?"

"It looks like it came off a table leg or something like that. It looks like a shaving from a lathe."

"What kind of wood?"

Haines inspected it. "Dark and tough," he said. "I know what it's not. It's not any kind of pine, or fir, or cedar, or oak unless there some specie that has a darker color. It's not redwood. I'm pretty sure its not mahogany and I know its not maple."

"Something exotic," Leaphorn said. "Maybe teak or ebony or something like that."

"I guess so," Haines said. "I have an idea that ebony is real black and teak's lighter. Maybe ebony. But I'm no expert."

"How often is this room swept out? Cleaned?"

"Every evening," Haines said. "Dorsey did it himself. He was a very neat man." He made a sweeping gesture around the room. "Normally if you walked in here when a class wasn't in session you'd find it slick as a whistle. No sawdust anywhere. Working surfaces all clear. Everything in its place. Not like this." He made a disapproving face at the cluttered room. "But after we found Eric's body, and the police came, they asked us to lock the room and not touch anything until the investigation was finished."

Leaphorn laid the shaving on the desk. "There was quite a bit of this dark stuff over by the lathe and some more of it over on the bench with the woodworking vice. So I guess it had to get there the morning he was killed."

"Yes," Haines said. "Eric always swept up. And he used one of those shop vacuums and a dust cloth. He said that was one of the things he wanted to teach the kids. You want to be a craftsman, or an artist, you have to be organized. You have to be neat."

"Did he allow some of the students to take out the projects they were working on?"

Haines looked surprised. "I don't think so," he said. "Maybe if they were sanding something. Something they could do at home. But the silversmithing projects, we kept them locked up in the store room."

Leaphorn touched the shaving with his finger. He said: "I searched through the storeroom, and every place in here I can think of. I can't find anything that looks like this wood."

"Oh," said Father Haines. He considered. "Maybe one of the students was working on–" He left the sentence unfinished.

"Maybe," Leaphorn said. "We'll talk to the students and find out what everybody was doing in woodworking. But Dorsey kept a list of what the kids were making. Nothing looked like it would be using a fancy wood."

"So you're thinking that maybe—"

"I'm thinking I'll take another look around Eugene Ahkean's place to see if I can find it there."

And he was also thinking that he would arrange to do a little crossing of jurisdictional lines. Dilly Streib could arrange it for him—and come along if he wanted to. They'd make a trip to Tano Pueblo just as Jim Chee had suggested in that memo he'd left. Leaphorn had decided as soon as he'd read it that he wanted to find out what was in the wagon the clown was pulling. What was it that had caused the people of Tano to quit laughing and suddenly become serious. And he wanted to see if he could find something made of heavy, dark wood in the place where Francis Sayesva stayed when he came home to Tano. Came home to educate his people, or maybe warn them about something. And to die.

15

SAMMIE YAZZIE SEEMED to be in charge of Radio Station KNDN when Chee pulled up off of Farmington's Main Street into the parking lot. He was about Chee's age, with a neat mustache, a short haircut and a harassed look. If he had enjoyed the excitement of broadcasting a confession earlier in the day it had worn off long ago.

"I don't know what else I can tell you. Like I told the deputy, and Farmington police, and the tribal policeman who got here this morning, the guy just walked in, and went to the open mike there and did his thing."

"I've got the police report," Chee said, displaying the copy he picked up at the Farmington Police Station. "It gives the facts: medium sized, middle aged male, probably Navajo, dressed in jeans and jean jacket and billed cap with CAT symbol on crown, wearing darkrimmed glasses, driving a dirty green pickup, possibly Ford 150 or Dodge Ram. Parked in front, walked in, went to the open mike, said he wanted to broadcast an announcement. Told to wait until end of record. Waited. Given signal. Then he made his statement, walked out. Drove away. Right?"

"Right," Yazzie said. "That's what happened. Except I think Ellie told the officers that she couldn't read the license plate when she went to the window to look. And the bumper sticker."

"Yeah. That's in here. He read again: "License obscured by dirt. Witness noticed sticker on tail gate: 'ERNIE'S THE GREATEST'. That's a funny thing to put on a sticker. You have any idea where it's from?"

Yazzie shrugged. "That's a new one to me. Maybe its one of those you get made up. Like, 'My kid's an honor student at Farmington High.' Or 'My kid can whip your honor student at Farmington High."

"Maybe," Chee said. "How about shoes? Boots?"

"You better talk to Ellie," Yazzie said. "She got the best look at him."

Ellie looked like she was about a year out of high school and was still enjoying talking to cops–especially a good looking young cop.

"Boots?" she said, and closed her eyes to show that she was thinking hard and had pretty long eyelashes. "No. He had on high top work shoes. I remember because I noticed he had tracked in dirt and I looked."

"Anything else? That might be useful?

"How would the boots be useful?"

"Well," Chee said. "What if he was wearing tall lace-up boots. That might tell us he worked for the telephone company. Or the power company. A lineman. Pole climber."

"Oh," Ellie said. "Or if he wore those big heavy shoes with the steel cap in the toe, maybe for the pipeline company."

"Right," Chee said, returning her grin. "Now if we're lucky you'll remember he had a patch on his jacket that said 'MEMBER SAN JUAN COUNTY SHERIFF'S POSSE', or Lions Club. Something easy like that."

Ellie displayed her eyelashes again, deep in thought. "No," she said. "I just remember he looked sort of nervous and scared, but that's not unusual. Lot of people are nervous when they pick up the mike. You know. About to broadcast on the radio. And he was kind of old."

Chee looked at the report. "It says middle aged here. Was he older than 'middle aged.'?"

"That's kind of old," she said, and shrugged. "You know. Maybe past thirty. And nervous."

It would be natural to be nervous, Chee was thinking, when you're going to tell the world you killed somebody.

"Nervous, you said. But he didn't ask anybody how to use the microphone? How to turn it on? How far to hold it from his face. Any of that?"

"I don't think so."

"He just picked it up and seemed to know how to do all the right things.?"

"Yeah," she said. "I didn't think about that. Some of the people who come in to make announcements need to be told. You know, they're from out in the country. Wanting to announce a funeral, or a sing, or a Girl Dance, or a meeting of the grazing committee at their chapter house. Something like that. And they don't know anything about using a microphone."

"One other thing," Chee said. "I understand these open mike announcements are taped while they're broadcast."

"That's a government requirement," Ellie said. "We have to do that. It's automatic."

"Could I get a copy?"

"We already made one for the Sheriff," Ellie said. "And for the Farmington cops."

"How about for me?"

Ellie inspected him, and giggled. "Why not?" she said. "You'll have to wait a minute."

145

While he waited, Chee peered out into the parking lot at his patrol car and the other vehicles there. Through the glass at this range he couldn't read the COURTEOUS DRIVING SAVES LIVES, nor the BUCKLE UP ITS THE LAW stickers on his own bumper. He made out the National Rifle Association membership sticker on the adjoining truck only because it was familiar. If Ellie had read the ERNIE sticker on the suspect's truck it must have been printed large. He'd ask about that when she got back, which was at that very moment.

"Here it is," she said, handing him a cassette. "No charge to a policeman."

"Thanks," Chee said. "You remember where the man's pickup was parked."

"Right there," she said, pointing. "The nearest spot."

"You're certain about what the bumper sticker said. The report says the truck was muddy. There was dirt on the license plate."

"Not on the sticker," Ellie said. "It looked brand new. And it was great big. The letters, I mean."

"Well," Chee said, "Thanks a lot." He handed her two cards, one identifying him as a Navajo Tribal Policeman and giving his office number, the other identifying him as a hataalii, and a singer of the Blessing Way and giving the number of the telephone in his trailer. "Home and office," he explained. "Would you give me a call if you think of anything else? Anything at all that might help me find this guy."

"The only other thing I can think of that was funny was the cap he had on." Ellie blinked at him, exposing eyelashes against a smooth cheek.

"Funny like how?"

"I don't mean ha ha funny. Funny strange. It was one of those baseball caps like everybody wears but it looked like somebody had sat on the bill. It went out straight from the crown and then it was bent up, like this. *Ellie raised her right hand to her forehead, palm upward.* She recreated with her fingers the oddly bent cap bill. "It looked like the bill was broken." She made a disapproving face.

"That was a good thing to notice," Chee said, smiling at her. "It's the sort of unusual thing which might help us find him. Can you think of anything else."

Ellie's expression said she was trying. She thought of something, considered it, looked doubtful, went back to thinking.

"You thought of something," Chee said. "What was it?"

She giggled. "I don't see how this will help. But I remember the funny way he smelled." She wrinkled her nose, and laughed. "He smelled like onions."

"I'll bet he'd been eating a hamburger," Chee said. "Maybe a Lottaburger. They have lots of onions." Which was the reason Chee favored them himself.

"No," she said. "It was morning. And it was his clothing, I think. Strong enough to make your eyes water." She was looking at the cards he'd given her. "You're a *yataali*," she asked, looking up at him. "Really? I didn't know you can be a medicine man and a policeman at the same time."

"I'm beginning to think you can't," Chee said.

16

ON HIS WAY OUT to his pickup Chee decided his next step would be to check places in Farmington where bumper stickers were printed. Probably he'd find no more than one or two. He'd ask at the police city station and check the telephone book. And when he'd found the one that had printed the ERNIE IS THE GREATEST business he would have another shot at finding the cold blooded bastard he was looking for. Then he'd complete this investigation. He'd make the arrest. He would impress Lieutenant Leaphorn, sew on his sergeant stripes, and add about five hundred bucks to his monthly income. Then he would be in much better shape to persuade Janet to marry him. In better shape, that is, if the Hunger People clan didn't link with one of his own and make her his sister and therefore sexually taboo. And if Janet would forgive him for the clumsy way he'd handled that business. If he'd done it as badly as he remembered, that didn't seem likely. Finally, there was the original question of whether a sophisticated, urbane, graduate of Stanford Law School and member of the bar would marry a sheep camp boy turned cop under any circumstances.

And what if she was a clan sister? What would he do then? that? Chee didn't want to think about it. He drove down Main toward the police station deliberately not thinking about it. Instead he got himself better organized mentally on the Lieutenant Leaphorn front. Leaphorn had made it abundantly clear that his help would not be welcomed by the B.I.A. nor by the Albuquerque FBI in the Sayesva homicide. Stay away from Tano was the Lieutenant's final instructions.

And then there was the matter of the Councilman Chester bribery business. He had rushed off without leaving Leaphorn any explanation of that tape he'd left in the tape player on the Lieutenant's desk. Not that much explanation would be needed. It would be clear enough to Leaphorn. Someone had tapped Jimmy Chester's telephone—or maybe Ed Zeck's. Ed Zeck was an old-time Indian Country lawyer—a regular lobbyist at tribal council meetings. Leaphorn would recognize his gravel voice. So you had a tape of Chester dunning Zeck for his bribe money. A very businesslike arrangement, so it sounded. It sounded as if Chester was accumulating interest on his twenty grand payoff. And apparently Chester had borrowed it from the bank to be paid back when Zeck delivered the money. Sort of an advance, or maybe a way to launder it. Such high finance, the way banks operated, was far, far from Chee's zone of expertise.

The Farmington police, it turned out, were way ahead of Chee. Chee was referred to Sergeant Eddie Bell.

"We handled that right after it happened," Bell said. "There're thirteen places in the yellow pages that do printing, an all but two will do bumper stickers if you want a thousand or so, and three of 'em would run off a single if you're willing to pay the preparation cost, and not a damn one of them remembered doing an ERNIE IS THE GREAT-EST job."

"Well, hell," Chee said. "You'd think somebody would remember an odd one like that. It would have to be one of those places that does singles, I'd think." This concept was new to Chee. He had admired thousands of bumper stickers, from assurances that God loved him, to recommendations for saving the planet, to obscenities, to dire warnings about following too closely. declarations of RED POWER, and even one which simply said: BUMPER STICKER. But he'd never given a thought to where they came from.

"Do they do that?" he asked Bell. "You just walk in and tell me what you want and they print you one."

"Sure," Bell said. Quikprint right down in the next block will run one off for you in five minutes. But its pretty expensive that way. Not like so much a thousand. So they don't do many and everyone we talked to says they thought they'd remember that ERNIE IS THE GREATEST. It's sort of weird."

"I guess he must have got it printed somewhere else," Chee said.

Sergeant Bell's expression said he thought that was a statement to obvious to need saying.

"We asked for checks of printers at Albuquerque, and Gallup, and Flagstaff, and Phoenix. They all came up blanks. But you know how that is."

"Yeah," Chee said. People tended to be way too busy to do other people's work. Or to do it well. He was disappointed and Bell saw it.

"Look. If you're going to keep working on this sticker business, be careful with it. It's an easy one to spot. If he finds out we're watching for it, he'll scrape it off. And if he doesn't scrape it off, we're going to have him sooner or later."

Now Bell also had said something too obvious to need saying. They were even.

151

And Chee was back to square one. The only thing he had that probably hadn't been worked by the State Cops, or Farmington police, or the San Juan County Sheriff, was the smell of onions. The man must have smelled strongly—not just onion breath. And it was, as Ellie had said, too early to be eating hamburgers. She's said it seemed like the odor came from his clothing and it must have been powerful.

Chee drove down to the Garden Spot Produce Company on West Main, checked the vehicles parked there without scoring a green pickup with an ERNIE IS THE GREATEST sticker, and parked himself. He'd scanned through the typed copy of his man's confession which Bell had given him. Now he got out the taped copy he'd gotten at KNDN and stuck in his player.

The voice was that of a young woman, talking in halting Navajo. Chee frowned. They'd given him the wrong tape. The woman was reporting the death of her maternal aunt, obviously reading something that had been written for her in English and stumbling over the translation. The family was getting together at the home of the deceased in Mexican Water to talk about what to do with her horses, and her grazing lease, and other property and there was going to be a funeral service at the Assembly of God Mission at Kayenta. The halting voice told Chee that the woman was born to the Streams Come Together People and born for the Towering House clan. But, Chee thought, whatever her clans, she had gone onto the Jesus Road. Before he could ponder that and whether it would effect the incest taboo, another voice came on.

"I tell the family of Hosteen Todachine that I am sorry. I heard the truck hit something, but I was drunk. I went back and I didn't see anything. I don't drink hardly ever so when I did drink that night I got drunk. I would have helped him if I knew he was there. Now I am sorry. I will send money every two weeks to help make up for the help he gave you. I want you to know I am sorry." End of tape. Chee rewound it and played it again. The words rushed out—a man tense with emotion and, understandably, in a hurry. He played it again. The speech sounded memorized, as if the man had written it out. He must have thought about it a lot. In this third time through Chee was impressed with the emotion. The man sounded as if he were holding back tears.

He switched off the tape, turned on the radio, punched the AM button. At the moment, KNDN was broadcasting a singer asking "why did you leave me Lucille, with three little children and a crop in the field." He turned the volume down a notch, and sat trying to visualize the man. Medium sized, medium aged, Ellie had said, wearing jeans and a jean jacket and a baseball cap with a long bill "bent up in the middle like somebody had stepped on it." On the tape he sounded like a childhood Navajo speaker—probably not boarding school. A lot of middle-aged Navajos had a limited vocabulary in their language because in those days the B.I.A. wouldn't let them speak it in school and that was the age period when you grow out of your childhood vocabulary. This man spoke it well. He knew the verbs to convert an English-language situation into fluent Navajo. Chee switched off the radio and went into the produce store. The clerk pointed him to a telephone. He called the Farmington Police number. Yes, Sergeant Bell was in.

"You know in that broadcast, the man said he was going to send money to the Todachine family." Chee said. "Do you know if he's done it?"

"He did," Bell said. "At least somebody did." He laughed. "Unfortunately, he forgot to put his return address on the envelope."

"Was it mailed around here?"

"Farmington postmark," Bell said. "Apparently he mailed it the same morning he made his little broadcast."

"How much?"

"Six twenties, two tens and a five," Bell said. "Wish he's sent a check."

"That'd be hundred and forty five dollars," Chee said. "Does that mean anything to you? The amount?"

"Not a damn thing," Bell said. "At least he didn't spend it getting drunk again."

"Well," Chee said. "Thanks. If I learn anything I'll let you know. But I haven't got much hope."

"Hey, by the way, did you hear it happened again. Down at your place this time?"

"What happened?"

"Somebody showed up at that open mike KNDN operates down at Kirtland. Down at Navajo Tractor Company by the highway at Kirtland. This guy walked in and broadcast a tape of one of your tribal councilmen talking about a bribe."

Chee sucked in his breath. "Did what?"

"I didn't hear it," Bell said. "But we got a bunch of calls about it and somebody went down to see about it. They told him this guy walked into the dealership there and got in line with the people waiting to broadcast their announcements. The microphone in a little box on the wall in the lobby and you just wait your turn. He said 'what you are about to hear is a telephone talk between tribal councilman so–and–so and such–and–such, the lobbyist for some company or other. And then he played this conversation. Held his little tape recorder up to the mike."

"Be damned," Chee said. "Who was it."

"Who knows. People come in every day during the noon hour to make announcements and nobody paid much attention. It happened a lot like the last one at the station in Farmington."

"Did you get a description?"

"Not much a one. White man. Maybe five eight or ten.

Maybe forty or forty five. Had a jacket on and a hat. Nothing on what he was driving, or how he got there. The manager said there's always a line of Navajos coming in to use the mike during that period for making announcements. The people working there are selling tractors, farm equipment and stuff and not paying attention to the mike. It's just a public service gimmick with the station. Probably they get a trade out on their radio advertising or something."

'That description doesn't narrow it down much." Chee said. It didn't need to be narrowed down for him. The man would be Roger Applebee. Applebee had found a way to use an illegal tape that couldn't be used in court.

He hung up and stood with his hand still on the telephone, considering his next step. Applebee's broadcast would stir up a lot of trouble, he had no doubt of that. But it wasn't his trouble. Not unless the Lieutenant changed his mind and let him investigate what was going on with the toxic waste dump business. That wasn't likely. His trouble was the Todachene hit-and-run. Chee's thoughts turned to the six twenties, two tens and one five, and to the voice of a man promising to send money every two weeks.

"Thanks for the telephone," he said to the clerk. "Could I ask you something sort of semi-personal?"

The clerk looked doubtful.

"Do you people working here get paid once a month, or once a week, or every two weeks, or what?"

"Once a week," the clerk said.

That took care of that.

The bins beside him were stacked with fruit. Oranges, then three varieties of apples, then pear, then bananas, then grapes. Bins along the wall held a mountain of potatoes, then yams, then lettuce, then cabbage, then carrots,then onions, then–"

The clerk was counting out change for a customer.

"Where do you get your onions?" Chee asked.

"Onions?" the clerk asked.

Chee pointed. "Onions," he repeated.

"I think they're local," the clerk said. "Yeah, we get them from N.A.I."

"From Navajo Agricultural Industries?" Chee said. "Right over across the river?"

"That's right," the clerk said, but Chee was already heading for the door. Why hadn't he thought of that?

17

EVEN BEFORE HE HAD finished reading Chee's memo, Lieutenant Joe Leaphorn had come to a couple of conclusions. The first was that he had guessed right about Chee. He was young, and still had the crazy idea that he could be both a yataali and a tribal cop simultaneously, and he had a tendency to do things his own way. But he was smart. And in this job, being smart was something you needed to be a lot. The second conclusion was that he should clear up this question of the link between Eric Dorsey and Francis Sayesva now, and the place to start was exactly in the unlikely place that's Chee's memo had suggested.

He picked up the cap he'd just taken off and headed for the door. The first step was to talk to Dilly Streib,. Streib would probably still be lingering over his breakfast at the Navajo Inn, where Leaphorn had just left him. He'd get Dilly to make the proper calls to assure that no jurisdictional toes were bruised. Then he'd make the long drive to Tano. Perhaps Dilly would like to go along.

Dilly wouldn't. He called the Albuquerque FBI office, and the proper people at the B.I.A. Law and Order Division to set things up across the jurisdictional boundaries. But as far as making the trip was concerned, he told Leaphorn: "Sorry, I got other sheep to shear."

"Maybe you've got the time to solve problems for people over in the Albuquerque office. Not me," Streib said. "Besides, my tailbone's hurting from all the driving we've been doing."

So, a little before noon Leaphorn arrived at Tano, stopped at the Pueblo administrative office, asked appropriate questions, and got directions to the house of Teddy Sayesva.

Teddy Sayesva showed no enthusiasm for giving a Navajo policeman the fifth repetition, as he put it, "of what damn little I know about how my brother got killed." But the Tano culture's demand for hospitality quickly overpowered his irritation. He prepared coffee in the pot on the cook stove, and then perched stiffly on the edge of a kitchen chair—a small, thin man with a burr haircut and wire-rimmed glasses which looked too youthful for a face that was lined and tired. No, he hadn't been at home when his nephew had come to see his brother Francis. He was a member of a kachina society and had duties to take care of at the society kiva. Except for the boy's visit, which he hadn't been home to witness, he could think of nothing unusual happening that evening.

He recited what had happened as if he'd memorized it. Francis had driven in from his home in Albuquerque early in the afternoon. As always during ceremonials he used Teddy's place as his home base. At supper he'd seemed preoccupied, maybe worried, but Teddy presumed that was because he had to go the next week to testify before a federal grand jury. Teddy paused after mentioning that and glanced at Leaphorn to see if it needed explanation. It didn't. Leaphorn had read of that in the FBI report. It seemed to involve an auditing technicality in a banking case with no connection to this homicide.

Leaphorn nodded. Teddy resumed his recitation.

Teddy had left for the pre-ceremonial meeting at his kiva. When he got home, Francis was in bed, sound asleep. He was still asleep when Teddy had left the next morning before dawn for prayers at the kiva.

"I didn't have any more chance to talk to him," Teddy said, looking down at his hands as he said it. "The last time I saw Francis he was sleeping." He pointed into the next room. "Sleeping in that bed there. Where we both used to sleep when we were boys."

"That would be a hard loss," Leaphorn said. He thought of telling the man of Emma's death, comparing the loss of the wife of your lifetime to the loss of a brother. But he could see no consolation in that. For either of them. Instead he said:

"FBI agent report indicates that you had no idea what your nephew brought over here that night to give to Francis. Is that correct?"

"No idea," Teddy Sayesva said. "The man told me it was supposed to be something long and narrow and wrapped in a newspaper. Like I said, I wasn't here when Delmar came with it. And I didn't see anything like that when I got back from the kiva. In fact I didn't see anything different at all."

He gestured, taking in the small, cluttered room. "Where would you put something in here where I wouldn't notice it? Right here in my own house. Any place he might have put it, we've looked. We didn't find anything."

"We think it might have been something made of wood. Of a heavy dark wood," Leaphorn said.

"Oh," Teddy Sayesva said. His tone indicated that this

interested him.

"Your nephew said this object, whatever it was, had religious significance," Leaphorn added. " That it had something to do with the ceremonial."

"Delmar told you that?" Sayesva's expression showed his shock. "He shouldn't—." He let the sentence hang.

Leaphorn cleared his throat. "Actually he told the officer that he couldn't talk about what was in the package. He said he couldn't talk about it at all because he was not supposed to talk about anything involving his religion to anyone not initiated into his kiva."

"Oh," Teddy Sayesva said. He looked relieved. "That's right. He couldn't talk about it if it concerned his religious duties."

"And he didn't talk about it," Leaphorn said. "When the B.I.A Officer told him he would have to take him in to Albuquerque to be questioned by the FBI if he didn't tell them what it was, then Delmar ran away."

Sayesva nodded, approving both Delmar's action and this Navajo's understanding of it. He got up, walked quickly to the door, opened it and stood for a moment looking out into the cold autumn sunlight. A pickup truck rolled down the alley past the porch. Teddy Sayesva waved, shouted something unintelligible to those who don't speak the language of Tano. Then he looked up and down the street again, shut the door and sat down.

"You're Navajo," he said. "Do you have a wife from any of the pueblos? Are any of your family married into our people?"

Leaphorn said no.

"I will have to tell you a little bit about our religion then," Sayesva said. "Nothing secret." He produced a wry smile. "Just former secrets—things that the anthropologists have already written about."

He got up, poured coffee from the steaming pot, handed a mug to Leaphorn, and sat again.

"You know my brother was the leader of our koshare society. Do you know about the Koshares?"

"A little," Leaphorn said. "I've watched them at kachina dances. The clowns, with the striped body paint, making people laugh. I know their duties are more than just to entertain."

"In our pueblo, and in some of the others, men who have jobs in towns and live away from us can't be members of the most sacred societies, the kachina societies. They can't spend enough time in the kivas. So they become koshares, and that is sacred too, but in a different way." He paused, seeking a way to explain. "To outsiders, they look like clowns and what they do looks like clowning. Like foolishness. But it is more than that. The Koshare have another role. I guess you could say they are our ethical police. It's their job to remind us when we drift away from the way that was taught us. They show us how far short we humans are of the perfection of the spirits."

He paused, an opportunity for a question. Leaphorn said: "An old friend of mine, a Hopi, told me their Koshares are like policemen who use laughter instead of guns and scorn instead of jails."

Sayesva nodded.

"You've been to kachina ceremonials," he said. "Lots of Navajos like to come to them."

"Sure," Leaphorn agreed. "We are taught to respect your religion."

"Then you've seen the koshare doing everything wrong, everything backward, being greedy, reminding us of how badly we behave. That's the purpose. If you had been to this last one, you would have seen the clowns come in. They work with the koshare, to help teach the lesson. This time one of them pulled in a wagon, and one of my cousins was there with the big billfold and the big dollars play-acting, pretending to buying sacred things. That's what my brother had decided to warn the people

161

about that day. Selling things they shouldn't sell. What Delmar brought him in that package, I don't know. But I think it must have been something to put into the little wagon. Something symbolic."

Teddy Sayesva looked at Leaphorn over his glasses. Shrugged. Sipped his coffee.

"Something made of dark wood and silver?" Leaphorn said.

Sayesva looked up from his cup, shook his head, produced a wry smile. "Silver, too? Black wood and silver?"

"We think so. We found a form for casting something in metal. About this big." Leaphorn made a small, round shape with his hands. "And with letters in it."

"Found it where?"

"In the school crafts shop at Thoreau."

"Where that man was killed?"

Leaphorn nodded. "Do you know what it was?"

Sayesva's expression said he knew, and that the knowledge hurt. But he didn't answer the question.

"Whatever it was, it seems to have been made in the shop that morning. We think Mr. Dorsey probably made it. We think it was taken about the time he was killed. Maybe before. Maybe after, but about that time. A friend of Delmar's says Delmar went to the shop about that time to pick up something the friend had made. When the friend came to pick up Delmar, Delmar had the package with him.

Sayesva shook his head, rejecting what he was hearing. He looked very tired. "You think Delmar killed this teacher?"

Leaphorn shook his head. "We have a suspect in jail at Crownpoint," he said. He's a Navajo named Eugene Ahkeah, a maintenance man at the school. He was seen leaving the shop about the time of the homicide. A box full of items stolen from the shop turned up under his house."

Sayesva looked relieved. "So you just want to know

what was in the package?'"

"Whatever you can tell us," Leaphorn said.

"I guess it was the Lincoln Cane," Sayesva said.

The Lincoln Cane. It took only a second for Leaphorn's memory to process that. President Lincoln had ordered ebony and silver canes made and sent them to the leaders of the New Mexico Indian Pueblos during the dark days early in the Civil War. They were intended, as Leaphorn remembered that episode in history, as a signal that Lincoln recognized tribal authority, to reward them for their neutrality and to keep them neutral. One of the Spanish Kings, probably King Charles if Leaphorn's memory served, had done the same two hundred years earlier.

"Not the cane itself, of course," Sayesva said. "I mean a copy of it." He nodded, agreeing with his own guess. "I guess my brother had a replica made. I guess he must have sent Delmar to get it for him."

Leaphorn waited. Teddy Sayesva was thinking, considering the implications of what he had concluded. Leaphorn gave him time to think. And then he said: "You think your brother had it put in the wagon? I heard that when the wagon was pulled around the plaza, past the crowd, the people quit laughing when it went by. I heard they got quiet. Serious."

"Yes," Sayesva said.

Leaphorn waited. "I thank you for what you've told me so far," he said. "Now we know what we're looking for. Sometimes that helps you find something, but it may not help this time. Whoever killed your brother may have taken it."

Sayesva acknowledge that with an absent nod.

"Your brother was killed for some reason. Could it be because he put the cane in the wagon. Would that suggest that it was being sold?"

Sayesva rose. "I don't think I know anything else to

tell you," he said. He moved toward the door but stopped short of opening it. "No," he said. "No. Francis wouldn't have got someone to make a copy of that cane." He shook his head, hand still on the door knob.

Leaphorn, who had been rising, sat down again.

"Why not?" he asked.

For a moment Leaphorn thought Teddy Sayesva's hadn't heard the question. He waited, aware of the autumn smells in this small, closed kitchen—the aroma of chili drying somewhere, or corn husks, of sacks of pinto beans and onions.

Sayesva left the door and sat down across the table. "Why not? Well, he and Bert Penitewa—Bert's the Governor–they were friends. They disagreed on a lot of things but they respected one another. He wouldn't insult the Governor like that. Putting that cane in the wagon like it was for sale was the worst kind of insult."

"Officer Chee said the wagon was full of things to be sold," Leaphorn said. "He thought it was sort of a general protest against people selling artifacts with religious value."

"Sure," Sayesva said. "The Koshare have done that before. Warned against selling sacred things, I mean. But the cane was another matter. They're aren't any rules, exactly about what the clowns can do, or what they can ridicule. But they do follow traditions. And traditionally, the clowns don't get involved in politics and they don't get personally insulting. Putting that cane in there was like accusing Bert of being willing to sell it- –and god knows what some collector would pay for something that old and sent out by Abraham Lincoln himself. It would be a personal insult because the Governor is the keeper of the cane. A sort of a sacred trust."

"So that broke with tradition. I mean putting the cane in the wagon?"

Sayesva nodded. "Everybody's been talking about it.

Maybe as much about that as about what happened to my brother. Francis was a valuable man. He didn't do foolish things. People wonder what he was telling them."

"If your brother didn't have that cane made, do you have idea who might have done it?"

Sayesva thought, shook his head. "No idea."

They sat, with Teddy Sayesva considering what he now knew along with what he had known before—considering how a cane taken from a murdered man's shop came to be made part of the symbolic cargo of a clown's toy wagon. Leaphorn was content to give him time. He let his eyes wander.

Sayesva's kitchen was the kitchen of a man who lived alone. Leaphorn saw the same untidy clues he saw on his house since Emma's death, the grimy stove, the cluttered sink, the unkempt shelves. He saw the sad look of loneliness.

"I talked to Henry Agoyo," Sayesva said, finally. "Henry is the chief clown—the one in charge of the team that does the skit." Sayesva hesitated, looked at Leaphorn, made a wry face, and continued. "I'm talking too much. About things we don't talk about. But something very strange has happened here. I think we should try to understand it. I talked to Henry. I asked him what he knew about putting the cane in the wagon. Why in the world did they do that? He said it wasn't planned that way. He said Francis brought it to him that morning—just a little while before the ceremonial started. He said Francis told him to put it in the wagon, and he didn't want to do it. But he said Francis seemed very upset. Disturbed. He said put it in and Henry said, 'Do you know what you're doing,' or something like that, and Francis said he wasn't sure, and maybe he was wrong, and he hoped he was wrong, but put the cane in the wagon."

Sayesva picked up his coffee cup, saw it was empty, put it down again. "Henry knew my brother real well,"

Sayesva said. "They were in the same class in school and they both drove trucks at the Jackswild Mine, before Francis went to the University to become an accountant."

"What does Agoyo do now?" Leaphorn asked.

"He runs a road grader for the county."

"He said Francis hoped he was wrong," Leaphorn repeated.

Sayesva nodded.

"Anything else. Could he tell you where the cane is now? What happened to it after the ceremonial."

"He said Francis came when the clowns left the plaza and said he had to have the cane, and took it out of the wagon."

Leaphorn connected his memory of what Chee had described with this new fact. There had been very little time between the end of the clowning skit and the death of Francis Sayesva in the room where he had gone to remove his costume. Only the few minutes Chee had spent running around looking for Delmar. Francis must have had the cane with him when he was killed,

He thought: *Find the cane, find the killer.*

"So putting the cane in the wagon was a last second addition," Leaphorn said.. "They hadn't planned it that way."

"That's what Henry Agoyo told me."

"You think probably your brother didn't know about the cane until Delmar brought it to him?"

"That's what I think," Sayesva said.

"So what was that shop teacher's motive for making it?" Leaphorn asked, as much to himself as to Sayesva. "And why was the shop teacher killed?"

Neither of them could think of an answer.

18

NOR COULD BERT PENITEWA, the Governor of Tano Pueblo.

Leaphorn had walked from Sayesva house, across the plaza and around a corner and down a narrow street walled with adobe houses. As Sayesva had told him, the Governor's home was the third on the left.

A middle aged woman answered the door, with a jacket on and a shawl over her head. Yes, Governor Penitewa was home. She was his daughter and she had to run to see about something a neighbor had asked her to do. But she ushered him in, invited him to sit on the sagging sofa, called her father, and left.

The Governor of Tano Pueblo was a short, heavy bodied man, probably in his late seventies. But like many of his race, he didn't show his age. His hair was thick and black, his face hardly lined and while his belly bulged over the belt of his jeans, his back still resisted the slump of the aged.

"I'm sorry Della had to leave in such a hurry," he said. "She makes much better coffee than I do and I want to offer you a cup."

"I'm afraid I've already had our quota for the day," Leaphorn said.

Penitewa gestured him back onto the sagging sofa by the front window and seated himself behind a table which seemed to also serve as his desk. Behind the desk, Chee could see into the bedroom from the Governor had emerged. To his left, a doorway opened into the kitchen. To his right he could see into what seemed to be another bedroom. This living room was small, crowded with worn furnishings, its plank floor covered with a good Navajo rug, its walls decorated with photographs and a framed print of Christ crucified, Beside the kitchen door a shelf held three kachina figures, a seed basket, two good examples of Acoma pottery and a plastic clock made to represent a coyote howling. On the wall behind the table where Penitewa sat two canes hung side by side. One was made of a light wood with a head of heavy ornate silver tied with a black cord and dangling a black tassel. The other was a simple ebony stick with a round silver head. The Lincoln cane.

"How about iced tea. I should offer you something," Penitewa said. "I presume this is an official visit from a representatives of the Navajo Nation. That hasn't happened at this Pueblo for many, many years."

Leaphorn wasn't quite sure how that remark was intended. As he remembered history, Tano had been hostile to the Navajos during what Frank Sam Nakai called "the Kit Carson wars." But then just about all of the Pueblos had joined the Americans in that campaign. Only Jemez Pueblo had remained forever friendly.

"I think the best we could call this visit is semi- official," Leaphorn said. "We had a teacher killed on our reservation a little while ago." He explained the evidence that the victim had made a copy of the Tano Lincoln Cane, that a Navajo suspected of the homicide was in custody and that Delmar Kanitewa had apparently brought the cane to Tano, had given it to Francis Sayesva and that it had subsequently been taken when Sayesva was killed.

Penitewa listened in silence, motionless, face impassive. But his eyes betrayed surprise and interest.

"So, that's it," he said. "I wondered where it came from."

"Apparently, that's it." Leaphorn said. "The evidence is circumstantial. But it's strong. We found shavings of ebony wood in the teacher's shop, and what seemed to be a mold to cast the silver head. The Kanitewa boy was there at the right time. He brought a package of the proper shape and gave it to Francis Sayesva. But, of course, we haven't actually had our hands on it."

"I saw it in the wagon," Penitewa said. "It was quite a shock. At first I thought it was the real one. I thought someone had come in here and got it down off the wall."

"Could that have happened?"

Governor Penitewa smiled at him. "It could have, but it didn't. I came right home to look and it was still on the wall." He turned and pointed. "There's the original. Would you like to see it?"

"I would," Leaphorn said. He glanced at his watch.

Penitewa hoisted himself out of the chair, took the black cane from the wall and handed it to Leaphorn.

The weight surprised Leaphorn. Ebony was a heavy wood indeed. He ran his hand down the smooth surface, looked at the tip—which seemed to be made of steel—and then at the head. Silver, inscribed **A. LINCOLN, PRES. U.S.A.** and **1863**.

Above that was the name of the Pueblo. He ran his thumbnail under the **L** and examined the nail. What it had scraped away looked a little like wax but it was probably something more professional than that. Probably some sort of molding putty sold in art supply houses for just this purpose.

Penitewa was watching him. "Are you are checking whether I'm a neat housekeeper?"

"No sir," Leaphorn said. He got up and showed Penitewa first the head of the cane and then the residue on his thumbnail. "I think someone stuck the head down into some sort of molding clay. I think they made an impression of it to make the copy. Could that be possible."

Penitewa looked surprised. "Who could it have been?" He sat again, put the cane on the table in front of him. "Lot of people, I guess."

"It's always left on the wall like that," Leaphorn said. "Or do you lock them up somewhere."

"It's the Governor's symbol," Penitewa said. "Who ever is Governor, it hangs on the wall in his office. It's the tradition. When I was a little boy, my great grandfather was governor. It hung on the wall in his house."

Leaphorn wanted to ask if anyone had ever stolen it, which would been a stupid question since there it was, in the Governor's hand. But Penitewa seemed to sense the thought.

"I think President Lincoln sent nineteen of them out from Washington—one for each of the pueblos. The Spanish started it in 1620." He pointed to the heavier cane. "Some of the pueblos got another one—three canes all together—one from the Mexican government when Mexico won its independence. And a couple of pueblos, so I'm told, don't have any anymore."

"Stolen?"

Penitewa shrugged. "Disappeared," he said. "Who knows what happened to them. But nobody has ever tried to steal ours."

"If someone made a molding of the head of this one, it probably happened fairly recently. Have you had any unusual visitors this month? Anyone you left alone in here long enough for that to be done? Anyone suspicious?"

Penitewa considered, shook his head.

"How about Delmar Kanitewa? We think he brought it from Thoreau to his uncle."

"Delmar," Kanitewa said. He thought. "No. He's been away living with his dad."

"How about Francis Sayesva?"

If the Governor needed to think about that, it had been long ago. His answer was instant.

"Francis was my friend."

"I heard that," Leaphorn said. "But I was told you disagreed about a lot of things. Where to put the grade school when it was built. Whether the pueblo should lease the old Jackswild mine for a landfill dump. Where to locate the new housing when the Bureau of Indian Affairs wanted them built. Things like that."

Kanitewa laughed. "Francis loved to argue," he said. "Somebody would want to do something, Francis was always the one to tell the council why not. Somebody want to stop something, Francis was there saying why to do it. But he was a good man. He was one of the valuable people."

"You don't think he had the copy made?"

"No. Not Francis."

"Teddy Sayesva said that Francis told Henry Agoyo to put the Lincoln Cane in the wagon. Teddy said this would be a terrible insult to you and that Agoyo didn't want to do it, but Francis told him to. Did you know that?"

"Of course I knew it. One of my nephews was the other clown helping with the wagon." The Governor smiled. "Tano is a small place, Lieutenant. Not many interesting things happen. Everybody was talking about that cane."

"Was it an insult? You said Francis was your friend. Why did he do it?"

The Governor smiled again. "If you had known Francis you would know the answer. He must have thought I was going to sell the cane. That would be terrible. So he was willing to do what ever he could do to stop it. Even if it was against an old friend. He was what you call 'an honorable man.'"

Leaphorn considered this. It demanded another question that was hard to ask. He cleared his throat.

"I am a stranger to Tano culture," he said, "But it would seem to me that if Francis was your old friend, and an honorable man, he wouldn't insult you that way in public if he didn't think it was true. Do you think he believed you were going to sell the Lincoln Cane?"

If the Governor was insulted by the question, he showed no sign of it.

"He must have believed it," he said. "That bothered me, too. It still does. I don't think he would have done it if he didn't believe I was about to betray the people."

Another hard question. "What would have caused him to think that?"

"I don't know," Penitewa said. "I am trying to find out."

He looked at Leaphorn. "It hurts when you think an old friend like Francis died thinking you were a traitor."

19

THE NAVAJO AGRICULTURAL INDUSTRIES project tended to affect Jim Chee is different ways—depending on his mood. If he drove past it in a "patriotic Navajo mood" it filled him with both pride and regrets. He was proud of what the tribe had done with its water rights from the San Juan River and an expanse of once-worthless sagebrush hills. His regrets focused on what might have been had not the whites wrested all the good rich bottom land away from the tribe.

On the north side of Highway 44, the ocean of sage brush stretched away into the Angel Peak badlands. On the south side of the highway where the NAI held domain, the black-grey-silver of the sage had been replaced by mile after mile of green, the shade depending on the crop and the season. Dense stands of corn stalks, alternated with thousands of acres of potato fields, followed by great circles of kelly green of alfalfa, and incredible expanses of onions, water melons, cantaloupes, cucumbers, sugar beets, whatever crop the market demanded. And all of this had been made possible by a rare and seemingly small Navajo victory over white land-grabbers. Chee had found an account of it in the depth of Zimmerman Library while a student at the University of New Mexico and had read it happily. Way back in Civil War times, and maybe before, the Navajos had built a header in the San Juan River to divert waters and irrigate their cornfields. Whites had already driven the Navajos off most of their rich bottom land farms along the river and seized it for themselves. They moved in on this irrigated land as well, even though it was part of what had by then been declared Navajo Reservation. But when the Navajos prepared to fight for their homes, the U.S. Army moved in and—for the first and only time—sided with the tribe and made the squatters move out. The old Cornfield Ditch was expanded into the Fruitland Canal in the 1930s, irrigating almost 1500 acres. More important, it maintained Navajo legal rights to the river water. While the whites had taken nearly all the good bottomland, the Navajo still owned water and an infinity of worthless high desert hills. Now, from planting season until harvest, that water was showered out over the desert through elaborate mobile sprinkler systems. It turned the hills lush and green and produced jobs for hundreds of Navajos.

When Jim Chee was feeling patriotic, he was proud of this—proud that his people were using their water and not letting it drain down into the Colorado to produce golf courses in Las Vegas and fill the hot tubs of Beverly Hills.

Today, however, he was feeling religious. When he felt that way, the NAI bothered him. He had stopped at the NAI administrative offices and got directions from a puzzled clerk, who obviously wondered about this policeman's interest in the processing of the onion crop. He turned off Highway 44 southward on the road to the warehouse complex where marketing and shipping were handled. He looked out at the stubble fields of autumn, at million dollars worth of mobile irrigation pipes parked for the winter and already being buried under the tumbleweeds blowing in from the desert; at the power lines which made it all work, and beyond this to the hills sloping southwards toward the Bisti Badlands and the De-Na-Zin Wilderness. The hills were still black and silver with sage—as nature had made them before the NAI bulldozers had ripped away plant life, and the insects and mammals which fed upon it, and the birds which fed upon them. He saw the hills as the great spirit Changing Woman must have seen them, She who had taught that the earth was our nurturing mother and that earth, and all that she produced, must be treated with respect. Was this business of reducing nature to great irrigated circles becoming the Beauty Way of the Navajos? This and the immense scar of the Navajo Mine, and the sawmill operations in the Chuska Mountains, and—.

What was wrong with him? Why this lousy mood? He knew why. Her name was Janet. But what was her clan? And what the hell was he going to do about it. He didn't know that. He couldn't decide what he would do until he knew for certain that he had to decide. First he was going to catch this hit-and-run son-of-a-bitch and then he was going to drive back to Frank Sam Nakai's place and find out what his uncle had learned. And if his uncle had learned nothing yet—had not yet gone to find the old man who was supposed to know—then he would take Hosteen Nakai to find the old man. Or if his uncle wouldn't go, he would go himself. He didn't want to wait.

But it is a policeman's fate to wait. The working day had not yet ended at the produce warehouses. He cruised slowly through the graveled parking lot, looking for a dark green pickup truck with an ERNIE IS THE GREATEST bumper sticker. There were seven greens among the ranks of trucks and cars, three of them about the right vintage to match the description. If any of them had even worn the bumper sticker it wasn't wearing it now.

Chee parked his own pickup where it was partly concealed by an old Chevy conversion van and glanced at his watch. Seven minutes until five when the warehouse closed. He sat, not thinking of Janet Pete. He switched on the radio, still tuned to KNDN. A group Chee remembered hearing at a Tuba City girl dance was singing a lament about a woman who loved them, but loving them or not, had still stolen their Chevy Blazer. All was in Navajo except the truck's trade name. The reader of the commercial which followed had a similar problem—there are no Navajo nouns for Purina Pig Chow.

A door at the side of the warehouse slid open. A man emerged wearing coveralls, followed by a procession of other men. Still more men emerged from around the building, with a scattering of women. Chee scanned them, studying them without knowing what he was looking for. A medium sized, middle aged, Navajo male. That narrowed it a little. It left out the women, and the very tall, and the very round and the young bucks who Ellie would definitely have been able to describe in more detail. Eight or ten fit the medium-middle category—probably more. One of them was standing beside the warehouse door, holding a clipboard, discussing something with two younger workers. Another was walking almost directly toward Chee. He gave Chee a glance and then climbed into the van and started the engine. Chee looked back at the man with the clipboard. Probably a foreman. He was wearing jeans and a jean jacket and a long-billed cap. The bill seemed to be bent sharply upward as if the cardboard stiffener in it had been broken.

"Aah," Chee said. He leaned forward. Staring. Too far away. He started the pickup engine and eased it forward into the stream of vehicles leaving the lot, then turned out of the traffic flow to coast past the door. The man was still talking to the two, his back turned. Chee drove past the doorway, circled and parked again where he could watch Clipboard. The man was still talking, his cap still met the description. But a bent-billed cap is scanty proof. The truck would be crucial to any chance of getting a conviction. Where had the man parked it?

At the warehouse door, the conversation ended. Clipboard disappeared inside. The two young men split. One disappeared around the warehouse the other walked along the wall toward Chee. He was grinning. Chee got out of his pickup, glad he wasn't wearing his uniform.

"That guy you were talking too," he said. "With the clipboard. Was that Billy Tsossie?"

"You mean the foreman?" He looked back toward the warehouse door, now closing. "No. His name's Hoski. Clement Hoski."

"Clement Hoski," Chee said. "Yeah, I thought he looked familiar. I need to talk to him. You know where he parks his truck?"

"I think he's in a car pool," the man said. "He comes in with a bunch who live out in NAI housing."

Clement Hoski emerged from the warehouse, shut the door behind him, and trotted to a white Dodge Caravan. He climbed into the back and it pulled away, spraying gravel.

"Thanks," Chee said. "I'll try to catch him."

The Caravan delivered the first two of its riders at a cluster of frame and plaster houses built for NAI on the hillside north of the marketing center. It pulled back onto the asphalt road. Chee gave it almost a quarter mile start. The empty road made undetected following difficult but it also made losing someone almost impossible. About three miles later the van pulled off on the shoulder. Chee slowed. Hoski emerged, waved at the departing van, and walked up the hill where, Chee guessed, his house must be located.

Right. As Chee drove past, Hoski was walking up a dirt road toward a plank house with a pitched tin roof. An outhouse stood some 50 yards down the hill, proclaiming that unlike the NAI houses this one lacked plumbing. A pole supporting an electric power line behind the house declared that it did have electricity. A pile of fire wood against the wall suggested that it wasn't served by a gas line. But where was the green pickup?

Hoski was out of sight now. In the house, Chee guessed. He drove past Hoski's access road and up the next hill. He stopped there, turned the pickup around and got his binoculars out of the glove box.

From here he had a better view across the fold of the hill. A basketball backboard and net had been mounted on the electric pole—suggesting that Hoski had school age children. He seemed old for that. Maybe someone lived with him. A single-wide mobile home sat on blocks behind the house. It was windowless and empty as far as Chee could tell through the binoculars. The green truck might be parked between that and the house. If it was, there would be no way to see it short of driving in there and looking. Why wait?

Chee started the engine and drove down the hill. But at the access road he parked again. Where was the truck? The truck was the key. When a fender hits a human hard enough to kill, there's always evidence. If he picked up Hoski without the truck, they'd have to release him. And if Hoski had any sense, he would then make sure that the truck would never be found. Chee thought.

A yellow van pulled up across the highway from him. It was small for a school bus but the legend on its side read: BLOOMFIELD SCHOOL DISTRICT. A boy climbed out. He was about fourteen, Chee guessed, a tall, skinny boy wearing a black jacket and blue pants and carrying a blue

backpack. He walked across the asphalt toward

Chee's truck, smiling.

"Hello," he said. "Hello mister."

"Hello," Chee said. What would he tell the boy he was doing, parked here? He'd say he was looking for someone.

"Is this your truck?" the boy asked, still smiling. "It's pretty."

The boy's eyes were a little too far apart, the bone structure of his face just a little wrong. The smile a little too innocent for fourteen. The bus was for Special Education kids. The kids with damaged brains, or bodies, or emotions, or sometimes all of those. And Chee recognized this boy's problem. He had seen this physical evidence before. Seen it too often. They called it Fetal Alcohol Syndrome—the doom the mother imposes on her child when she drinks while pregnant. It was another of the reasons Chee hated alcohol, hated the people who made it, and advertised it, and sold it, and poisoned his people with it.

"It's my truck," Chee said. "But it looks prettier when I get all the mud washed off it."

"I think it's pretty now."

"I think maybe I'll get it painted. Would green be a good color?"

"Sure," the boy said, his smile unwavering. "Green's good."

Chee was aware that he was not feeling good about this. But he said: "Do know anybody who owns a pickup that's green?"

"Sure. My Grandfather. His pickup is green."

"Where does your Grandfather live?"

The boy pointed over the hood, at the house of Clement Hoski.

"Have you come to see your Grandfather?"

"I live there," he said. "Me and Grandfather Hoski, we live there." The boy laughed, a sound full of absolute delight. "Sometimes he lets me do the cooking. I cook eggs in the morning. And I make oatmeal. And I make

179

tortillas. And Grandfather Hoski is going to show me how to make a pumpkin pie, and mutton stew. And how to roast pinon nuts."

"Your mother and dad? They live there, too?"

The boy looked puzzled. "They're gone," he said. "It's just me and Grandfather. He's my friend. He goes to work and I go to school and then when we get home he teaches me how to read, and about numbers, and then we play games, with cards, and at the end of the week we do things together. We hunt rabbits and sometimes we go look at things."

"In his pickup truck green?"

The boy laughed, utterly delighted. "It's Green. He lets me drive it. When we are way out on the dirt roads. He says I'm going to be a great driver."

"I'll bet you will be," Chee said. He took a deep breath. "Where does he keep it?"

The boy looked at Chee, puzzled.

"The truck. Where does he keep the truck?"

"Up there behind the house. It's there between our house and the old empty place where we keep things. You want to go see it? I'll show you. It's pretty."

"Your name's Ernie, isn't it."

"Ernie," he agreed nodding. Grandfather had my name printed and put it on the back of our truck. You want to see it?"

"Not now," Chee said. "I want to think about it."

20

JOE LEAPHORN HADN'T had much sleep. He had stayed up late—sitting in what they had called their guest bedroom in the days when Emma had been alive and they had entertained guests. Now it had become, slowly and with no real planning, Leaphorn's office away from his office. The guest bed had become the flat surface on which things which needed to be spread could be spread. On it, Leaphorn had arranged airline timetables, railroad time tables, maps of China, maps of Mongolia, both Chinese and ex-Soviet Union, an assortment of the odds and ends one needs to plan a trip when you're half afraid of taking it. Contrary to Leaphorn's nature, this business had become rushed and hurried—last minute planning. In just three days he would meet Louisa at the Flagstaff airport. They would fly down to Phoenix, thence to Los Angeles, and from there it would be off to another world—to Peking. (*Beijing*, Leaphorn thought. I have to remember that.) Louisa had made reservations for them at the Tianlun Dynasty for the three days they would be there. ("*They're so expensive,*" *Louisa had said.* "*I thought we could share a room.*" *And into the silence she had added;* "*It has two beds in it.*") The three days were to allow him time to work his way through any bureaucratic snarls which going north into Mongolia might entail, and to allow her the time she need in the Beijing libraries, and to meet with the folklorists with whom she had been working. ("*And to allow us a little time just to be tourists.*" *She had reached over and squeezed his hand as she said it, looking intensely happy. As happy as a child. He had been touched, and was touched now, remembering it.* "*You've got to see Mao's Tomb, the old Summer Palace and the Friendship Store. The world's wildest variety store.*" He looked at the map again. After Beijing he would head northwestward to Urumqi and Turpan, where Louisa had written to a linguist and other scholars and made reservations for him, and she head south to Xian, and Nanjing, and more meetings with her fellow citizens in the small world of folklorists. Then they would meet again in Shanghai for the trip home together.

He had spent almost two hours reading through the guide books she had loaned him, working out the best schedule he could—disgruntled because it had to be based mostly on guesswork. And then he had started packing. "*Layers,*" *she had advised him.* "*That's the secret in China. It seems like it's always cold outside and too hot inside. So take sweaters, and long johns and some stuff you can peel off. And don't take too much because it's easy to get stuff washed. And you are the right size. You can buy Chinese clothing.*" *She had studied him, smiling.* "*In fact, I think you could pass for Chinese. Especially up in the north where you'll be.*"

He had pushed the maps aside to make room for his suitcase, folding in shorts, and undershirts, and socks and in the process, uncovering his pajamas. Emma had bought them for him. She had bought him his first set for his birth-day two weeks after their marriage, looking at him shyly as he opened the package, wondering how he would take this hint. He had worn pajamas for years in deference to Emma's modesty, and gradually had become used to them, and to receiving a gift-wrapped new pair whenever a present was appropriate and the previous pair had worn thin. But Emma had died. There had been no more new pajamas then. No more wearing the old ones. Putting them on had provoked far too many memories.

He had picked them out of the drawer, inspected them and found them in fair condition. A little tight around the stomach, as he remembered, but he had lost a little weight eating his own cooking. One room with two beds. He'd folded them in. And then he had been over-powered by the desolation of this empty, silent house, and the knowledge of loss and loneliness. He had gone out into the darkness, and walked up the gravel street. When he became aware that his feet were hurting, he sat on a boulder where he could watch the last half of the moon rising over the ridge east of Window Rock, and the occa-sional car rolling down the highway toward Fort Defiance. Finally, when even the highway was silent and the moon was high and the cold had seeped up his pantlegs and down the back of his jacket, he got up and walked stiffly home.

In his office now he felt the lack of sleep. He glanced at his In Basket. It had collected a stack of notes and mail in the days he'd spent working at Thoreau and Tano. But that stack could wait. So could everything else except the Eric Dorsey homicide. He had just two days left to work on that before he left.

He picked up the telephone receiver and buzzed Chee's number. He'd talk to Chee about what he'd learned at Tano. If nothing else it would help him judge Chee's intelligence. The memo Chee had left him showed good instincts. He'd sensed that the people at Tano had seen something Chee had missed. Maybe the boy would come up with something from the Lincoln Cane business.

But Chee didn't answer his telephone. Leaphorn buzzed Virginia.

"Just a minute," she said. "I think there's a note in the overnight file." The minute passed. "He called in. He said he's been working on that Todachine vehicular homicide case. He said he has to take the rest of the week off, He's going to charge it to his annual leave time." Virginia's tone had become disapproving. "I didn't see any paper-work on that," she said. "Did you put through the paper-work?"

"Did he leave a number where I can reach him?"

"There's not a thing about that here," she said. "You want me to call the Shiprock office."

"Please," Leaphorn said. "And let me know." It wouldn't do any good, but it would get Virginia off his tele-phone.

He hung up, feeling sleepy and disgruntled. This absence-without-permission business exactly fit Chee's reputation. When the kid had worked out of Tuba City, Captain Largo use to complain about the trouble getting him to follow regulations. At Crownpoint it had been the same story. There his brains had gotten him acting sergeant stripes when he was still green, and his habit of doing his own thing had gotten him busted just as fast.

Ah, well, Leaphorn thought, it was worth the gamble. In this office it didn't matter so much. Less routine and more innovative thinking required. Maybe he could get Chee saddle broken just a little bit, just enough to keep him. But where the hell could he be. Could Chee still be trying to work as a hataali? Maybe that was it. Maybe Chee had found a customer and was off doing a curing ceremonial someplace. If he was still doing the Blessing Way—the full eight days of the ceremonial—that could become a real problem.

His telephone buzzed.

"Leaphorn," he said.

It was Virginia. "The Chief wants to talk to you. Line two."

He punched two.

"Yes sir," he said. And then he listened, placid at first, then frowning.

"Yeah," he said. "Yes sir. I didn't actually hear it but I read about it. I was over at Flagstaff. There was a piece about it in the Arizona Republic. Hell of a funny . . . " He stopped, interrupted. The frown converted into consternation.

"In the tape player on my radio?" He looked at the radio. The tape player was empty. "Let me get this straight," Leaphorn said. "Sergeant Roanhorse was walking by my office and he heard this tape playing in my office. And that was the day before it was broadcast by KNDN? Is that what you're telling me?"

Leaphorn listened. "Be damned if I know," he said. "There's no tape in there now. Did somebody come in here and take it?"

Listened again, the frown resolving itself into an stolid anger. "All right," he said. "I'll be right down."

He trotted down the stairs. The Chief's door was open. Bennie Redhair, who served as the Chief's secretary and gofer, was sitting behind his desk looking very, very nervous. His smile at Leaphorn came out more like a grimace. Beyond him in the inner office was Councilman Jimmy Chester, wearing a black hat with a silver band, sitting across the desk from the Chief. Councilman Chester glowered at Leaphorn. The Chief's expression, as he motioned Leaphorn in, was a mixture of worry and puzzlement.

"Close the door behind you," The chief said. Leaphorn closed it.

When he came out it was almost thirty minutes later. He climbed the stairs slowly and eased himself into his swivel chair—staring at the radio. How could this have happened? The specifics were obvious—to him if not to Councilman Chester and the Chief. Someone had come in, put a tape of that telephone wiretap in his radio tape player and turned it on. And left it turned on for a while, apparently, because Roanhorse's report said he had heard parts of it at least twice. Once walking down the hall, and once on his return trip. Then, after the notorious broadcast over KNDN up in Farmington had stirred up an uproar, Roanhorse remembered what he had heard. He'd reported it. A check was made and the tape was found, still in Leaphorn's radio.

The question, of course, was who, and why. Leaphorn hadn't the faintest idea of how to answer either question. The councilman had no such problem. He knew the answers. Leaphorn was the who, and the why was to destroy the councilman's reputation. Just why would Leaphorn want to do that? Because the Councilman, as chairman of the Justice Committee, had opposed the idea of setting up Leaphorn's separate Division of Investigation. And because he suspected Leaphorn was one of the tree huggers fighting the waste dump proposal. And because way back years ago one of Leaphorn's maternal uncles had lost a grazing rights dispute with the Councilman over in the Checkerboard Reservation. And what was to be done about this misconduct? The Councilman wanted Leaphorn charged with illegally tapping his telephone, a third degree felony. He wanted Leaphorn dismissed from the Navajo Tribal Police for using his office to interfere in the politics of the Navajo Nation.

It ended, as such affairs always seem to end, with an unhappy compromise. The Chief would assign Captain Dodge to handle an investigation—to determine exactly what had happened and to collect the evidence needed to prosecute the guilty party.

"Investigation," Councilman Chester had snorted. "That can drag on forever."

They had thought about that for a moment, with Leaphorn thinking that Chester, having presided over many of them himself in thirty years on the council, should know.

And so it was decided that Captain Dodge would be given ten days to wrap it up and report.

"And how about him?" the councilman had asked, nodding toward Leaphorn.

The Lieutenant, said the Chief, would be ordered to cooperate fully with the investigators, to make himself available at all times, to provide all information available.

"Come on," Councilman Chester had said. "Give me a break. He's one of the top brass around here. What kind of cooperation is Dodge going to get in this department with him looking over everybodys' shoulders?"

"Lieutenant Leaphorn will be off duty until this investigation is completed," the Chief said.

And with that Councilman Jimmy Chester left, slamming the door behind him.

"That mean I'm suspended?" Leaphorn asked. And, of course, that had been exactly what it meant.

He sat now thinking of what this suspension would mean. For one thing, all of this meant he couldn't follow his instinct to cross-examine everyone in the building. Surely someone would have seen someone come up here and get into his office. And if they hadn't, that too would tell him something. But he couldn't do that now. Captain Dodge would be doing it. Leaphorn wished someone a little brighter had been picked. Why Dodge? He was always reliable. And come to think of it, he was also one of the Towering House clan. And so was Councilman Chester. Which explained why Chester had seemed moderately satisfied with the deal, and why the Chief had picked Dodge.

Where the hell was Chee when he needed him? Leaphorn got up and peered absent mindedly out into the parking lot. No sign of Chee's always muddy pickup truck. What if Chee had done it? Leaphorn considered that. Chester had labeled Leaphorn a tree hugger, but it was Chee who wanted something done to stop the waste dump, and Chee who wanted this office to go on a corruption hunt. Chee was always in and out of his office, but so was Dodge, and Virginia, and Roanhorse and just about everybody else. Chee had the opportunity. How about motive. Leaphorn considered that.

The young man resented him, that was plain, but Chee also respected him. Liked him, too. And he was way too damned smart to do an illegal wiretap and then be so careless with it. It wouldn't be Chee. How about Roanhorse. Nope. Roanhorse was a friend, sort of a protege, and a member of Emma's clan. Dodge? Maybe. But only if Councilman Chester had somehow engaged Dodge in some sort of weird conspiracy to discredit Leaphorn. He could think of no possible scenario for that.

And so he dropped it and did what he had been dreading to do. He picked up the telephone, got an outside line, gave the operator his ATT calling card number, and dialed Professor Louisa Bourebonnette.

She would understand why he couldn't go, but she would be disappointed. "I like to travel," she had told him. "But it can really remind you of your loneliness. When you're tired, and you're having trouble with the language and you've gone all day with not a soul to talk to, then it really hits you."

The telephone in Louisa's faculty office rang, and rang, and rang. No classes this morning, he remembered. She would be at home. He dialed again, thinking how he would put it. He would want her to know he simply had to cancel until this was over. With even a hint of a criminal investigation aimed at him, he couldn't leave, and he certainly couldn't leave the country. But he wouldn't want her to worry. He'd already done too much to take the fun out of this trip for her.

On the fourth ring, her answering machine kicked in—her pleasant voice telling him to leave a message after the tone. Well, maybe it was better this way.

"Louisa," he said. "This is Joe. Bad news. I'm sort of suspected of being involved in that Councilman Jimmy Chester telephone tapping thing. The one in the paper where it sounded like he was soliciting a bribe. I'm under orders to stay here until its cleared up. If it can be cleared up today or tomorrow morning I could still make it, but that's about one chance in a million. So If it doesn't drag on too long, I'll try to catch a later flight and join you in Beijing."

He paused, searching for something to say. "Louisa. I feel terrible about this. I'm really going to miss you." He paused again. To his surprise, he found himself thinking that he might say a lot more than that. He might say I think I love you, or maybe even I love you. But then he ran out of time and the answering machine clicked off.

21

LEAPHORN HUNG UP the telephone and looked at his watch, unusually conscious of time. He might be finished with the Navajo Tribal Police. If the person who had set him up had planned it carefully he might never really be cleared of doubts. In that event he would resign, and if he did, he wanted no loose ends left behind him. He had a possible hook now on the Eric Dorsey homicide. At least he thought he did. He wanted to know.

For Captain Dodge, he typed one of the detailed memos for which he was noted. In three precise single spaced pages he provided a chronology covering his every step, answering every question he thought Dodge would be asking, suggesting people Dodge might want to contact. Finished, he read it through carefully, thought a moment, and stuck the final page back into the type- writer.

"I will stay out of this office, of course, until this mat- ter is resolved, but I will check in with you periodically in the event I am needed."

He signed it, stuck the sheets into an envelope, dropped his office key into it, sealed it and addressed it to Captain Dodge.. On his way out, he handed it to Virginia.

Virginia looked uncharacteristically solemn. She glanced at the envelope, and up at Leaphorn, raising her eyebrows in an unspoken question.

"I'm going to tell you something," he said. "And then I am going to ask you for a favor."

"Something bad has happened, hasn't it," she said.

"Bad enough," Leaphorn said. "Sometime today, or maybe it won't be until tomorrow, the word is going to start leaking out that I've been suspended. What I want–"

Virginia's expression stopped him. It went from shock, to sorrow, to anger and the intensity of it surprised him. Virginia is my friend, he thought. Why hadn't he appreciated that before? Why was he so blind about such important things?

"Suspended," she said.

"It has to do with that Councilman Chester telephone call. The one that was broadcast."

"That son-of-a-bitch," she said. "I thought it would be him." We'll get it worked out," Leaphorn said. "But until we do I could use you help."

"Anything," Virginia said.

"About tomorrow, I'd guess, you're going to he hearing rumors about this. Captain Dodge is going to have to be asking around, questioning people, so it won't be hard to figure out that an investigation is going on and that I'm the target of it. Word will be leaking out. What would help me a lot would be if you could sort of slow it down. When people call to ask, could you laugh it off. Could you maybe make them think it's just another rumor."

"I'll tell 'em it's a damned lie," Virginia said. "I'll tell 'em nobody would be that crazy. Not even this bunch." She held her hand out to him. It took him a second to understand the gesture, then he took it, and felt his hand being squeezed.

"Joe," she said. "Go in beauty."

He called the Crownpoint office from home. Lieutenant Toddy was out in his car but the dispatcher said he would get the message to him.

"It's meet Lieutenant Leaphorn at Saint Bonaventure Mission in an hour? That right? And bring the key to Dorsey's office and his Dorsey file."

"Right," Leaphorn said. It would take him more than an hour to drive from Windowrock to Thoreau. But he could count on Toddy being a little late.

But Toddy was waiting there when Leaphorn arrived. He was sitting on the little foldout doorstep of the dilapidated little trailer which had been Dorsey's home and office—drinking a Pepsi and looking bored. He broke the seal which secured the door, unlocked it, and held it open for Leaphorn.

"You know Streib already searched this place," Toddy said. "I don't think he found anything interesting."

"He didn't know what to look for," Leaphorn said.

Toddy suppressed a grin and restored his expression to almost neutral. "That's supposed to be better isn't it? Didn't I hear somebody saying that just a little while back? 'If you know what you're looking for, then you look for something specific and you don't see something that might be more important. Somebody was saying that."

"Well," Leaphorn said, grinning himself. "Whatever you say. But this time we're a little wiser. We know that Dorsey made an ebony cane with a silver knob—a copy of the antique cane the Governor keeps at Tano Pueblo. Let's forget that stuff somebody told you and look for anything that would tell us who he made that cane for."

"Or the cane, itself?"

"That'd be nice. But apparently the Kanitewa boy got his hands on it and took to Tano and gave it to his uncle,"

Leaphorn said. He was looking around the tiny room, barely high enough to stand in and not much longer than the fold-out cot against the opposite wall. Everything was tidy, everything neat, nothing relaxed, nothing comfortable. A tiny table, a single chair, a narrow fold-down cot with a filing cabinet at its foot, a small desk. On the wall, a framed family photograph—mother, father, three boys and a girl. Beside it, another framed photo of a bearded young man with a sweatband holding back long hair. Down the wall a bit, a picture of St. Francis of Assisi. Leaphorn paused to read the poem under it.

He had conversations with the crows,
This brother to the moon
All he asked of his Lord
Was to be God's fool.

"This shouldn't take long," Toddy said, "searching this place."

It didn't. Leaphorn started at the desk, which he guessed Dorsey must have made himself. It was fitted carefully in the space between the entrance and the sliding door which opened into the a space which held a shower, a toilet stool, and a wash basin. Four wooden desk organizer boxes stood in an exact line on the desk top, labeled UNFINISHED BUSINESS, GRADED, UNGRADED, and TO BE FILED. The "graded" and "ungraded" boxes were empty but the other two held neat stacks of papers.

If anything relating to the cane was here at all (and suddenly that seemed unlikely) it should be in the unfinished business box. After all, when Eric Dorsey left this tiny room never to return the business of the cane was in fact unfinished. But if there was nothing there, he would sort through the grey metal three drawer file which occupied the space at the foot of the narrow bed. He would search everywhere. It was the only lead he had, the only chance.

He found what he wanted right on top of the stack in the UNFINISHED BUSINESS box, as if Dorsey might have dropped it there just before he left for his shop. Streib must have looked at it, but there it would have meant absolutely nothing.

It was a sheet of poor quality typing paper. On one side a poster advertising a meeting had been printed. On the other someone had neatly penciled in sketches of the Lincoln Cane and had scribbled a scattering of explanatory notes on dimensions and tapering and a line of jottings on the margin.

"I think this is what we're looking for," he told Toddy, displaying the sheet. He sat on Dorsey's neat bed to study it.

The drawings were the sort Leaphorn had himself once made in woodworking shop long ago when he was a student in a Bureau of Indian Affairs boarding school. Little lines marked margins, and numbers between arrows marked dimensions in inches. One sketch was of the cane itself. The other was of the head, with the details of the legend carefully drawn in: A. Lincoln, 1863, and—as Leaphorn's had expected—TANO. Across the page was written: Misc. File. Notes, in what Leaphorn presumed was Dorsey's tidy handwriting, ran down the right margin of the paper:

> ebony—get dark as possible
> tip—cast iron. neat fit. try farrier at Farmington.
>   grind.
>
> head—buff. avoid dust.
> $450, $250 advance.
> delivery on/before Nov. 14.

November fourteen. The day Eric Dorsey died.

Leaphorn turned the paper over. The back was blank. He handed it to Toddy. "It looks like Dorsey got cheated out his last two hundred," he said.

There was nothing else related to the canes in the either of the baskets. The contents of the file cabinet dealt mostly with classwork, warranties on power tools, operating instructions and orders for supplies. Leaphorn checked through those, sorted out invoices from Albuquerque Specialty Woods. An invoice on a September 13 shipment listed: "One ebony, 2x2x36."

He showed it to Toddy. "Here's when he bought the wood," Leaphorn said.

Toddy grunted.

There were other Specialty Woods invoices in the file. Leaphorn checked through them, backward in time, in his advertised mode of just looking without knowing for what.

"Be damned," he said. "Look at this."

"Well, now," Toddy said. "It looks like Mr. Dorsey was in the cane making business."

The form principally covered an order of walnut, mahogany and clear white pine. But the last item read: No. 1 Ebony blank 2x2x36."

Leaphorn looked at the date. The shipment had been made more than two years ago.

No more ebony purchases showed up in the other invoices. Leaphorn found the MISC FILE folder in the back of the bottom drawer. In it was a thick packet of letters secured with a rubber band, copies of correspondence about an overdue Visa Card payment, notes which seemed to deal with Christmas presents and assorted sheets of paper bearing notes. One bore a neat pencil sketch of a Lincoln Cane.

Leaphorn extracted it. On this sheet the instructions had been typed. They gave dimensions, details of the finish of the silver head, of how the cast iron tip should be ground. The dimensions of the letters to form the legend

were specified in millimeters. And now the legend read:
A. LINCOLN 1863 PICURIS

Picuris. Leaphorn had been there long ago. A tiny
place beside Santa Barbara creek in the Penasco Valley
north of Santa Fe with nothing much left of what had been
a thriving Pueblo but a few melting adobe walls. Leaphorn
flipped through the bundle of envelopes. Thirty seven letters, the first of them with the same return address in Fort
Worth, Texas, the rest from the Veterans Administration
hospital there, and all with the name "George" above the
street number. They had come about a week apart at first
and then less frequently. Leaphorn returned them to their
hiding place in the bottom drawer.

He handed Toddy the Picuris Lincoln Cane sheet.

"I'd say he made two of them," Toddy said. "And the
second one he finished right on the deadline."

"Yeah," Leaphorn said. "That was the date, wasn't it?"

"It was. So now we know Dorsey not only got killed.
He got screwed."

"Out of his final payment," Leaphorn said. "That's
right. He just had twenty something dollars in his billfold.
But maybe he got paid in advance."

Toddy shrugged. "No difference, now," he said. "You
finished here?"

"I think so," Leaphorn said. "Has Streib released this
stuff so his kinfolks can claim it? Is somebody coming
after it?"

Toddy was looking at the family photograph. "I guess
this one is him," he said. "The oldest boy." He moved from
the photograph to the framed motto. "Did you read this?"

"No," Leaphorn said.

"I think its out of the Bible. Maybe one of the psalms."
Toddy read it, in the voice one reserves for reciting
poetry:

'One thing I will ask of the Lord,

This will I seek after;
That I may dwell in the House of the Lord
All the days of my life.'

"I think it's one of the Psalms of Solomon, or maybe it was David."

"It's a lot like some of the verses from our Blessing Way," Leaphorn said. "You notice that?"

Toddy's expression said he hadn't. But now he did.

"I see what you mean," he said. "The House Made of Morning Mist, the House made of Dawn." He turned and looked at the motto. "May I always walk with beauty before me."

"But is Dorsey's family coming to get his stuff?" Leaphorn repeated.

"No," Toddy said. "Nobody seems to want it. Let's get out of here."

22

FATHER HAINES HAD his coat on and his hat in his hand when Leaphorn tapped at his office door.

"I just wanted to know if I could borrow a telephone," Leaphorn said. He displayed his ATT Calling Card. "I need to make some long distance calls."

"How about mine," Haines said. He pointed to his desk and glanced at his watch. "I have a meeting in Gallup so just make yourself comfortable."

Comfortable it was. From its looks, Haines' chair had been made about fifty years ago and heavily used. It's seat was well padded leather. It swiveled, and tilted and felt generally substantial. And the Haines telephone was one of those heavy black rotary dial jobs made way back when Ma Bell ruled.

Leaphorn used it to dial information and get the number of the Clark Gallery in Santa Fe. Desmond Clark was in, and wanted to know how Leaphorn was doing, and when they were going to go deer hunting again, and why didn't Leaphorn retire, and how his health was holding up. Past all that old friend exchange, they came to business.

"You know all about the Lincoln Canes, I guess," Leaphorn said. "What would one be worth to a collector, and who would buy one. Fill me in on all that."

"That's easy," Clark said. "Nobody would buy one. Everybody would know it was stolen property. You couldn't display it. Or brag about it."

"How about the Zuni War Gods," Leaphorn said. "Somebody bought them, knowing they had to have been stolen. And the Hopis have had lot of stuff disappear and then it turns up in collections. And—."

"Okay," Clark said. "I see what you mean. The underground market. Let me think about it a minute."

"Think," Leaphorn said, and waited.

"I believe Ole Honest Abe sent thirteen of those out during the Civil War. Thirteen or fourteen. So they're extremely rare, and they're extremely unusual and they look great. Ebony and silver you know. And everybody's favorite national hero had them made with his name on them. So if you were a Lincoln man, or even a Civil War buff, one would be worth a ton. I'd guess bidding would start at a hundred thousand. Maybe better. But a stolen one–. I don't know. I guess dealers who know the Lincoln trade could find a buyer. My field is Native American collectibles. I wouldn't know."

"But you think as high as a hundred thousand?"

"If it was a legitimate sale. Certified authenticity. All that. Say for example Taos Pueblo decided to sell its cane. All legal and everything. I'd say that would be low. You'd have the Indian buffs and the Lincoln buffs and the Civil War crazies all competing for it. But now you've got to tell me why you're asking."

"In a minute," Leaphorn said. "Let's say it wasn't a public sale. Let's say a dealer just approached a collector and said he had acquired one and wanted an offer."

"The collector calls the cops."

"Let's say he was a unscrupulous collector."

"He still calls the cops," Clark said. "Even quicker. He figures it's a sting. He's being set up."

"Okay," Leaphorn said. "How about another possibil_ity. Haven't some of those canes disappeared? Down through the generations. Got lost or something? What if—
."

"Aah," Clark said. "That opens a new can of worms. Yes. I'm no authority on these Lincoln Canes. You could find out in the library. But I think some of the pueblos don't have them any longer. Some of them went through pretty troubled times, you know. Like little Pojaque, and Teseque once, and Picuris."

"So lets say somebody who really knows about such things gets his hands on one of those lost canes. Could he sell it?"

Silence while Clark considered. Then he said: "I doubt it. Probably not."

"Why not?"

"He'd wouldn't have any documentation. There are a few dealers who could do it, I think. People with such reputation for absolute integrity that their word would be accepted." Clark considered what he had just said for a moment. "Well," he added, "I'd say their word plus a longish letter explaining the chronology of where the cane had been, whose hands it had passed through and how it had come into their possession."

"Who are these honorable dealers?" Leaphorn asked. "Besides you, I mean."

Silence again. Leaphorn wondered if that had been taken as sarcasasm. "I didn't mean that the way it sounded, he said. "This is nothing to joke about."

"Okay," Clark said. "Maybe Clark galleries, although we don't do much of that big money rare stuff. Let's me think who else." Silence again, and then he named an old but small gallery in Taos, another Santa Fe trader, one in Albuquerque, one in Gallup. "And a few independents, I think. I'd say Elliot Pew down in Tucson, and J.D. Regis in Albuquerque, and Archer Davis in Santa Fe, and maybe old man Fishbien, if he's still in the business." Silence again. "It's a short list. And there's a lot more honest dealers. But the thing is it takes years to get that word-is-his-bond reputation. And collectors, they're paranoid. If one of them gets screwed, or thinks he did, he spreads the word in that very small world and right away you couldn't see a five dollar gold piece for three dollars. You're dead. Nobody'll touch anything you're selling."

"How would I find out if anybody has one of those missing Lincoln Canes?"

"You probably can't," Clark said. "But if you want to try I'll give you a name of a guy in Chicago. A guy named Everson. He buys some little stuff from me but mostly he's into Lincoln. For about forty years. He'd be as likely to know as anyone."

The telephone in Chicago was answered by a man who switched Leaphorn to a woman. She identified herself as Mr. Bundy's assistant, listened to his identification, took down Desmond Clark's name and put Leaphorn on hold.

"This is Bundy," the next voice said. It was an old voice, with the sound of smoke damage and too much whiskey.

"I'm Lieutenant Joe Leaphorn, Navajo Tribal Police," Leaphorn said. "Mr. Clark thought you might be able to help me track down some information."

"If I can."

"You know about the Lincoln Canes given to–."

"Of course," Bundy said. "What's your question?"

"It concerns the one Mr. Lincoln sent to Picuris Pueblo. Have you ever heard whether it has turned up in any collection, any museum?"

Silence. Then a hoarse, hooting laugher. "Excuse me," Bundy said. "I'll be damned."

"You've heard something?" Chee asked.

"I thought it was bullshit," Bundy said. "Just a rumor I heard last summer." He laughed again. "We have a little meeting, we Lincoln people. Annual get together. Have a speaker in from one of the history departments, compare notes. One of my friends there said he'd heard that a fellow, Florida fellow I believe it was, down in Miami, had bought the Picuris cane. Said it had turned up somewhere out in the West. I didn't believe it."

"Do you know the man's name?

"No. I guess I could try to find out but it's probably going to take a day or two. What's this about? Is it important?"

"It's a about a murder," Leaphorn said, and gave Mr. Bundy his home telephone number.

Then he sat, rocked back in Father's Haines swivel chair, thinking about it. How about Asher Davis, he thought. Perhaps Asher Davis had killed Dorsey. He put together a scenario which would explain how he might have been motivated to do it.

But that left two big questions. Could there possibly have been two killers with separate motivations–making the link of the Lincoln Cane irrelevant? If so, who had killed that Koshare? And why" But that was more than two questions. And there was another one. How could he find a single shred of evidence to connect Davis to the Dorsey homicide?

23

THEIR HOUSE HAD NEVER seemed emptier. Leaphorn had walked into the kitchen intending to put something together for his supper. Perhaps he would boil some water in the coffee pot and open a one of those little sacks of dried soup. But as he walked across the linoleum tile, he became aware of the sound of his footsteps. That hadn't happened to him since the days after he had returned from Emma's funeral. He had left her mother's place out beyond Rincon Largo and come home with a sense of failure—rare for him and thus all the more disturbing. He had fled on the second day of what Emma's clan called "the time of blackening"—when everyone wore at least a symbolic smudge of soot to make themselves invisible to the *chindi*.

It had simply not been possible for him to think of the wife of his lifetime as a malevolent ghost. Emma existed in his mind (and would always exist) as someone laughing, beautiful, gentle, full of joy—someone who loved him even when he least deserved it. And so he fled–skipping two of

205

the four days of silent, passive family grief which the tradition of Emma's clan demanded. It's purpose was worthy— lending the thoughts of those who loved her to accompany Emma on her four day journey into what someone had called "that last great adventure." But hungered for isolation he become acquainted with his own sorrow. To get it, he had been willing to suffer the disapproval of Emma's very traditional people. It was a weakness he had always regretted and often remembered. He remembered it now as he stood beside the sink—reminded by the sound of his own footsteps in an empty kitchen.

He turned on the tap, watched it fill his glass, and took a small sip. The sound of crows overhead came through the window. They gathered each twilight in the cottonwoods around the Navajo Nation Administrative offices for their nightly roost—a precise reminder of the earth's turn away from the sun, of the inevitability of darkness. Where the devil was Jim Chee? He took another sip of the cool water. Supper could wait. He looked at his watch. The plane he would have taken had this Chester problem not developed would be landing in Los Angeles just about now. If all went on schedule Louisa would have a bit more than an hour and a half to get to the International terminal, show the proper people her passport and what ever other formalities were required. She would call him. Probably she would call him. Perhaps she would be angry at his desertion; perhaps she would be offended, her feelings hurt. He doubted that. She seemed a very sensible person. Logical mind. Practical. She would have understood that circumstances made it impossible for him to go. He stood by the sink, holding the half-empty glass, wishing he could remember exactly what he had said in that message. Had he been specific enough? That brought him to the question that he had been keeping buried somewhere. Why hadn't she called him? Perhaps she had. He had left his office after he'd deposited his message on her machine and he hadn't been back. If she'd called him at home, there was no machine to record it.

He put down the glass and walked into the living room. He would turn on the television and watch the news. He would not think of Louisa Bourbonnette. Instead he found himself watching a car dealership commercial and thinking of Chee. Had he and Emma had a son he might have been like Chee, a complicated mixture of intelligence, romanticism, idealism, logic and idealism, If Emma had been his influence he would been, like Chee, at least trying to maintain his traditionalism. Had he taken after his father, he would have been—like Chee seemed to be—incompetent to understand women. Clearly the boy had his troubles there. Clearly he was enamored of that young lawyer. Miss Pete. Judging from signs of unhappiness Chee had been showing that must not be going well. Abruptly, it occurred to Leaphorn that this might explain Chee's disappearance. Perhaps the rift had been healed and the lawyer and the cop were off somewhere enjoying each other's company.

The door bell rang.

That had been an unusual sound in this house for a long time. Leaphorn put the glass on the counter. Who could that be? Maybe Dilly Streib had uncovered something he wanted to tell him. Maybe Virginia had suggested that Streib drop by. Or maybe, with the same circumstances, it was Jim Chee. Where had Chee been? He'd have to make sure this absence without explanation business didn't happen again.

Janet Pete was standing at his door, her little Ford Escort parked on the street. Miss Pete looked tired, slightly disheveled, glum and nervous.

"Well," Leaphorn said. "Good evening. Come on in."

She followed him into the living room. "I apologize for coming like this," she said. "Intruding into your privacy, I mean. But I couldn't get you at your office and Virginia said you might be here, and you wouldn't mind."

"It's perfectly all right," Leaphorn said, This is another coincidence, he thought, happening to me, who does not believe in them. I am worrying about Chee and this young woman and she appears to talk about him. It will be something personal. So what can I tell her?

He smiled at her. "Could I get you something to drink. "Something legal, of course. Possession of which is not prohibited in the Navajo Nation. I think I have some sort of sodapop in the refrigerator. Or I could put on some coffee if you'd like it. And meanwhile, have a seat."

"Oh, no," Miss Pete said. "Nothing for me." But she sat in the chair he indicated. "I can only stay a moment. Just long enough to represent a client."

"Ah," Leaphorn said, and sat across from her, thinking this was his week for guessing wrong. "Which client?"

"I represent Eugene Ahkeah," she said.

"So I heard."

"We had a long talk today," Janet said. "Over at Crownpoint." She hesitated.

She will tell me something, or ask me a favor. Or perhaps both, Leaphorn thought. But she's making this visit on an impulse. Worst possible time, right at supper. She hasn't thought it through. She may change her mind.

"Does Mr. Ahkeah have something to tell me?" Leaphorn said.

"No," she said. "Well, not exactly. I guess I do." She laughed, shook her head. "Your assistant, Officer Chee, suggested that I tell you my client is innocent. After today, I'm sure he is. He didn't kill Eric Dorsey. He didn't steal all those items you found in the box under his house."

"Chee said you should tell me Ahkeah was innocent? When? Did you see him today?"

"He was just joking," she said, surprised at his intensity of his tone. "It was last week."

"Not something he knew, then," Leaphorn said, making a gesture of dismissal. "We've been working on separate things and I haven't seen him for a few days. I thought perhaps you were bringing me a dispatch from wherever Chee is spending his time these days."

Miss Pete looked faintly alarmed. "I think he has some days off," she said.

"Correct," Leaphorn said. "And he's taking them."

Miss Pete had collected herself. "This may sound unprofessional—my coming to you instead of going through the usual legal channels. But I know going to the U.S. Attorney wouldn't do any good, and I'm not sure what you will say and so the worst I can do is waste some of our time." She paused, picked up the handbag she'd placed on the chair beside her, and put it in her lap.

Leaphorn waited.

"I realize you have a lot of circumstantial evidence," Janet said. "The stolen materials under his house, principally, although no search warrant was issued as far as I can find out so far and that probably won't be admitted in court. I guess you can probably place him at the scene of the homicide at about the right time, and perhaps you have some other evidence. But given time I think I'll be able to show he was set up, that the crime was actually done by the man who made that anonymous telephone call about the box under Ahkean's house."

She paused, awaited a Leaphorn reaction to all this, received a smile and a nod instead of the argument she'd expected, and hurried on.

"There's simply no motive for Ahkeah to have done it. The prosecution will argue that the motive was theft. He needed to get money to buy whiskey. But he didn't sell the stuff. He didn't buy whiskey."

She paused, waiting again for the counter argument.

Leaphorn nodded.

Miss Pete flushed slightly. She picked up the purse and put it on the chair beside her and cleared her throat.

"Totally aside from his innocence, Mr. Ahkeah is certainly no risk to become a fugitive. He has no connections off the reservation. He doesn't have any money, no way to run and no place to hide. He doesn't even speak very much English. There's really no reason to hold him in a cell under a bond he can't possibly raise."

Miss Pete stopped, looked at him, waited a response.

"What would you like me to do?"

"I came to ask you if you would ask Mr. Streib to recommend to the court that Mr. Ahkeah be released on his own recognizance."

Leaphorn thought a moment. "All right," he said.

Miss Pete looked startled. She picked up the purse and put it down again. "All right? You mean you'll do it?"

"I'll call him this evening," Leaphorn looked at his watch. "I'll give him time to eat his supper. I think he'll go along with it. Mr. Streib is usually pretty reasonable."

He was watching Miss Pete, who was struggling to replace the amazement on her face with something less revealing. She won the battle, and then produced a nervous laugh.

"You know," she said, "Jim said: 'Tell the Lieutenant Ahkeah is innocent and he'll turn him loose.' I thought he was just kidding."

"He was," Leaphorn said, smiling at her. "It just happens that I agree with you. Even if Ahkeah did it, he isn't going to run anywhere that we can't find him. And you may be right about him being not guilty."

Miss Pete had recomposed herself. "I wish the police would concentrate on finding who it was who set Ahkeah up. I think that's what happened. Whoever killed Mr. Dorsey saw Ahkean at the Bonaventure mission. They noticed he was drunk and decided he'd be perfect as the fall guy."

"Possibly," Leaphorn said. He was thinking, I like this young woman. I like the way she works for her client and maybe I will be needing a lawyer myself if they decide to charge me with concealing evidence of an illegal wire tap. And he was thinking that he could see now why she appealed to his assistant.

"Do you know where I can find Jim Chee?"

Miss Pete looked surprised. "No."

"Or how to get a message to him?"

"No."

Leaphorn allowed himself to look disappointed, which was easy, because he was.

"I thought you might," he said. "I have gotten the impression that Jim counts his time wasted when you are not near by."

It seemed to Leaphorn that Miss Pete looked sad to hear this.

"We've been friends a long time," she said. "He tells me his troubles. I tell him mine." She dismissed all this with a shrug, but her expression cancelled that.

"It's good to have someone you can talk to like that," Leaphorn said. "I apologize. I must be sounding like an overaged cupid. I guess I read Jim all wrong. We have an old hit-and-run case—totally hopeless—but the chief wants it solved and there's probably a promotion there for whoever can nail the guy. I think Chee's working on it hard because he thinks with sergeant stripes he would look to you more like a worthy marriage prospect."

Miss Pete's expression, *if Leaphorn read it right, went from irritation, to surprise, to sorrow.*

She exhaled, picked up the purse again, and put it down.

"I don't normally behave like this," Leaphorn said. "Normally I'm pretty good at minding my own business. 'Herd your own sheep,' as my mother used to teach us. I'm Jim's boss and I like him, and I worry about him some-times."

"I worry about him too," she said. "But I think you

have sort of misinterpreted things." She produced a weak smile. "So did I. 1 was thinking in terms of Romeo and Juliet. The wrong families and all that."

It took Leaphorn a moment to understand. "Clans," he said, and made a wry face.

"Well, actually I think the clan business is all very ambiguous. Only my father was a Navajo. And its hazy on his side, too. But Jim, you know, I think maybe he's not the marrying kind. So, even a hazy, ambiguous clan taboo can be useful."

"Uumm," Leaphorn said. What in the world was he doing, he thought, behaving just as Emma would behave, trying to be a matchmaker. This was absolutely none of his business. But he had found that he liked Janet Pete. He hadn't expected to like her. And when you looked past his various flaws, you had to like Jim Chee, too. So, to hell with it, he would continue interfering. Emma wouldn't believe he was doing this, but she would certainly approve.

"There something hard for normal people to understand about Jim Chee," he said. "He's an odd sort of idealist. He wants to become a practicing *hataalii*, He wants to be a bonafide traditionalist. To be singer of the curing ceremonials. Not just to be a shaman, but to a really effective one." Leaphorn paused, looking for some general statement to sum this up, and his own attitude toward it. "It makes any sort of taboo more powerful than it would be to me—and probably to you." He made a wry face. "Office Chee wants to save his people from the future."

Janet Pete had listened to all this intently, without fiddling with her purse. Now she picked it up, and got up, and said: "I have to go."

Leaphorn escorted her to the door. " Well," he said, "I guess Office Chee will show up again someday."

"I guess so," she said, and turned to look at him. "Were you serious about calling Mr. Streib."

Leaphorn looked at his watch. "Right now," he said.

24

JIM CHEE, born for the Slow Talking Dinee', born to the Bitter Water Clan, whose real, ceremonial and secret name was actually Long Thinker, awoke on the floor of Gracie Cayodito's hogan just when dawn was invading the extreme eastern edge of the night. He was awakened by the voice of his uncle, who was standing outside the east-facing door of the hogan, signing his blessing song to the new day.

As Chee lay there, stiff from a night on this unyielding bed and still only half awake, a second voice joined the husky baritone of Frank Sam Nakai. This one was older, cracked and scratchy—the sound of Hosteen Barbone shouting his greeting to the great *yei* Dawn Boy. Normally, Chee sang his own dawn prayer a bit later, after he'd started the coffee perking and the Eastern sky was red with morning. He groaned, pushed himself upright, tucked in his shirt and fished out from under it the buckskin medicine pouch which contained his corn pollen.

When in Rome, he thought, one does as the Roman's do. He didn't want to worsen the bad impression he had already made on these old men.

But now, with the sun up and the town of Window Rock in view through his windshield, he was pretty sure the perfect knowledge he'd displayed of the morning blessing hadn't made any difference. The problem was the generation gap. The problem was theological. The problem was how one defined the concept of *hozho,* that idea of harmony which was the very root and foundation of the Navajo religion. This kind of problem wasn't what he wanted when he'd gone back up the mountain to find his uncle again. He'd been in a crazy mood. Having that hit and run case turn out the way it did had been the last straw. Too much ambiguity, uncertainty, indecision. He wanted no more of that. He would go to the mountains and get a ruling on whether he could marry Janet Pete and still be a Navajo in the traditional sense. That took him through Farmington, right past the Quikprint shop. He slammed on the brakes, backed, pulled into a parking place. He had three different bumper stickers made, timing the process. It took almost thirteen minutes and, yes, it was expensive. Then he drove faster than the law allowed, making up for the lost time.

He'd wanted a favorable ruling. He imagined the scene—an old, old man recounting the history of the Hunger People from the clans day one, proving that these people had never joined with his own ancestors, never made common cause, never did any of those things which would make them linked in blood. Then he would tell Janet. And what would she say. *So what? You think you can tell me I'm taboo. Like maybe I had AIDS. And I don't meet your high Navajo standards. And then you can come back and say I passed your test. Well, screw you old friend.* Or maybe the ruling would be negative. Even a negative ruling was better than this ambiguity. With that he could at least make a clear cut decision.

But the great conference at the Cayodito hogan had drifted away from anything specific into the misty world of Changing Woman, First Man and First Woman, Talking God and the great galaxy of other *yei*.

Frank Sam Nakai had heard Chee's truck coming up the muddy road and was standing in the doorway of his hogan.

"I have been asking and I have found the man who will know about the Hunger People and your own clans," his uncle had said. "He lives over by Crystal. We will go and listen to what he will tell us."

The man who would know was named Barbone. Like Nakai he was a hataalii, and like Nakai he was called "Hosteen" in respect of his years and his wisdom. But, of course, when they turned off the pavement of Navajo Route 32 and jolted down the road past the old Crystal trading post and up the crooked tracks into the aspen grove where Barbone had built his hogan they discovered that Hosteen Barbone was not at home. His daughter, who seemed to Chee to be about seventy five, said he had gone to the place of Gracie Cayodito to decide what sort of ceremonial was needed to cure a Cayodito grandchild of an illness.

On the road again, eastward out of the Chuskas to Route 666, north to the Two Grey Hills turnoff, then back into the Chuskas on the road which led—when and if weather permitted—to the Toh- Ni Tsa forest fire lookout tower. A badly used Chevy Blazer and a pickup truck were parked at the Cayodito place. Gracie was there. So was Hosteen Barbone, looking old enough to have a daughter over seventy. Beside Barbone, against the south wall of the hogan, sat a woman who looked even older than Barbone. Old Woman Mustache. Chee had heard of her somewhere—had heard that she was the wise person of the Streams Come Together Clan.

About an hour into the ensuing discussion, Chee decided that Old Woman Mustache was either mute, or had fallen asleep. Hosteen Barbone covered the genesis of the Hunger People, how the clan had formed and gotten its name during *Naahondzibd*, the "Fearing Time" when the American Army had joined the Mexicans and Utes in the war against the Dinee', and the men were afraid to leave on a hunt because they might return to find their hogans burned, their wives slaughtered and their children taken by the soldiers to be sold in the slave market at Santa Fe.

"They say that's when the Hunger People began. They say that Kit Carson came through there, came through about where Many Farms is now with horse soldiers and some Utes. They killed the people they caught there, and took the horses, and burned up all the corn and pinon nuts and blankets, and gathered up the children to sell them in Santa Fe. My grandmother said they got a hundred and fifty dollars for her. A rancher way down the Rio Grande bought her and had her baptized but she ran away and got back to the Jemez Pueblo and they sent her back to where her family was but her family was all gone. They say that only one man in that camp had a gun and when he tried to fight the soldiers with it, it wouldn't shoot. The soldiers killed that one and just a few people got away up into the mountains. And they found other people hiding there, mostly women and children. They say they were from all over. From other camps where the soldiers had come though and cut down the orchards, and burned the food and stole the horses. A lot of them starved or froze to death during that winter, but Carson never did capture them so they didn't go on the Long Walk to Bosque Redondo. They say that when the Americans released the Dinee' from that prison and they came back to Dine' bike'yah, these people had their own clan. They say that since they came from all over they couldn't name them with the place they came from, so everybody called them the Hunger People."

Hosteen Barbone had given them the beginnings of the Hunger People, as he had heard it. Now he would give them the rest of that clan's history. And when that was finished, they would hear from Gracie Cayodito, and perhaps from Old Woman Mustache if she wasn't asleep.

Chee had been raised among the traditionals, among the sheep camp and hogan people. He knew how to sit comfortably and be patient. If he was lucky, Barbone's account would never, in any way, link the Hunger People with the clans of his own mother or father. And so he listened, trying to keep track of contacts and relationships between maternal clans, paternal clans, offshoot fragments of clans. The only bad news he heard seem vague and ambiguous.

Barbone fell silent. The silence extended long enough to signal that his account was finished. He had talked about an hour, Chee thought, but he resisted the impulse to confirm this with a glance at his watch. Into the silence Old Woman Mustache spoke.

"Too much talk about those father's clans," she said in a voice that was very old but surprisingly clear. "Remember in the Fourth World when the women got tired of the men and went across the river and pleasured themselves. Remember what the Holy People taught us then. That men have their things to do, and women have their things to do and one of the woman's things is the family. Remember what they taught us then. The mother's clan, the clan you're born to, that's the one that is important."

Having said that, with long pauses for breathing between each sentence, Old Woman Mustache closed her eyes and rested. Gracie Cayodito spoke next.

She began with the self-effacing "They say," by which traditional Navajos pass along information without making any personal claim to it. In the case of Gracie Cayodito the form did not represent any self-doubts. She took them through the histories of Chee's two clans. Since her sources of data considered the Bitter Water dinee' one of the original four formed by Changing Woman herself, she took them back to the mythic days when the spirits called Holy People still walked the Earth Surface world with the humans they had formed. Gracie Cayodito covered this history with relative speed, but digressed often into the heresies being committed by the contemporary shamans who violated the old rules of ritualism, and, with hard looks at Jim Chee, produced the horrors produced by violations of the incest taboo.

"People who have sex with their sisters," she said, looking at Chee. "That causes craziness. That causes people to jump into the fire."

But, alas, when she had finally finished, whether Janet Pete was indeed his sister remained unclear in Chee's mind. What was crystal clear was that Cayodito felt even stronger than Hosteen Barbone about adapting ceremonials as old as the dawn of time to the terminal years of the twentieth century.

Then Hosteen Frank Sam Nakai spoke—not long, but long enough to underline the important points.

First, nobody could tell for sure whether or not this daughter of the man from the Hunger People was a clan sister of this son of the Slow Talking People and the Bitter Water Dinee', and second, the Beauty Way of the Navajo people was being undermined by young shamans who were too lazy to learn the rules the Holy People had taught, or too willing to do ceremonies the wrong way and thus adapt them to the world of the beligaani.

Chee parked his muddy pickup in the "Police Cars Only" area at the office and waited for the place to officially open at 8 a.m. He would check in with Leaphorn and then...But no. He'd forgotten. Leaphorn would be gone. Off on his great China trip. Gone for a month. Chee felt a

twinge of guilt. He should have checked in with the Lieutenant yesterday. Should have told him goodby and gotten
his final instructions. Leaphorn would probably want him
to do something about the Jimmy Chester-Ed Zeck telephone call. He'd probably want to talk about how they
could get some evidence against Chester that could be
used in court. Probably want to bring in Dilly Streib.
Maybe help set up an FBI sting operation.

He glanced at his watch. Couple of more minutes and
Virginia would be there. If he'd guessed right about the
Lieutenant, there's be an envelope awaiting him, full of
instructions on what to do and how to do it. He allowed
himself a final review of what last night's session meant to
him. Whether Janet was his clan sister, even vaguely,
remained in doubt. BUT, BUT, BUT. There was no doubt at
all that for Hosteen Barbone and Gracie Cayodity and,
much worse, Frank Sam Nakai, his own "little father,"
mere absence of proof was not good enough.

And how about Old Woman Mustache? When Frank
Sam Nakai had finished his summation they had all sat in
silence for a while, watching the fire burn down under the
smoke hole. And then the Old Woman had spoken:

"You have wasted words," she said. "Two much talk of
men and the man's clan. Nothing matters but the mother's
clan."

But what the devil did that mean to him? Janet's
mother was a white. There was no mother's clan. He
climbed out of the truck, and slammed the door behind
him.

Virginia looked no happier than he felt.

"Where have you been?" she demanded. "Lieutenant
Leaphorn was looking everywhere for you."

"Took my days off," Chee said. "Did he leave anything
for me."

"Not with me," she said, and glared at him.

Nor, to Chee's surprise, was there a fat envelope in

his In Basket. There was absolutely nothing in it. Leaphorn's office door was closed, which wasn't unusual. It was locked. Unusual but understandable under the circumstances. He wouldn't want to leave it open for a month.

Chee trotted down stairs, past Virginia's now-vacant desk, and out to his car. This felt odd. With Leaphorn in China for a month he was totally on his own. Well, not quite. He probably should report to the Chief, as the Lieutenant did. But that could wait until he had a little time to think. To do that he'd go home. Maybe he'd even get a little sleep.

He pulled his truck out of the lot, stopping to let the northbound traffic pass. The third car looked like Leaphorn's. And Lieutenant Joe Leaphorn was driving it.

25

WHEN JOE LEAPHORN realized that the dirty pickup truck tagging behind him belonged to Jim Chee and saw, through the mud- speckled windshield that Chee was driving it, his instinctive reaction was pull of on the shoulder and starting asking questions immediately. But he resisted that impulse. He wanted more privacy. He turned down his own street, pulled into his driveway and turned off the ignition. By the time Chee had parked on the street, Leaphorn was standing beside his truck.

"Where have you been?" Leaphorn asked, pleased that he'd kept the emotion out of his voice.

"I thought you'd gone to China," Chee said. It was the wrong thing to say. Chee realized that instantly from Leaphorn's expression. "I had some days off," he added.

"You've been out of communication for two days," Leaphorn said. "You know the rule about that."

"Yes sir," Chee said.

Leaphorn stared at him. "Are you telling me that

since I was supposed to be in China you could take off without going through the procedure?"

"No sir," Chee said. "I forgot. I had other things on my mind."

"Like what?"

Like Janet Pete, Chee thought. Like not being able to be with her. Like hurting her by telling her she was taboo. But to hell with Leaphorn. That was none of his business. "Like I think I may have solved that Todachine hit-and-run case," he said. And as soon as he said it, he regretted it. "And like what to do about Ed Zeck and Councilman Chester," he added, hoping that would change the subject.

"Ed Zeck and Councilman Chester," Leaphorn said, with a question in his voice.

"Yeah," Chee said. "What did you think of that tape? The one I left in your tape player?"

Through years of police work, of questioning people who he didn't want to show his reaction to their answers, Joe Leaphorn had learned to control his expression. He could hear the best news, or the worst, behind the same bland and neutral face. But not now. His cheeks flushed, blood rushed to his forehead, the lines around his mouth tightened.

Jim Chee was looking at Leaphorn enraged.

But it only lasted a moment. Relief replaced fury. The veils of mystery had fallen away. He wasn't the victim of some unknown malice, the target of a shrewd and secret enemy. He was victim of simple-minded boneheadedness. No more suspension, or risk of dismissal, or hiring a lawyer to defend against a charge of conspiracy to suppress evidence. All of that could be fixed tomorrow morning. Leaphorn felt weak with relief. He leaned a hand against Chee's truck. And then he remembered what this boneheadedness had cost him.

"Why did you leave that tape in my player?" His expression was neutral again, but the voice was cold.

Chee hastily explained how that had happened, and why the call telling him the Todachine suspect had confessed over KNDN up in Farmington had caused him to rush away without an explanation.

"I wanted to get right on that before it got cold," Chee concluded, and looked at Leaphorn to see if explanation had created the mollifying effect desired. If it had, he couldn't read it in Leaphorn's expression.

Leaphorn stood there studying Chee, saying nothing.

"About the Chester tape," Chee said. "You were asking me if I knew of any evidence of bribery. I know it can't be used—the tape I mean. It must have come from an illegal telephone tap. But maybe it will persuade the federals to so something."

"What do you know about how it came to be broadcast?"

"Just what was in the police report," Chee said. "This middle-aged, middle sized man walked into the Navajo Tractor Sales office. The radio station has an open mike there for announcements. He got in line with the other people and when his turn came he held the tape player up to the mike and broadcast it and then he just walked out."

"You had nothing to do with it?"

"No Sir," Chee said, loudly. "Nothing. Absolutely nothing."

"Know anything more about it?"

"No sir," Chee paused. "Except I guess Roger Applebee did it. The lawyer lobbying against that toxic waste dump." He told Leaphorn how he'd met Applebee while having lunch with Janet Pete and what Applebee had said about getting some concrete evidence. "It can't be used in court, of course. But maybe he thought it would cause the FBI to get interested. Maybe to set up a sting. Something like that."

"I doubt it," Leaphorn said.

Chee was surprised. "Well," he said. "They're into that sort of thing now, the federals are. Running stings. They've been nailing politicians here and there for accepting bribes. And twenty something thousand dollars is a lot of money."

Leaphorn studied Chee a moment, sighed, and made a decision. Under the circumstances, when he was Chee's age he might have done what Chee had done.

"Councilman Chester and Ed Zeck have been in the cattle business for about twenty years," he said. "They run bred heifers on Chester's grazing lease and a Bureau of Land Management lease that Zeck holds. The twenty something thousand dollars is exactly what it takes to pay off a Farmington Bank of New Mexico loan Chester signed to buy the heifers. Zeck sold them to the feed lot people, but he hadn't deposited the check."

"Oh," Chee said.

"Only thing wrong about the deal was the price of beef went down and they lost a little money on the project," Leaphorn said. "But Dilly Streib is going to want to talk to you about an illegal wire tap, and maybe about that radio broadcast."

"Sure," Chee said. He wanted to ask Leaphorn why he was wearing civilian clothing on a work day. Maybe he'd misunderstood. Maybe it was today that Leaphorn was leaving for China.

"Call Streib and tell him," Leaphorn. "And call Captain Dodge and explain the tape business to him. And let's get back to business."

"Yes sir," Chee said.

"The Todachine thing. Have you found him?"

"Well," Chee said. "I think I have the driver spotted. But I need to find the truck before we have any evidence. I haven't located it yet." He stopped, hoping Leaphorn wouldn't press him for details. Leaphorn didn't.

"Let that go for awhile. We want to pick up that Kanitewa boy and find out if he saw anything that day at Eric Dorsey's shop." He told Chee what he had learned about the Tano Lincoln Cane and the Picuris Lincoln Cane and what he had learned about collectors of historic rarities, and his conclusions about Asher Davis.

"It's like your Todacheenie suspect, though," Leaphorn said. "We don't have any concrete evidence. Just circumstantial stuff. Unless the Kanitewa kids saw something helpful."

Chee cleared his throat. "You mean," he said. "Asher Davis killed Eric Dorsey?"

"Except we don't have any evidence."

"Lieutenant," Chee said. "Asher Davis was out on the Hopi Reservation when Dorsey was killed. He was out there with Cowboy Dashee, buying stuff from Dashee's relatives. About the time Dorsey was killed they were eating lunch with Dashee's uncle at the Hopi Cultural Center."

Leaphorn lost his neutral expression again. But only for a moment.

"Well, now," he said. "That's interesting."

Chee cleared his throat again.

"Lieutenant, was I wrong about you taking leave and going to China? Did I get the date wrong?"

"No," Leaphorn said. "I had to call it off. I got suspended and I had to stay for the hearing."

"My God!" Chee said. "Suspended! Why would you get suspended?"

Leaphorn told him.

26

"THE OLD BATTLEAX did a lot of talking," Harold Blizzard said. "She'd talk about absolutely everything except where she was hiding the kid."

"I can see I'm going to have to go out there myself," Chee said. "You just don't seem to be catching on about how to interrogate people."

"I can interrogate people all right," Blizzard said. "Normal people, I have no problem. It's you Navajos. You know that stereotype about us Indians being taciturn?" Blizzard raised a huge palm toward Chee and growled "Ugggh" to illustrate his point. "Well that's based on the rest of us Indians. Cheyennes, Cherokees, Choctaws, Comanches, Chippewas, Modocs, Kiowas, Seminoles, Potts, Hopis. Normal Indians. But whoever decided Indians were silent hadn't run into you talkative Navajos."

"You're telling me she didn't just flat out deny she knew where Delmar could be located? Is that right. She just wasn't willing to tell you?"

Blizzard used his big right hand to demonstrate lips flapping. "She'd just talk about what a lousy job we policemen did in protecting people, enforcing the laws and all that. And how would she know Delmar would be safe if we had him in our custody? And how she knew we wouldn't post a guard on him, or anything like that. And on, and on."

"Did you ask her why she thought he needed a guard?"

"Sure, I did. And she'd then just give me five more minutes about how lazy we cops were. And then I'd tell her she was judging us by the performance of you guys." Blizzard cut off own chuckle and Chee's response to that by signalling the waitress and pointing to their coffee cups.

"Hey," he said. "There's your lawyer lady. We're going to need another cup."

There, indeed, was Janet Pete, standing in the entrance of the Navajo Nation Inn coffee shop, looking hesitant. She saw that Chee had seen her, and turned away. Pretending, it seemed to Chee, to be looking for someone.

"Hey, Janet," Blizzard shouted. He stood, waving. Harold Blizzard was far too large, far to loud to be ignored.

Janet came. She looked at Chee and looked away. "Hello Harold," she said. "Hello Jim."

Chee stood and pulled back a chair for her.

"I met a friend of yours the other day," Blizzard said. "Jim's friend, too, I guess. Fellow named Asher Davis. He said if he wasn't about sixty pounds overweight, you two could provide him a perfect alibi in that homicide over at Tano Pueblo."

"Oh," Janet said. She glanced at Chee, and away.

"He's on the list the feds gave me of people to check out. About number sixty or so."

"I guess he's right," Janet said. "He went there with Mr. Chee, and Cowboy Dashee and me. And when we decided to watch the ceremony from the roof, he decided he was too heavy for it to hold him."

"That was before the clowns came out with the wagon load of stuff?" Blizzard asked. "Or was it after?"

"I think it was before," Janet said. "Yes it was right at the very beginning."

"That's the way I remember it, too," Chee said. He was thinking Leaphorn told Streib about the Lincoln Canes, and Streib told the Albuquerque FBI, and Blizzard knows his business better than I gave him credit for. "Are you thinking of Davis as maybe a suspect?"

Blizzard gave him a stern look. "Just my native curiosity," he said.

"I understand Davis looked good for it after the business of the Lincoln Canes came out," Chee said. "But it turns out he was with an Apache Country deputy sheriff over on the Hopi Reservation when Eric Dorsey was killed."

Blizzard looked surprised, then angry. "God dammit," he said. "What don't anybody ever tell anybody anything."

"I had no idea Davis was a suspect," Janet said. "And wait a minute. I thought you were talking about the Sayesva case. What's the Dorsey killing have to do with that? Which one are you talking about?"

"Nobody tells me about anything either," Chee said. "I've been out of touch. I just heard about the phony Lincoln Canes this morning."

"Phony Lincoln whats?" Janet said. "I still haven't heard about them."

And so Chee explained, skipping—Navajo fashion— back to the very beginning with the Spanish King Charles sending canes to the Indian Pueblos in the 17th Century, from there to 1863, thence to Leaphorn's discovery of the sketch on Dorsey's desk. He concluded finally with the presumption that the package Delmar Kanitewa had taken to his Koshare uncle was a copy of the Tano cane and the Koshare put in the wagon to warn against selling of pueblo artifacts.

"I'd never even heard of Lincoln Canes," Janet said, looking thoughtful. "Is it your official 'theory of the crime' now that this cane ties the two homicides together. Same killer for the man who made it and the man who used it?

"I'd say so," Chee said. "More or less."

"How's it work?" Janet asked.

"Sort of like this," Chee said, happy that Janet was once again talking directly to him and even looking at him. Maybe we're almost back again to being old friends, he thought. And maybe that was all he could ever hope for. "Somebody hires Dorsey to make the Picuris cane, knowing he can sell it to a collector of Lincoln rarities because the cane from that Pueblo disappeared generations ago. So he has Dorsey make such a cane, not telling Dorsey what it is or about the fraud. Then he decides to try again with the Tano Cane and gets Dorsey to make it. Delmar Kanitewa shows up at the shop while Dorsey is finishing it. He shows it to the boy since he's a Tano kid. Delmar tells Dorsey what it is."

Chee paused, looked at Janet. "You have to understand this Dorsey is a genuine straight arrow. Into doing good. Now he figures something crooked must be going on and he's being used. Probably he figures the real cane is going to be stolen and this one used to replace it so the theft won't be noticed. So he gives it to Delmar to take to his uncle with a warning about the impending theft. And then the guy who commissioned it shows up to collect it, and Dorsey jumps on him about it and the guy kills Dorsey to protect his secret."

Blizzard made a wry face. "It sounds too damned complicated," he said. "I like 'em simpler. Like the janitor walks in drunk and tries to borrow money and gets turned down and gets made and knocks off Dorsey and steals some stuff."

"I don't like that Blizzard theory at all," Janet said. "But I don't know about the other one either." She thought. "How could this guy sell the second cane? Nobody would buy it. Collectors know about these things or they wouldn't be collecting them. They'd know that Tano Pueblo still had its Lincoln Cane. And so they'd know that one they'd bought was a fake, or, worse yet, the one they bought was stolen."

"So they couldn't brag about it. Or show it off." Blizzard said. "So why buy it?"

"And why use Dorsey."

"He had connections with some traders," Chee said. "We know that because he was helping some of the Navajos out on the Checkerboard get better prices for their stuff." He paused remembering what the old woman with the ill husband had told him. "Including some old stuff that the real collectors go for."

"Okay, but I still see holes in it," Janet said.

"I have trouble with it, too," Chee admitted.

The waitress arrived bringing Janet a cup and a coffee refill for Chee and Blizzard.

"You know," Blizzard said. "I think maybe all three of us are in the same boat I was in at that Cheyenne Autumn movie the other night. I couldn't understand why all the Navajos were hooting and blowing their car horns. Different culture. Different perceptions. There's probably some Tano Pueblo connection here we just don't fathom." He made a wide, Blizzard style gesture with his hands. "Different value systems, you know. Hard for us outsiders to comprehend."

"Yes," Janet said in a voice almost too low for Chee to hear. "Hard to comprehend."

"Janet," Chee said. He reached his hand toward her.

"There's something I'd like to explain."

She put down her cup and sat back, not looking at him.

"Well, now," Blizzard said, hastily. "I've got work to do." He picked up the ticket. "You get the tip," he said to Chee. "See you later, Janet." And he was gone.

"Me too," Janet said. "I've got to go."

"Where," Chee said.

"First to Crownpoint. The federals are releasing Ahkeah and I have to do the paperwork."

"I'm going that direction," Chee said. "Could I give you a ride."

"I have to go on from there up to Aztec. I have some business at the San Juan County courthouse."

"That's right on my way," Chee said.

"I'd better take my own car," she said. "You'd have to wait for me." She got up, dropped a dollar on the table. "My share of the tip."

"Janet," Chee said. "I want to talk to you."

"I'm not sure I'd care for that."

Chee sat looking up at her. He could think of nothing to say. But his expression must have said something to her.

"What could we talk about?" she asked. "Do you think we can go back to being friends?"

Chee shook his head. "I doubt it. I don't think I could."

He put his hand out. She looked at it. Then took it. Her finger tips felt soft and warm against his skin.

"Just a few hours," he said.

"What do we talk about?"

"The weather. The landscape. Old times, maybe, if we're careful how we handle it. And I think maybe I want you to help me make up my mind about something."

She extracted her hand.

"Not about Navajo clans," he said. "About something

you must have studied in law school. Justice. Retribution. Social revenge. Ethics. All that."

She managed a smile. "I'm good at that kind of talk,"

In fact they talked very little on their way to Crownpoint.

South of Gallup Chee pointed to the places along the red sandstone cliffs of Mesa de los Lobos where various movies had been shot. He explained that Thoreau was pronounced "threw" because the village had been named after a railroad engineer and not the poet-essayist. He pointed southward to Little Haystack Mountain and told her how a Navajo prospector named Paddy Martinez had found a vein of radioactive pitchblende near there and opened the great Ambrosia Lake uranium mining district. He told her, finally, about the chain of events which had gotten Leaphorn suspended, and caused the Lieutenant to miss his trip to China.

"It was a stupid thing to do," he said. "Leaving that tape in there, I mean. Leaphorn didn't make much out of it, but I feel terrible about it."

"I didn't think I would like that man at first," Janet said. "But I really do. I think he's a kind person. I used to just think he was smart."

"He's smart, all right."

"That's what he thinks about you, too."

"Why do you say that?"

"The way he talked about you."

"What do you mean? When did you talk to him?"

"I went to see him about Ahkeah. Exactly like you told me to do."

Chee took his eye off the road to stare at her. She was looking amused. "I told you to go see Leaphorn? When did that happen?"

"Don't you remember? I told you Eugene Ahkeah was not guilty. You said go tell Lieutenant Leaphorn that and he'd turn him loose. So I did. And he did."

"Did you really," Chee said. "Wow."

"I think it was just good timing. He'd figured out someone else had done it."

"But what makes you think he has this high opinion of me," Chee said. "I don't often get that impression."

"The hit-and-run case. He thinks you can solve it."

"No he doesn't. Or he didn't. He doesn't think anyone can solve it."

"He told me that, too," Janet said. "No clues. But really, he thinks you can do it."

Chee took his eyes off the road again. She was looking straight ahead so all he could see was her profile. Hard to understand, but a beautiful profile.

She spent only a few minutes in the Crownpoint station and emerged with Eugene Ahkeah in tow. Ahkeah looked tired and disheveled. "I told Mr. Ahkeah we'd give him a ride home," she said. They did, dropping him off at his mobile home.

"Blizzard was kidding me about Navajos being talkative," Chee said. "He should meet your client."

"He's resentful," Janet said. "He thinks he was arrested just because he was handy."

"Well, now," Chee said, feeling a touch resentful himself, "there was the matter of finding all that stolen stuff under his house."

"Yes, but–" Janet said, and stopped. "Let's not argue."

They drove in silence through the rolling, autumn grassland. It is eighty one miles from Crownpoint to Farmington and there were days when Chee had made the drive without seeing another vehicle. Today they had met a car and two pickups before they were ten miles north of Crownpoint.

"Heavy traffic day," Chee said, hoping to restart a conversation.

"You wanted to ask me about something. Remember?"

"I do," Chee said. He fished the tape out of his glove box and put it into the tape player and pushed the "PLAY" button. "But first I want you to listen to this."

Janet listened.

"That doesn't happen very often," she said. "I heard about this but it didn't seem real. Did he send any money?"

"Six twenties, a ten and a five," Chee said. "In the U.S. Mail."

She thought about that. Shrugged. "And nobody recognized him of course, or he'd be in jail by now. How about the description?

"The usual. Middle aged, middle sized, average looking Navajo male, wearing average looking Navajo clothing. He was wearing one of those long-filled baseball caps with the bill bent, and he smelled like onions, and he drove a middle aged, middle sized middle green pickup truck with a bumper sticker which said Ernie is the greatest."

"Smelled like onions?" She looked at him, eyebrows raised with the question.

"Middle of the morning," Chee said. "Too early for your Lottaburger onion fix."

"Now you see why I think Lieutenant Leaphorn things you're going to nail this guy?" She was smiling at him.

Which Chee enjoyed. But this was not the time for basking. He said: "This stopped being a tough one as soon as he walked into that radio station. It's not tough now. Now we catch him because of that bumper sticker."

"Surely he'd have gotten rid of that. He'd have soaked it off as soon as he got home."

"I don't think so," Chee said. "Neither do the Farmington police, or the New Mexico state cops. He'll keep driving that pickup out on the highway and sooner of later a cop drives up behind him and sees it."

Janet looked unpersuaded. She shrugged. "I defer to

your experience in such matters. As for me, I'd have painted over it, or something."

Chee thought about that. "No," he said, looking at her. "I have a feeling you'd turn yourself in."

They were driving almost due north through a landscape devoid of humans and the signs which humans leave. Jim Chee loved for its emptiness. It's beauty had always stirred him and it now stirred him out of his pessimism. Things will work out, he thought. Somehow they'll work out. They passed the junction which offered thirty miles of dirt road and the White Rock Chapter House to the left, and the much shorter dirt road to the Lake Valley Chapter House to the right. Behind the grassy hills to the right, Kenbeto Wash, and Bettonie Tsossie Wash, and Escalvada Wash and Fajada Wash all got together after draining thousands of square miles of mountain slopes and mesas, and moved enough water to be called the Chaco River. On this afternoon of a dry autumn, the Chaco bridge crossed a broad expanse of sand on which dust devils were being produced by the autumn breeze (or, as his mother would have assured him, by those playful *yeis*, the Blue Flint Boys).

Janet broke the long silence. "Why do you think I would give myself up?"

"I'm going to answer that the Navajo way," Chee said, and laughed. "That means you have to be patient, because its very round about. It's all about culture."

"I don't want to talk about culture," she said.

"For convenience, let's call our hit and run driver Gorman. Let's says he's a widower. Doesn't drink much, usually. We'll follow the script in the radio tape but give him more of a personality. He's a hard worker. All the good things. Something comes along to be celebrated. His birthday, maybe. His friends take him out to a bar off the reservation. Driving home he hits this pedestrian. Like in the tape, he hears something and backs up. But he's drunk. He doesn't see anybody. So he drives away. Now I'm a member of the Navajo Tribal Police, also deputized by a couple of the counties in Arizona and New Mexico, sworn to uphold the law. My boss wants me to catch this guy. So one day I catch him. What do I do?"

"Is that the question?" Janet said, surprised. "That's what you want to ask me?"

"That starts it," he said.

"Well, its not pleasant, but its not too hard either. You just think about why you have laws. Society puts a penalty on driving drunk because it kills people. It puts a penalty for leaving the scene of an injury accident for pretty much the same reason. So what you do is arrest this guy who broke those laws and present the evidence in court, and the court finds he was guilty. And then the judge weight the circumstances. First offense, solid citizen, special circumstances. It looks like little likelihood the crime will be repeated. And so forth. So the judge sentences him to maybe a year, maybe two years, and then probation for another eight years or so." She studied him. "You agree?"

"That was phase one," Chee said. "I'm going to make it harder for you now. "We'll give this guy some social value. Let's say he is taking care of a disabled kid. Maybe a grandchild whose parents have dropped him on our Gorman while they do their thing. Maybe a broken family. Father took off, mother a drunk. You make your own plot. Now what do you do?"

"Come on, Jim," she said. "Why not make him a biologist? He's about to unlock the secret of the AIDS virus. But he can't leave his laboratory even for one minute to be arrested or his test tubes will all dry up and his cultures will die. It doesn't change the basic principle. Society passes laws to insure justice. The guy broke the society's laws. Justice is required."

"Okay," Chee said. "Now we get to the next phase. More complicated. We'll say this bird is a Navajo and the guy he killed was a Navajo."

"What's the difference?" Janet asked. "He violated the laws of the Navajo Nation, too. If you have justice, it spells out the punishment in advance. It tells you if you do this harm to society, then society does this harm to you. We'll lock you up, for example. Of fine you. The idea is prevention."

"Right," Chee said. "Now we enter phase two of this problem."

"We just finished phase two," Janet said. "But it's better than talking about culture."

"Okay, now for phase three," Chee said. "We're dealing with justice. Just retribution. That's a religious concept, really. We'll say the tribal cop is sort of religious. He honors his people's traditional ways. He has been taught another notion of justice. He was a big boy before he heard about 'make the punishment fit the crime' or 'an eye for an eye, a tooth for a tooth.' Instead of that he was hearing of retribution in another way. If you damage somebody, you sit down with their family and figure out how much damage and make it good. That way you restore *hozho*. You've got harmony again between two families. Not too much difference from the standard American justice. But now it gets different. If somebody harms you out of meanness—say you get in a bar fight and he cuts you, or he keeps cutting your fences, or stealing your sheep—then he's the one who's out of *hozho*. You aren't taught he should be punished. He should be cured. Gotten back in balance with what's around him. Made beautiful again—." He glanced at her. She was looking straight ahead, apparently listening.

"Beautiful on the inside, or course. Back in harmony. So this hypothetical cop, that's the way he's been raised. Not to put any value on punishment, but to put a lot of value on curing. So now what are you going to do if you're this cop?"

238

Leaphorn waited for an answer.

Janet looked at him, raised her hand. "I want to think about this one," she said. "Time out."

They were driving past the Bisti Badlands now, looking into the edge of a wilderness eons of time had uncovered alternating layers of grey shale, pink sandstone, yellow caliche and black streaks of coal. Wind and water had played with these varied level of hardness and carved out a weird tableau of gigantic shapes—toadstools and barrels, gargoyle heads, rows of fat babies, the raw material for the most frantic imaginations.

"Wow," Janet said. "This country is always ready to surprise you."

"Okay. Time back in," Chee said. "What's the answer."

"If this is hypothetical, it's just partly hypothetical," she said. "You agree with Leaphorn. You think you can find him and you're getting ready for it."

"Either way, what's the answer?"

"It's hard to apply normal city street law school solutions where you're looking at this," Janet said.

"Maybe the landscape is part of the answer," Chee said. "Maybe it makes the answer a little different."

"Yes," she said. "I see what you mean." She looked at him a while, her face sad. "Maybe the hypothetical cop would have to quit being a policeman," she said.

Chee made a left turn onto the dirt road which led, if you followed it long enough, across the southernmost boundary of the Navajo Agricultural Project, and if you followed it ten miles more, and made the proper turns, to the house where Clement Hoski lived.

"I've thought about that. It's one solution."

"What's another one?"

He didn't answer for a while. "I'll show you," he said.

He stopped at the same placed he'd parked before, and glanced at his watch. It was a little too early for the school bus. As before, Clement Hoski's green pickup truck was not visible—either away somewhere or parked behind the house.

"What are we doing here?" Janet asked. "And I'll bet I know the answer. Your hit-and-runner lives right there. And you want me to see he's a real, live fellow human with all sorts of good traits." Janet's tone said she wasn't happy about this. "You're forgetting my job. Right now I have about seven or eight clients who are genuine humans, and I like them even though they robbed somebody, or cut somebody. You have to believe in justice or you get out of the business."

"I don't disagree. The question is belagaanii justice, or Navajo justice. Or maybe it's do you try for punishment or do you try for *hozho*."

Janet looked at him, and then straight ahead out of the windshield, her face grim. "We are about to talk about culture," she said. "Let's not. Let's talk about where you've been the last couple of days. I get the impression the Lieutenant was trying hard to find you. Aren't you supposed to check out, and leave a number and all that?"

"I was unhappy," Chee said. "I had acted like a damn fool and I felt like I'd earned your contempt and all of a sudden I had to go someplace and see if I could find some wisdom so I went to see Hosteen Frank Sam Nakai."

"Your uncle," she said. "Your teacher. The hataalii."

"I think probably my former teacher," Chee said. "I think I am considered sort of a semi-heretic."

Janet was no longer staring out the windshield. She was looking at him. Concerned.

"Aw, Jim," she said. "Really. I know you were close to your uncle. What happened?"

"We'll it got complicated. We had two other shamans involved—man and a woman, and an old, old, old woman who sort of represents my clans accumulated memory and wisdom. We talked for three or four hours and the upshot of it all is I don't think I'm traditional enough to meet their standards."

Janet looked stricken. "It was because of me, wasn't it?"

"It was because of how you understand the Beauty Way," Chee said. "This business of *hozho*. The way I understand it—." He paused. The way he understood *hozho* was hard to put into words.

"I'll use an example. Terrible drought, crops dead, sheep dying. Spring dried out. No water. The Hopi, or the Christian, of maybe the Moslem, they pray for rain. The Navajo has the proper ceremony done to restore himself to harmony with the drought. You see what I mean. The system is designed to recognize what's beyond human power to change, and then to change the human's attitude to be content with the inevitable."

"A lot like psychiatric therapy," Janet said.

"Well, sort of," Chee said. "Now another example. Now we are engulfed by, buried under, modern American materialism. The eight hour day, the five day week. But your curing ceremonials, most of them anyway, can only be performed in the "season when the thunder sleeps." The cold months. Not normal vacation times. And most of the most important ones are supposed to take seven or eight days. So I think the concept of *hozho* means you adjust the ceremonial system like you adjust everything else. You keep it in harmony with the inevitable."

Chee's passion on this subject was showing in his voice and Janet's expression made him aware of it.

He made a wry face and shook his head. "Well, that's why we Navajos have endured. Survived with our culture alive. This philosophy of *hozho* kept us alive. And some of the shaman I know, mostly the younger ones, they split a long ceremony over two weekends, so working people can take part. That's the way I'd do it. And Hosteen Nakai knows it, and its poison to him, and the other two. They say done that way, the ceremony does more harm than good."

"They won't let me vote," Janet said. "But I would agree with you. They sound like some fundamentalist Christians. Can't see the metaphor in the gospel."

Chee didn't comment. The school bus was coming over the hill.

"You went up there to see about me, didn't you? To find out if I was taboo?"

Chee nodded.

"What did you find out?"

"Just a second," Chee said. "I want you to meet somebody."

Ernie had climbed off the bus. He stood looking at Chee's pickup, then walked toward them, grinning.

"Who?" Janet said.

"Ernie," Chee said. "Ernie who is the greatest."

Ernie was standing at the Janet's window, looking at her and then at Chee.

"Hello," he said. "I saw mister before. You came back didn't you? Now do you want to see grandpa's pickup truck?"

"Not today, Ernie," Jim said. "But we want to talk to you a little."

"It's green," Ernie said. "Real pretty."

"Is that backpack full of your homework?" Janet asked.

"I have to draw pictures tonight," Ernie said. "When Grandpa gets home from work, he helps me."

"After he cooks supper?"

"After that. Now he lets me peel the potatoes. And he let me cook the oatmeal yesterday. And he lets me drive the truck." Ernie turned away from the window and pointed at the dirt road which wandered toward infinity behind Clement Hoski's place. "Down there," Ernie said. "He keeps his foot on the gas but he lets me steer."

"I'll bet that's fun," Janet said.

Ernie laughed, his face contorted with delight. "Lots of fun," he agreed.

"I brought something for you grandpa," Chee said. He opened the glove box, took out a Quikprint sack and extracted from it a bumper sticker. He unfolded it and showed it to Ernie.

"What does it say?"

"It says, I have the world champion grandson." Chee said. "That's you. You're the grandson, and your grandpa knows you're a champion."

Ernie reached across Janet, took the sticker and inspected it. "Grandpa's teaching me to read," Ernie said. "But I don't do it yet."

"It's hard," Janet said. "You really have to work at it."

"Now here's what you have to tell your grandpa. Tell him he has to take off the bumper sticker that's on his truck now or put this one on over it. It would be better to scrape off the ERNIE IS THE GREATEST sticker though."

Ernie looked sad. "I like it," he said.

"Can't leave it on though, and this new one is better. It says you're the champion." Chee reached across Janet and took Ernie's hand. "Now this is important, Ernie. Remember this. Tell your grandpa he might get arrested if he has that old sticker on his bumper. Tell him a lot of people saw it at the radio station.

You got that?"

"Get arrested because a lot of people saw it at the radio station," Ernie said.

"Right," Chee said. "Will you tell him that?"

"Okay," Ernie said. "You want to see the truck now?"

"Maybe later, Ernie," Chee said. "Now we've got to go to Aztec."

They drove up the hill and over it in silence. Then Janet said: "Fetal alcohol syndrome, wasn't it?"

"Looks like it to me."

"When did you get the bumper sticker made?"

"Yesterday."

Silence again.

"I asked you what you found out from the three shamansabout me. You said 'just a second.'"

"They didn't know."

"So maybe I'm taboo?"

"I told you how they were. I got the history of my clans and the history of your dad's clan, with nobody knowing of any linkage. But since they didn't know there wasn't one, maybe there was. It was that kind of thinking. And Janet, you know, I don't care what they think." He was looking straight ahead, gripping the windshield. "Not if you don't. I mean if you're taboo for me, I'm taboo for you. I know you're not my sister because if you were I wouldn't have fallen in love with you, and I wouldn't be thinking about you all the time, and longing for you, and—"

"You said there was an old, old, old woman there. The wise woman of your clan. What did she say?"

"Well," Chee said, and laughed. "We were talking all the time about your dad's clan, of course, since your mother isn't Navajo. And she said we were wasting everybody's time because only the maternal clan really mattered."

"Stop the car," Janet said.

Chee pulled off on the shoulder. "What," he said.

"I want to go back to that 'what to do,' question. About which justice you use on your hit-and-run case. I want to talk about that?"

"Okay," Chee said. "What?"

"First, I want to tell you I decided I'm a Navajo. And I love you for how you handled that. And second I want to tell you I called my mother. And she told me her clan, and my clan, is MacDougal, and we have this funny red and green and black tartan, and the MacDougals are in no way linked to anybody named Chee."

"Not yet," Chee said, and pulled her to him.

27

NORMALLY JOE LEAPHORN was good at waiting, having learned this Navajo cultural trait from childhood as many Navajos of his generation learned it. He'd watched his mother's flocks on the slopes above Two Grey Hills, and waited for roads to dry so he could get to the trading post, and waited for the spring to refill the dipping pool with the water he would carry to their hogan, and waited for the nuts to ripen on the pinon where his parents had buried his umbilical cord thereby tying him forever to the family home of Beautiful Mountain. But this morning he was tired of being patient and especially tired of being patient with Officer Jim Chee.

He paced back and forth across the grounds of the St. Bonaventure Mission School, fully re-instated and wearing his Navajo Tribal Police uniform again. At least Chee was finally following orders to keep his whereabouts known. Chee had called to inform the night shift dispatcher that he'd be reachable at the San Juan Motel in

Aztec. Indeed, he had answered the phone there when Leaphorn called him at six a.m. That had been a pleasant surprise.

"Chee," Leaphorn had said. "I'm driving over to Thoreau. To the Bonaventure Mission. Come on down and meet me there and we'll see if we can find something to wrap up this Dorsey business."

Chee had said yes sir, but where the hell was he now? It was maybe a hundred and thirty miles down from Aztec—two and a half hours driving time if Chee kept to the speed limit—which Leaphorn doubted. Give him fifteen minutes to dress and check out and he should have reached Thoreau an hour ago. Leaphorn had watched the school's teachers arrive—mostly healthy looking whites who looked like they were just a year or so out of college. He'd watched the mission's small fleet of castoff and recommissioned school buses discharge their loads of noisy Navajo kids. He'd watched relative silence descend as classes began. He had read every word in last night's edition of the Navajo Times. The top headline read:

COUNCILMAN DENOUNCES LOBBYIST

Chester Claims Nature First
Lawyer Aired Illegal Tape

The story beneath it said that employees at KNDN had tentatively identified Roger Applebee, Santa Fe attorney and lobbyist for the environmental group as the man who had walked in and broadcast the troublesome telephone call. It quoted Captain Dodge as saying that the investigation was continuing. Dodge said that a photograph of the lobbyist had been shown to employees at Navajo Tractor Sales, where the broadcast had originated. He said that the man who broadcast the tapes "generally resembled the photograph of Applebee" except for the hair.

"The suspect might have been wearing a wig," Captain Dodge said. Applebee, of course, "could not be reached for comment."

Leaphorn examined the Applebee photograph which accompanied the story. He had caused Leaphorn a hell of a lot of trouble but he was a decent looking fellow. The only thing certain was that Dodge was doing his job, which was to get Councilman Chester cooled down and defused. Leaphorn was very much in favor of that. He also approved Dodge's silence on the matter of the tape left in his tape player, on Leaphorn's brief suspension, and on Jim Chee's boneheadedness. Let the department lick its wounds away from the public gaze.

With even the want ads read, he'd unlocked Dorsey's office and spent thirty minutes planning the methodical search he and Chee would make of every thing Dorsey owned. But where was Chee?

Here was Chee now, driving onto the gravel of the visitors' parking area, looking sheepish.

"I guess you stopped off for breakfast," Leaphorn said. "Or had car trouble."

"No sir," Chee said.

Leaphorn looked at his watch.

"I had to detour over to Window Rock," Chee said.

"Why?"

Chee hesitated. "I had to drop somebody off."

"You pick up hitchhikers?"

"This was a lawyer," Chee said. "Had some business at the courthouse in Aztec."

"Which–" Leaphorn began, and then decided he didn't need to ask which lawyer. He kept his expression absolutely neutral. "Let's get to work," he said, and ushered Chee into Dorsey's cramped quarters.

"This place was originally searched by Dilly Streib and Lieutenant Toddy. They were looking for nothing in particular, just anything that would shed a little light. Then Toddy and I took a second look at it. We were specifically looking for anything that would explain why Dorsey made that Lincoln Cane. Here's what we found."

He picked the sketch of the cane of the top of the Dorsey's correspondence basket and handed it to Chee.

Chee examined it, glanced up at Leaphorn. "Looks like he made a couple of them," he said.

Leaphorn nodded. "I've had time to do some checking. The genuine Picuris Pueblo cane seems to have disappeared back in the nineteenth century. So I'm told it could be sold to a collector if you found one whose's conscience wasn't too well developed."

"That sounds reasonable," Chee said. "Is that why you were thinking Asher Davis?"

"But as you pointed out, he has an airtight alibi for the killing," Leaphorn said. "And I'm told he has a gilt-edged reputation for integrity. His word is his bond. A lifetime of being the trustworthy trader."

"All too rare," Chee said.

"Which makes it valuable," Leaphorn said. "The second one makes it all the more curious. It's seems to have been a copy of the Tano cane. I guess you can sell anything, but the buyer would know it was stolen or, worse, a fake."

"What we're looking for in here is anything that will give us any hint of who hired Dorsey to make those things? " Chee asked. "No question it was the same man? "

"No question in my mind," Leaphorn said. "You'd have to put more faith in coincidence than I can muster."

Chee examined the sketch again. He saw nothing that Leaphorn hadn't explained. He turned the sheet over. Dorsey had made his sketches on the back of eight by eleven inch poster, which proclaimed the SAVE THE JEMEZ movement. It asked one and all to join a boycott of stone washed bluejeans. The printed material explained that such jeans were faded with perlite from strip mines, and said strip mines were ruining the Jemez Mountain forests and the Jemez River. Nothing had been written in the margins unless the writer used invisible ink.

"You go through everything on the desk," Leaphorn said. "See if I missed anything. I'll start on the bottom drawer of the file cabinet and work upward."

They worked. Twenty five minutes passed. A bell rang somewhere followed by the sounds of kids running, yelling, laughing. Another bell. Silence descended. Chee had finished with the desk top, with Dorsey's brief case, with a careful shakedown of Dorsey's meager wardrobe of shirts, jeans, underwear and sweaters. Leaphorn was sitting beside the file cabinet, the middle drawer open.

"Nothing so far," Chee said. "How about you?"

"Did you find that hit-and-runner?" Leaphorn asked.

"What?"

"The Todachine case. You told me you thought you had a line on him."

"Oh, yeah," Chee said. He laughed, and it sounded almost natural. "One of the witnesses at the radio station had a good look at his pickup truck and she said he smelled like onions. I went out to the onion warehouse at Navajo Agricultural products. But no such truck."

Leaphorn leaned back in his chair, grunted, stretched his back, looked at Chee. "Onions. Did you try that produce place in Farmington? Or the grocery stores?"

"I checked the produce place."

"Keep trying," Leaphorn said. "That funny bumper sticker ought to make it easy."

"Right," Chee said. "If he doesn't get the truck painted. Or something."

Leaphorn arose and stretched. "Let's take a break. Did you bring any coffee?"

Chee shook his head, which was aching from lack of sleep and caffeine deprival. He hadn't had a cup of coffee since dinner last night. Dinner with Janet. Dinner with—

"You look happy,"Q Leaphorn said.

"Um," Chee said. "If there's a place to get a coffee in Thoreau I've never noticed it."

"I should have brought my thermos." Leaphorn said.

"They probably have a teachers' lounge or something where they have a coffee pot and–" Chee's voice trailed off. He turned back to the desk, recovered the sheet bearing the Lincoln Cane sketches, looked at it again and handed it to Leaphorn.

"Was Dorsey an environmentalist?"

Leaphorn looked at the poster, and at Chee. "By God," he said. "Do you know when this Save the Jemez thing was going on?"

"Last year," Chee said. "I'd say about the right time."

Leaphorn picked up the telephone, dialed the intercom Office number. "Mrs. Montoya," Leaphorn said. "Do you know if Eric Dorsey belonged to any environmental groups? Nature First, Sierra Club, Nature Conservancy, any of those?"

He listened. "Do you know if he had any interest in that sort of thing?" Listened again. "Okay, thanks. Yes, I'd like to talk to him."

Leaphorn waited. "Father Haines?" he said. "It's Joe Leaphorn. I'd like to talk to you if you have the time."

The glass coffee pot on Father Haines' hot plate was about two thirds full. He motioned them to chairs and said: "What's up."

"We have some more questions about Eric Dorsey," Leaphorn said. "Maybe you can help us."

"Sure," Haines said. He noticed that Chee was staring at the coffee pot, face full of yearning. "But how about a cup of coffee first?"

"Not a bad idea," Leaphorn said.

It took a moment for Haines to rinse two cups and do the pouring.

"I guess you noticed that Eric's parents still haven't claimed his possessions." Haines said. He sighed. "Those poor people. The world is indeed full of sin and sorrow."

"I was going to ask you if Mr. Dorsey had any interest in environmental problems. Air pollution, saving whales, strip mining, water pollution, nuclear problems, anything like that."

"I don't think so," Haines said. "All he cared about was people. Nurse the sick, feed the hungry, clothe the naked. That was Eric's mission."

"You're pretty sure, I gather."

Haines laughed. "I think you could say I'm certain. A lot of these volunteers here are socially active in various ways. I guess you have to be to work for three hundred bucks a month and live in the kind of housing we provide. And so you hear a lot of talk about such things. Pollution from the Four Corners Power Plant, and the damage done to the Taos Mountains by Molycorp, and how you can't see across the Grand Canyon any more because of the smog in the air, and the dangers of disposing of spent uranium fuel rods. All that. But Eric never seemed particularly interested. He wanted to talk about how to get a water supply out to the hogans, or get the kids inoculated. People things."

"Do you remember if he showed any interest in that Save the Jemez movement?" Leaphorn asked. "That was when people were putting on the pressure to stop strip mining of perlite up above the Jemez Pueblo. They use the stuff to give bluejeans that wornout look. Stonewashed, they call it, so the plan was to get people to boycott stonewashed jeans."

"Really?" Haines said, grinning broadly. "No," he said, the grin developing into a chuckle. "I can just imagine Eric's reaction to something like that. After he got over

251

thinking it was just silly, he'd begin worrying about who would feed the miners' kids if the boycott worked and they shut down the mines."

"Did you ever see one of these before?" Leaphorn asked, handing Father Haines the poster.

Haines read it. "By golly," he said. "They really do wear out those bluejeans before they sell them. I thought you were kidding."

"Maybe some of the other volunteers were involved with this movement," Leaphorn said. "Were any posters like this stuck up around here?"

"No." He shook his head and laughed. "This one I would remember."

"Would you have any idea how this got to Dorsey's room? Or why he'd keep it?"

Father Haines had no idea. They finished their coffee, walked back into the cool autumn sunlight and stood beside Chee's pickup, talking. Leaphorn stood beside the cab, his back as straight as the crease in his uniform trousers. Chee dropped the tailgate and sat on it. He was tired. And happy. Almost no sleep last night. Ah, Janet, he thought. Why did we waste so much precious time? But Leaphorn was reviewing things. He should be listening.

"Add it up and what do you think?"

"I think I'd get on the telephone and see if I could find out if Nature First was involved with the Save the Jemez venture," Chee said. "And if it was, I would begin wondering why in the world Roger Applebee would be getting into the phoney cane business."

"Yes," said Leaphorn. "Exactly. Why would he?"

They considered that. Chee had difficulty keeping focused. He would find his concentration broken by visions of Janet. Everything about her, top to bottom. Of Janet in his truck driving north from Hoski's place, of Janet's face while she weighed his solution of the Hoski problem against the belagaani law school solution. Of her voice as she said: "I am a Navajo." His memory regressed to the drive-in theater at Gallup, to Janet sharing Blizzard's puzzlement at the hilarity CHEYENNE AUTUMN was causing among the assembled Navajos. Of Janet puzzled by a culture that was her's by blood but not by memory. He went back to the roof in Tano, Janet jean-clad thigh pressed against his, Janet asking "what's going on" when the clown's wagon brought silence to the crowd and his own sense of shared puzzlement.

Leaphorn was saying something about linkages.

"Hey," Chee said, loudly. He got down from the tailgate and stood facing Leaphorn. "I think I know why Applebee would have wanted that Lincoln Cane made."

Leaphorn looked at him, waiting.

"Just a second," Chee said, thinking it through. "I'm beginning to see why you want all those details in your reports."

"I'm glad to hear that," Leaphorn said.

"And why you use those pins on your map, linking things together. If you can find the link everything makes sense."

"All right," Leaphorn said. "Let's hear it."

"Why did Applebee get the cane made?" Chee said. "For the same reason he got Chester's telephone tapped."

Leaphorn considered. "Maybe. Chester was up for reelection. So was the Governor. I see where you're going but you have some problems with it."

"I do," Chee said. "But now I understand why the crowd got so silent when the cane went by in the clown's wagon. Those Tano people weren't seeing an artifact for sale. They were seeing the cane as a symbol of the Governor's authority. They saw the koshare accusing the Governor of corruption, of selling them out on the toxic dump issue, I'll bet."

Leaphorn was smiling slightly now. "Of course," he said. "That makes sense. But we still have problems."

"I know it," Chee said. "Like who killed the Koshare. We know it wasn't Applebee. I guess Janet and I are both his alibi. I know we both saw him out there in crowd on the plaza about when Sayesva was being killed. She pointed him out to me. Going to introduce us, because I'd just written that letter to the Navajo Times about the waste dump plan. I didn't put anything about Applebee in my report."

"Well, there was no reason to do that?" Leaphorn said. "You can't provide a inventory of the crowd. Now we can see it matters. Can you think of anything else that might matter, knowing what we know now?"

"Nothing," Chee said.

"Applebee and Davis were both at the Tano ceremonial," Leaphorn said. "Along with a few thousand other people. But did you seen anything that might connect them?"

"Wait," Chee said. "Sure. Davis told us they were old friends." He stopped, remembering. And Leaphorn stood, willing to wait. Patient again.

And Chee extracted from a memory trained by a culture which had kept its past alive without a written language, an almost exact account of what Asher Davis had told them of the Applebee- Davis friendship.

Leaphorn considered, shook his head. "Another link," he said. "Can you see how it helps?"

"No," Chee said. "Not yet."

"I guess we're finished here, anyway." Leaphorn said. "I'll take care of reporting this to Dilly Streib. He might have some ideas. You can get back on that hit and runner and the other stuff on your list."

Chee was backing out of the parking area when he stopped. "One thing I might add to that report from Tano," he said. "We can't provide an alibi for Asher Davis there. He was off buying stuff. But as far as I know he could have gone back down that alley and done the job."

"We have all the wrong alibis for the wrong people in the wrong places," Leaphorn said.

"And one more thing," Chee added. "I remember when I met Applebee in the coffee shop, he mentioned he sometimes collects old Navajo stuff."

"But no mention of collecting Lincoln Canes, I guess," Leaphorn said.

And Jim Chee drove away, smiling and happy. But that, Leaphorn understood, had nothing at all to do with canes or inconvenient alibis.

28

BACK IN DORSEY'S CRAMPED quarters Leaphorn called Dilly Streib. He explained he was once again officially in the law enforcement business, officially unsuspended. He told Streib of the poster and what they had learned in Dorsey's quarters.

"Uh, huh," Dilly said. "I don't see making much out of that. It could have come from anywhere. It's doesn't look to me like it's going to be much help."

"Maybe not," Leaphorn agreed. But it was all the help they had. And when Dilly was off the line, he called the Santa Fe office of Nature First. A woman who sounded young and Eastern answered. Yes, that was an attractive poster and yes Nature First had produced and distributed it. That boycott was one of their more successful ventures. Stone washed jeans had declined in popularity and the market for Jemez Mountains perlite had significantly diminished.

So there was the possible connection, nebulous and

insignificant as it was, between two Lincoln Canes and two murders and Roger Applebee.

But Applebee couldn't be the killer. Chee was watching him in the Tano Plaza while Sayesva was being killed.

Davis could have killed the Koshare. But he was away on the Hopi Reservation when Eric Dorsey died.

But they were friends, Applebee and Davis. How about some sort of a conspiracy?

Joe Leaphorn sat in the chair Eric Dorsey no longer needed and considered. A bell rang somewhere. A door opened and was slammed. The air smelled of dust and of the long, dark days of winter. Leaphorn methodically worked his way through a variety of possibilities and hit a variety of dead ends. He got up, stretched, glanced at his watch. Past time for lunch but he wasn't hungry. He pulled back the curtain on Dorsey's tiny window to inspect the weather. Clouds building up. Tonight it might snow. Just about now, Louisa would be in Honolulu. He let the curtain fall and sat down again. Concentrate. Work them out one at a time. And start with Dorsey, where his own jurisdiction was involved. Forget the Koshare for a moment. Without that, the solution to the Dorsey homicide seemed clear enough. But even as he was thinking that, Leaphorn's lifelong Navajo conditioning to look for harmony in all things bore its fruit.

Suddenly he saw the connections, how it happened, why it had happened. The irony that resulted produced a brief, bleak smile.

Leaphorn picked up the telephone Eric Dorsey would never need, called Virginia, and got the number of Councilwoman Roanhorse. She was at home.

"No," Leaphorn told her. "I'm not going to ask you where he is. I'm asking you if you have a copy of today's Navajo Times."

She did.

"Now," Leaphorn said. "All I want you to do is ask the

boy to take a look at that photograph of Roger Applebee on the front page. If he saw that man going into the wood-working shop at St. Bonaventure when he was coming out of the shop. I'll give you my telephone number here and I just ask you to call me back and let me know. That's all I'm asking."

Leaphorn listened.

"If he recognizes Applebee, then we take Applebee in custody, get Delmar to identify him officially and for-mally on the record before Applebee can get bonded out. And then you don't have to worry about Delmar's safety any more."

Leaphorn listened.

"He'd be safe because we'd already have the formal identification. Why hurt him? Nothing gained, a lot to lose."

Leaphorn listened.

"If he doesn't recognize Applebee, then you just keep on hiding the boy if you want to."

"Okay, I'll hold on."

Leaphorn held on. He glanced at his watched. A minute passed. Two more. The next voice he heard was a boy's.

"That's the man," Delmar Kanitewa said. "That's the one I saw. I was coming out. He was going in. I held the door open and he said thanks."

"You had the cane? Did he see it?"

"It was wrapped up in newspapers."

"Why did the teacher give it to you?"

"Well, I went in to get a bracelet this friend of mine. Felix Bluehorse had made it for his girl friend. And I saw the Lincoln Cane like the one hanging on the Governor's wall. The teacher was wrapping it up but he left it on the bench there when he went to get the bracelet and I looked at it, and I saw it was our cane. Or maybe a copy of it. And so when he came back with the bracelet, I asked him about it, and he said he was making it for a guy, and I asked what the guy was going to do with it, and he said he didn't know, and then when I explained to him what it was, he got mad."

"Mad?"

"He got furious. Hit his fist on the bench. Said 'dirty lying son of a bitch. Things like that. It was scary. Then he finished wrapping the cane and handed it to me and told me to take it and give it to the people at my pueblo. So I took it to Tano and gave it to Uncle Francis."

"I'm going to send a patrol car out to your grand-mother's house to pick you up," Leaphorn said. "We want you to identify this guy for us."

"Sure." Delmar said. "Like in a police lineup?"

"Exactly," Leaphorn said.

He called Dilly then. While he hadn't really expected Dilly to be happy with a speculative theory about Lincoln Canes, he did expect Dilly to be overjoyed with a witness who could put a suspect at the scene of the crime, up close and personal. He was right.

"I'll call Albuquerque," Dilly said. "They'll get the warrant and pick him up. And we'll take the kid off your hands, too."

"If I were you I'd give Eugene Ahkeah a look at him, too. I guess Ahkeah was drunk, but Applebee must have seen him since he picked him for the frame. And so Ahkeah–"

"Must have been around there, too," Dilly said. "And before you suggest it, yes we will indeed dig out the vari-ous fingerprints we collected from the shop, and from the stuff under Ahkean's place and check them against Applebee's, and so forth."

"Great," Leaphorn said. "Now it's your turn. You tell me who killed the koshare. Applebee has a perfect alibi for that one. He was in plain view when it happened."

"Oh," Dilly said. A long pause. "Who did the Sayesva

homicide then? What do you think?"

"I think I'm glad that one happened outside my juris-diction," Leaphorn said. "You and I can let your Albu-querque office and the B.I.A cops worry about that one."

Why waste time saying more than that? He had no evidence and no way he could think of to get any. Maybe it would surface, maybe it wouldn't. But Leaphorn wanted to understand it. So he sat in Dorsey's chair, surrounded by Dorsey's silence, and Dorsey's loneliness, and worked out how it had probably happened.

Asher Davis, the trader with the gilt-edged reputa-tion, needed money. Or received an offer. Or saw an opportunity to make some really big money. Davis knew Dorsey, had probably got better prices for artifacts Dorsey wanted to sell for his old people. Would Dorsey make him an ebony cane with a cast iron tip and a silver head with A. Lincoln, the date and Picuris Pueblo inscribed upon it.

A sudden thought struck Leaphorn. The date that first cane was ordered would have been just a week or so after Governor Penitewa of Tano announced he favored the deal for the Continental Collections dump site. Apple-bee again. Applebee seeing a need, when the Governor's election time neared, to destroy the man. Applebee sug-gesting to his old friend Davis, the cat's paw, the ideas of having a Lincoln Cane made. Let's see if that shop teacher can actually make a credible Lincoln Cane. Do a Picuris. If it looks right, you sell it. We split. And thus Applebee would be ready when the time was ripe to have a Tano cane made.

What had Davis told Chee about his relationship with the lawyer? He'd said that Roger had all the great ideas, but Davis was the one who got suspended.

So the Picuris cane is made, delivered, and sold. Asher Davis has put his solid gold reputation on the gam-ing table. Nothing goes wrong. Not yet. It goes wrong later.

It goes wrong with the second cane. Applebee handles this deal himself. Why? Because phase two is going to be so risky to that precious Davis reputation that even Applebee wouldn't try to talk his big stupid friend into doing it. There's about to be a phoney Lincoln Cane out in the public eye and its going to be part of a scandal. And even if the scandal isn't good enough to ruin the Governor it will ruin Davis. It sure to become known to the insiders in the small world of collectors.

How could it not destroy Davis? Leaphorn looked for an answer to that. Exactly what had Applebee planned to do with that duplicate cane?

Obviously, the whole purpose was to discredit Governor Penitewa. Probably like this. From what Sayesva's brother had said, something had already happened to make Sayesva suspicious of his old friend. Something that Applebee had done. Something that fit the pattern of his behavior. Like the taping of the Chester/Zeck telephone call. Like the faked phone call to the principal about a gas leak. Like the anonymous tip which sent Lieutenant Toddy searching under Ahkeah's home. Perhaps a faked letter. An anonymous telephone call, God knows what. With the suspicion planted, Applebee intended to pick up the cane and deliver it to the Sayesva as proof of whatever he had already caused him to believe. That the Governor intended to sell the genuine cane and replace it with the copy? That, and maybe more than that.

Had Applebee only know it, Dorsey had done him a favor by sending the cane home with Delmar. That must have made it all the more persuasive to Sayesva. Here was a copy of the symbolic cane, handed him by his nephew, along with the account of an angry artisan, tricked into making the fake and wanted no part of such a plot. It was easy enough to see why Sayesva was convinced that the Governor was a traitor.

But back to Applebee. Why the homicide? It could have been self defense—at least in part. Fighting off an attack by the angry Dorsey. But Dorsey had been struck from behind. Self defense at another level, then. Dorsey left alive would mean Dorsey exposing his plot, discrediting the Nature First campaign, discrediting Roger Applebee.

And so Dorsey had to die. And did die. And that left Applebee home free as always. The next afternoon, Asher Davis saw the faked cane in the wagon. He knew his cane maker had been murdered the day before. He must have seen Applebee's hand in this. Must have known the reputation he had treasured was as dead as Dorsey if the fake cane came to public light. He had to get his hands on it. He had to bury it so deep it would never be found. Maybe he didn't mean to kill Sayesva.

Davis would lose his reputation now. But maybe he'd get away with the murder. Unless Applebee took him down. And Applebee was a goner. The FBI was slow sometimes, and burdened by its bureaucracy, but once it got pointed in the right direction if got the job done. They'd match prints, and find forensic evidence, and maybe more witnesses and Applebee would do enough years to add up to life. Davis? He never had been Leaphorn's problem. Let the feds work it out.

Time to go home. He got up and pulled back the curtain for another look at the weather. Getting dark now. Cloudy. Snow by morning, he guessed. What did he have to eat at home. Out of milk, he remembered. Eggs but no bacon. Maybe a can of chili left, and about a half loaf of bread, but it was already stale yesterday morning. He really didn't want to go home. The house would be cold. The bed would be cold. His footsteps would echo.

Where was Louisa now?

He turned out the light and locked the door that was no longer Dorsey's door. Leaving Honolulu by now, he thought. In the air. He imagined himself in the seat beside her. He imagined himself holding her hand. He imagined listening to her telling him what to expect in China. He imagined–"

In the darkness, a woman was walking across the gravel toward him. Louisa.

"Joe Leaphorn," she said. "You are one hell of a hard man to locate."

Lieutenant Joe Leaphorn was absolutely speechless.

"You leave me a message on the machine. But then you're not at your office, and you're not at home and don't seem to be anyplace at all. But Virginia, bless her heart, finally . . .

"What are you doing here?" Leaphorn asked. "Why aren't you on that—"

"I can always go to China," Louisa said. "You said you were suspended. I thought maybe you might need somebody."

"I do," Leaphorn said. He realized that his voice was shaking. But it didn't matter. "I need you."